DEATH IN THE FEARFUL NIGHT

George Bellairs (1902–1982). He was, by day, a Manchester bank manager with close connections to the University of Manchester. He is often referred to as the English Simenon, as his detective stories combine wicked crimes and classic police procedurals, set in quaint villages.

He was born in Lancashire and married Gladys Mabel Roberts in 1930. He was a devoted Francophile and travelled there frequently, writing for English newspapers and magazines and weaving French towns into his fiction.

Bellairs' first mystery, *Littlejohn on Leave* (1941) introduced his series detective, Detective Inspector Thomas Littlejohn. Full of scandal and intrigue, the series peeks inside small towns in the mid twentieth century and Littlejohn is injected with humour, intelligence and compassion.

He died on the Isle of Man in April 1982 just before his eightieth birthday.

Death in the Fearful Night

George Bellairs

ipso books

This edition published in 2016 by Ipso Books

First published in 1960 in Great Britain by John Gifford Ltd.

Ipso Books is a division of Peters Fraser + Dunlop Ltd

Drury House, 34–43 Russell Street, London WC2B 5HA

CONTENTS

CHAPTER I
THE AFFAIR AT FREAKE'S FOLLY

The Gamekeeper from Huncote Hall was a tall, thin, sad-faced man, dressed in a sports-coat, soiled flannel trousers and gumboots and he had a drooping ragged moustache. He had an aggressive manner, too, as though everyone he spoke to were a trespasser on the estate and ready to argue about being ordered off. His intimates, however, knew that it was his compensation, his answer to the outside world for his inferior position at home, where his domineering wife ruled him without mercy. His name was Woodcock.

Woodcock was standing in the middle of a crowd of people all of whom he treated with the same lack of concern. The spectators were made up of policemen, journalists, plain-clothes men, and the idle and the curious from miles around. He was telling Superintendent Littlejohn, of Scotland Yard, the story he'd been retailing to everybody else for the last four days.

"It was like this ..."

It was late autumn and past the harvest. There was a scent of damp air and dead leaves about, but above the trees of the clearing in which they were all standing, the sky was clear and blue.

"I got up at half-past five and came in this direction from the Hall. The missus wanted some mushrooms..."

He gave the crowd a searching, sidelong glance, as though expecting his wife to be a part of it and ready to set about him as she often did in public.

"The best fields for mushrooms lie between here and the town. So I crossed the home farm meadow and took the short cut past Freake's. You have to be up good and early for mushrooms. Everybody's after 'em."

"What time did you pass Freake's?"

The question came from a tall, fresh-complexioned, irritable man in the uniform of a Police Superintendent, Herle, of the Midshire County Constabulary. He was self-conscious and held himself like a soldier on parade.

The gamekeeper made little spitting noises, as though trying to clear his lips of bits of tobacco.

"I told you before. It was about half-past six. The clock in the house stood at that as I went in."

He glanced across at the shabby building to the right of where they were standing. It was a queer edifice of stone, the back in ruins, the front turned into crude living quarters with deep narrow windows and a tumbledown door. There was a ruined tower, like that of a sham castle, overgrown with ivy, at the far end of the frontage. It had been erected during the Regency to house an eccentric member of a wealthy land-owning family and still carried his name, Freake's Folly.

"Go on."

"I didn't pass within sight of the house; I kept in the trees. It didn't do to let Bracknell see you on his property. I'd no rights there, but, as I said, it was a short cut."

He paused for effect. The reporters standing round knew what was coming, but they looked as eager as though they were hearing it for the first time.

"I wouldn't 'ave stopped if it hadn't been for the dog. He was chained-up in the kennel there but, instead of barkin' his head off, as he usually does if anybody comes within miles of the place, he was howlin' just like a baby cryin' ..."

Another pause. Woodcock passed the back of his hand across his mouth this time.

"I stopped and peeked at him through the trees. He took no notice of me. Jest kept turnin' up his muzzle to the skies and yowlin' like he was heartbroke. It was then I see the door was open, too."

"The dog were took to the kennels at Fenny Carleton and bit the R.S.P.C.A. man on the way. So savage, he were, they 'ad to put 'im to sleep..."

A spectator in the front row said it *sotto voce* to his neighbour. Woodcock turned and fixed him with a stare until he grew silent.

"I thought to meself perhaps Bracknell might be ill or somethin' else wrong, so, after a bit of thinkin', I went to take a look. There wasn't any sign of him through the windows and in between the dog hollerin', everything was as silent as the grave..."

He paused again and the silence seemed to return. It was as if they were all holding their breath waiting for what was coming.

"...So, I went in. There, in the livin'-room, was Samuel Bracknell, stretched his full length on the floor, with a knife in his back. It turned me up good an' proper, I can tell you."

He surveyed the surrounding faces, as though expecting applause, but none came. He looked disgusted.

"That was last Saturday. I guess whoever did it's got far enough away by now."

He said it for the benefit of the police, who, he thought, hadn't appreciated enough his share in the affair. True, he'd pocketed quite a few five-bobs from the newspaper men who had questioned him and another few shillings from the swarms of motorists and cyclists who'd been buzzing round since the day of the crime. But the police hadn't even thanked him.

"Thank you, Mr. Woodcock," said Littlejohn.

That was better! The Superintendent was even offering him a cigarette from his case and lighting another himself. Woodcock smiled maliciously at P.C. Gullet, with whom he carried on a perpetual feud.

Gullet shepherded the crowd away, somehow including Woodcock in it, too.

"Move along, there. Don't h'impede the investigation."

The retreating Woodcock protested, waving the cigarette which Littlejohn had given him in Gullet's face as though it were a passport.

"I'm a witness... I'm part of..."

"Move on."

The reporters had been in and around the town of Carleton Unthank for the past two weeks, for the death of Samuel Bracknell was the third in that short time. First, a girl of twenty-three, returning home after choir practice; then, a few days later, a postman's daughter, aged seventeen. Both had been killed with a knife.

Now, Bracknell, in just the same way. A man between forty-five and fifty.

The police had drawn a blank on the first two investigations, but now the newspapers had something fresh to report.

THE MIDSHIRE MANIAC
County Police Send for Scotland Yard
Superintendent Littlejohn at Carleton Unthank

Littlejohn and Cromwell had arrived that morning. Carleton Unthank was a pleasant market town, joined to nearby Fenny Carleton by a string of ribbon building, and the whole forming a community of about ten thousand people. The local police headquarters were at Carleton Unthank and Superintendent Herle had been sent there by the county constabulary to take charge of the case.

Over a cup of tea, Herle had earlier put the two London detectives in the picture.

"On the night of September 21st, Nancy Tooley, a good-looking girl of twenty-three, a farmer's daughter and engaged to be married, left the choir practice at Carleton Unthank Church at ten o'clock. She hadn't far to go and had ridden down on her bicycle. Her fiancé, also a farmer, had been to a meeting of the local agricultural committee, and kept later than usual, so she had gone off home alone. Her friends said she was a bit annoyed when she found her young man wasn't there to meet her as usual, so she flounced away in a bit of pique. She was found in the small hours, one-thirty to be exact, in the ditch off the by-road leading to her father's farm. She'd been stabbed in the back with this..."

Herle opened a drawer and produced the weapon. It consisted of a blade about six inches long, broad at the base where it entered a black hardwood handle into which it was firmly held by brass rivets; the rest worn and tapering down to a fine point at the end of a keen edge. It was like a well-used butcher's knife.

"Medical evidence gives the time of Bracknell's death at between eight and nine o'clock. The method was the same in each; a deep stab in the back. Medico-legal reports say the same knife was used each time, but the wounds indicate that in the case of the women, the murderer seized them from in front, held them to him, and stabbed them. With Bracknell, however, the blow was delivered from behind. In each case the heart was pierced. The knife was withdrawn and carried away in the first two murders; in the last one, it was left in the wound. There was no sexual crime against the women; they hadn't been interfered with at all and there were no signs of a struggle."

Herle had six files on his desk. He turned one over and consulted the next.

"Then, on the night of September 27th, Marlene Turville, a postman's daughter at Carleton Unthank, left home at eight o'clock to attend a harvest social in the church school. She was a nice, quiet girl of seventeen, who'd a matter of a quarter of a mile to walk to the social. She was found, murdered, a mile out of Fenny Carleton in the opposite direction from her way to the school. A search-party found her about midnight."

He turned to the next file and told the story of the third crime, committed on September 29th, two nights after the second.

"It might have been that Bracknell, who was a queer, isolated chap, came across someone acting suspiciously, or in the vicinity of one or both of the bodies on the nights in question. He may have spoken about it to them or else accused them outright. The murderer was obviously the same in each case. Perhaps a homicidal maniac. He was bound to kill again to shut Bracknell's mouth. The difference was he left his knife at Bracknell's place. He may have been scared off by something."

"And the rest of the files?" said Littlejohn, finishing his tea and lighting his pipe.

Herle smiled.

"The first murder caused a sensation, but the second created panic. The three remaining files are of unsuccessful attempts or false alarms. Two were followed by suspicious characters; the third was actually accosted, but pushed the man aside and ran away. We expect many more. One of the complaints was from a girl who was brought here by her mother, who did all the talking. Another by a girl who had hysterics and had to be given sal volatile and have her face slapped. The other...well...she thoroughly enjoyed it. She was the type. Proud of it, and got an immense thrill out of retailing all the details."

"Any clues?"

"You couldn't exactly call them clues. Merely events. Nancy Tooley had, as I told you, been to choir practice. She had her music book with her when she left the church. It was rather large and bound in soft morocco leather. She had it in the carrier basket on the front of her bike. In checking her belongings and examining the body and the bicycle, we couldn't find the tune-book. The murderer seems to have taken it with him."

"Any fingerprints?"

"None. Not a single one, either on the knife or on anything—such as the bicycle—connected with the victims. Marlene Turville carried a handbag, with money and cosmetics in it. That had vanished. Nancy didn't have a handbag, but kept her lipstick and powder in the pocket of her raincoat. They were still there. It therefore might be that the murderer was out for loot. In other words, handbags. He perhaps mistook the soft-backed tune-book for a handbag. It was dark, remember. In such a case, the attack might have been made to get the girls' cash and when they resisted or screamed, the murderer just killed them. As for Bracknell, the same motive. The intruder at Freake's Folly could have been after money..."

Littlejohn shook his head.

"Is that likely, Herle? Why tackle young country girls when there are better fish available in the neighbourhood? Why carry a knife, thus making the affair murderous and premeditated, instead of merely hitting them hard with his fist if they resisted? It's all too hit-or-miss and as far as the carrying of a weapon goes, highly dangerous."

"Perhaps so. There was another funny thing about Marlene's death. It might have nothing whatever to do with the case, but about a foot away from the body on the grass verge, there was an orange and a little further on, a swede turnip."

"Queer clues?"

"Yes. Marlene was on her way to a social in connection with decorating the church with fruit, vegetables and flowers for the following Sunday. The crime was committed on Thursday. She hadn't any offerings with her because her father had taken her heavy basket of stuff down to the school earlier in the evening. It contained neither swedes nor oranges. Where did the two beside the body come from? Or was it pure coincidence?"

"I can't say, but we'll remember it. And that's all?"

"Yes. We've questioned everybody we could about the movements of the two girls and Bracknell prior to the murders. A complete blank. No fingerprints. No reasonable motives. The local people are sure there's a maniac hiding in the woods, and the newspapers, I must say, have done nothing to allay their fears. They've had a field-day and stirred-up a perfect frenzy of terror. In Carleton Unthank, the men have formed a squad of vigilantes and no women go abroad at night without escorts. In the daytime, the children have guards to and from school. The police have come in for torrents of letters, suggesting things and showering abuse. The whole area is crawling with guards and pickets from the former special constables, the British Legion, and the Oddfellows. ... So, the murderer avoids them and goes to a forsaken spot like Freake's Folly and kills the tenant there ..."

"Freake's Folly?"

"It was built about 1800 for the father of one of the ladies of Huncote Manor, a mile or so out of town. His name was Freake and he went a bit queer, to put it mildly. A sort of alchemist, or something. Contemporary prints show it was a kind of sham castle with a tower which still remains. He studied the stars from the top of it."

"Is it a farm, now?"

"Yes and no. It has thirty acres with it. It was carved out of the home farm of Huncote Manor. It's approached from the main Fenny Carleton-Leicester highway by a side-road called Dan's Lane. Old Freake's name was Daniel. When Dan's Lane ends, there begins a small forest of oaks and beeches. The house is in the middle of these in a clearing and from a distance seems totally buried in them. The forest ends and about twenty acres more of cleared land runs parallel with the boundary of Home Farm. The Folly is about half a mile across the field to the home farmhouse."

"Has it been occupied ever since it was built?"

"No. It stood empty, I gather, for a long time after the death of old Freake. Then, one or two good-for-nothings of the Huncote family lived there ... Remittance men, you might call them. In its day, it was a fine house. Panelled beautifully, they say. But all the good stuff of the interior was rifled in the early part of the century, when it was deserted till 1914; then the War Office used it for storage. There was talk of pulling it down or felling the timber, but nothing came of it. Then, about 1954, Bracknell took it over. It still belonged to a member of the family at the manor who emigrated to Australia. He came back on a visit and decided to stay, so settled-in at Freake's Folly, which he seemed to fancy."

"Why did they never join the land to the home farm? It would have paid better than leave it derelict, wouldn't it?"

"No farmer would want that adding to his fields. It's poor, barren and swampy. Bracknell did very little with it, except chase off trespassers. He even forbade the keeper and agent from the hall to come near. The hall is now let to the county as an old-folk's home. He was a recluse and a bit of a mystery. I suggest we go down to the Folly and see for ourselves. You'll find it an ideal setting for a murder."

"So, we've really got to start from scratch?"

"Yes, sir. I'm sorry. That's why the Chief Constable thought it better to enlist your help. You might bring a fresh slant and new techniques on a case like this. We've worked hard with no results. You can imagine what checking-up for miles around on sales of oranges and swede turnips must have been like! And all no good. Everybody seemed to have appetites for and be buying-in swedes and oranges about that time."

"We'll do our best. Do *you* believe in a maniac who suddenly wandered in the district and murdered for the sake of it?"

"No, sir. I don't."

Herle met Littlejohn's look with a straight clear stare.

"I don't. It's someone who in his relations with everybody else except his victims, behaves just like you and I. He lives in these parts and it might be anybody. It might even be me!"

There was a small pleasant hotel, the *Huncote Arms*, in Carleton Unthank, run by a sloppy little man called Russell, who had hair like a shaving brush and a front tooth missing. "The pair of you are very welcome," he told Cromwell, who made arrangements for the rooms. "It's time this case was settled and the murderer hung. We've sold a barrel of beer less every week since this 'orrible business started. People just won't come out after dark. One of the reporters of a London daily called it *Unthank, the Town of Fearful Nights*. My missus is scared to death, too. She's gone home to her mother at Upton-on-Severn ... If things go on like this, we'll have to put up our shutters ..."

"Don't do it whilst we're here, will you?"

The place was spotlessly clean, the beds were comfortable, and Mr. Russell said he'd been a chef at a large London hotel until he decided to take it easy. A buxom, healthy, young blonde, called Bertha, showed them their rooms and generally seemed to run the business whilst Russell did all the talking. Cromwell wondered whether the murderer or Bertha had been the cause of Mrs. Russell's flight to the Severn.

CHAPTER II
THE HOUSE IN THE WOOD

"We'd better have some lunch first, and then, if you like, we'll go and take a look at the scene of the crime..."

Herle was certainly a glutton for work. Littlejohn and Cromwell had left London by the early train to Leicester, changed to a diesel to Fenny Carleton, and arrived there just after eleven. At the police station, Herle had talked solidly for an hour and a half in his pleasant countryman's voice, telling them all about the crimes and what the local police had done in the way of investigations.

"If you like, you can take the files with you, sir, and look them over at your leisure in the hotel to-night."

He was even assuming the London men were going to work overtime!

"I'll lend you a brief-case to put them in."

Littlejohn had first turned over the pages of the swollen dossiers with such a bewildered expression on his face that Cromwell had to suppress a smile. Stacks of paper-work reflecting a very thorough enquiry by the local men. And all the roads had converged in a dead-end. For a detective who soon got bored by typewritten records and by dictating notes for the archives, and who usually scribbled little *aide-mémoires* on old envelopes from his pocket, it was a nightmare.

"We'd better have some lunch..."

What a relief!

There was a little old inn in Fenny Carleton which, although it now belonged to a brewery and had been modernised to the extent of installing a lot of cocktail-bars, phoney antiques, and silly little table-lamps, nevertheless possessed an amiable old waiter with a bald head, sideboards and flat feet, who knew how to be civil and prompt with the service. Like the farmers, the police cut out the smoked salmon and scampi and left them to the local tycoons and went straight ahead to excellent roast beef and then a magnificent Stilton cheese.

"It won't take us long to Freake's Folly."

Herle couldn't seem to take his mind from his job, so they all went off straight after coffee. Littlejohn hadn't even time to fill and light his pipe after the meal and had to do it in the car on the way.

And then, a reception committee of more police, newspaper men and local idlers was waiting for them. They wouldn't have been surprised if the spectators had raised a cheer as Herle drove them into the clearing.

"Anything fresh?" asked a reporter in a slouch hat and dirty raincoat.

"Give us a chance," said Cromwell reproachfully.

Three rooms of the half-ruined house had been occupied and were all on the ground floor. The shutters of these had been flung back; the rest, upstairs and downstairs, were closed. The trees round the place kept it in semi-darkness indoors and outside in a dull melancholy light. There had been a courtyard and a small garden in front, but now rank grass grew from between the stones and covered them, and the soil of the one-time flower beds—from one of which still rose a huge old rosebush gone wild—was sour and uneven.

Here and there were dumps of rubbish. Old iron, an antiquated mowing-machine, a rotten barrow, and an old plough. In a tumbledown shed, the door of which was open and askew, stood an out-of-date saloon car and behind it in the gloom a farm-wagon with one wheel off and the rest with the spokes half out. The remainder of the buildings consisted of derelict stables and pigsties and an outdoor brick oven with the rusty door hanging off. The background to all this ruin consisted of a wing of the house which had collapsed from neglect, with the tower on which Freake, the alchemist, had spent his nights, hanging dangerously over it all.

The air smelled of dead leaves, mould, and rotten wood. The weight of the high trees oppressed the courtyard.

Inside, the odour of damp and decay persisted, like an aura of impending catastrophe. In one living-room some semblance of comfort had been established. There was an old carpet on the floor and a threadbare rug before the fire. Here and there, pieces of what might have been someone's cast-off furniture. A commode with drawers, the brass handles of which were verdigrised. A huge oak chest, black and worm-eaten. A table, a couple of horsehair-seated dining-chairs from which the stuffing was leaking, and a soiled wing-chair in faded red plush beside the wide fireplace. The room was moderately tidy, but the paper on the walls was peeling off and patches of damp showed on the outer ones. A paraffin lamp with a half-broken mantle stood in the middle of the table.

On the floorboards near the door, the police had outlined the shape of a body in chalk.

Across the hall, which was red-tiled and uneven, was the bedroom. Another chest, an old dressing-table with a broken marble top, and a walnut bed which resembled a huge boat. The bedclothes had been stripped from it, revealing a stained and uneven box mattress. The floorboards were bare and there was an old rug by the bedside.

"Upstairs is completely empty and full of dust and cobwebs. We've looked it well over," said Herle.

The staircase had been a fine one and the graceful handrail followed about eight steps and then turned at a landing. Some of the spokes of the balusters had been broken or had disappeared. There was no carpet on the oak treads. Behind the stairs, the kitchen, a damp, dark room almost like a cave, with an old sink and a neglected oil cooker on which stood a kettle and two pans. There was a rusty iron oven and boiler flanking a disused grate. The place seemed little used.

Beyond all these were doors leading into the interior, which became more and more ruined and barren at each step until, finally, the roof and walls were falling-in and the daylight began to illuminate it through the gaps.

Littlejohn followed Herle about disconsolately. The dead man had been discovered here and lived here before his murder. So, what? The records said the place had been searched, but beyond a few books, bills, and letters of no account, nothing personal had been found; nothing at all to throw any light on the crime. There had been a few pounds and an old watch and ring left untouched on the dressing-table. No fingerprints, not a trace left behind by an intruder, not a clue as to the past and present life of the dead owner of Freake's Folly.

Samuel Bracknell had kept himself to himself. Hardly a day had passed without his being seen in the town where he bought-in his food and other necessities. He had been civil enough and had exchanged the time of day with people he met or with the shopkeepers whom he patronised. He had read a lot, too, and borrowed books at the public library. These, according to the librarians, questioned by the indefatigable Herle, had been volumes of local history and antiquarian lore about the Carletons and their neighbourhood. He seemed to have spent his life quietly, loafing the days away, doing little useful work about his land and property.

Littlejohn had gathered an impression that Bracknell had not been a man in keeping with his tumbledown home, which, however, he had tried to keep tidy, in spite of its unprepossessing condition. The police file had been liberally laced with photographs of the corpse, clothed, unclothed, in the place where it had been found, and on a slab in the morgue. It revealed, even in death, a large, clean, well-built, swarthy man, with a short beard, strong features, intelligent head and large Roman nose. The police photographer made a gruesome hobby of fashioning death-masks of his subjects and that of Bracknell might have passed for one or two of the Huncote family, whose busts and effigies littered the parish church of Carleton Unthank.

The dead man, too, had not been as shabby as the Folly he occupied. The clothes in his wardrobe were of good material and he had patronised good tailors. The suits, although well-worn, were neat and well-kept and the same applied to the small quantity of linen found in drawers and chests.

But Littlejohn was irritated by the crowds outside the Folly, controlled, more or less, by the bobby, but noisy, eager and curious, as though Scotland Yard were about to solve the crime any minute.

Superintendent Herle was crowding him too much. This decent, energetic, impatient officer had had his fill of the Freak's Folly affair. His reputation was beginning to suffer owing to the complete absence of any progress. His other business was piling-up, too, and he hoped to be rid of the murder case quickly now. He overdid his eagerness and Littlejohn, who relied so much on imagination and background, could not get in the mood on which his work always depended.

"I'd like a quiet walk round the neighbourhood to begin with, Herle," he said at length. "And I do wish you'd have all this mob of spectators cleared away..."

Herle looked amazed.

"I thought..."

"Don't take it badly, old chap. I merely want to get a quiet idea of the surrounding in which Bracknell lived and where the two dead girls spent their lives. This part of the country is quite new to me. I'd like to get to know it a bit."

"You mean, you won't need me with you all the time?"

There was relief, almost appeal, in Herle's voice.

"Not at all, Superintendent. I know you've a lot to do, and whilst we enjoy your company..."

"I'm up to the neck in other jobs!"

"All the routine work has been most carefully done and will save us a lot of time and worry. The files have given us an excellent start. You're quite handy at Carleton Unthank and if I need any help—and I'm sure I shall—I'll get in touch with you right away. Meanwhile, Cromwell and I will take up where you left off..."

Not long after, they parted at the end of Dan's Lane and Herle drove away. P.C. Gullet, too, had nimbly cleared off all the sightseers and newsmen and Freake's Folly had lapsed into a sombre silence again. Gullet remained on guard there, shortly to be relieved by a man from Fenny Carleton.

"And now, sir," Gullet ventured to say, saluting respectfully and nervously fiddling with his helmet until it dropped into its proper position in the deep furrow which circumscribed his head. "Now sir, you'll be able to 'ave a nice quiet little browse over the scene of the crime, as I expect you want to do."

He was an avid follower of Sherlock Holmes, the volumes of whose adventures on his bookshelves at home were falling to pieces from constant use.

Gullet was a sturdy middle-aged man, the father of a family of which he was very proud. One of his sons taught science in a university, and his elder daughter was a ballerina. His other son was an air pilot and his youngest girl travelled all over the world with her boss, who was a London financier and never stopped dictating letters to her in 'planes, trains, over meals, and even from his bed. The Gullet family had lived in Carleton Unthank for over four hundred years and had always been regarded as a cut above the ordinary. Every winter, P.C. Gullet himself gave a lecture to the Women's Institute on some aspect of crime or the law and terrified all the members to death ...

"I don't think we'll bother going over the place again, Gullet, thank you. And really, there's not much point in your staying here on your own to guard it. There's nothing anyone's likely to disturb. You can lock the door, give me the key, and go home and get a good tea. 'Phone your relief, too, and tell him the same. I'll put it right with headquarters."

Gullet gulped, locked the place, and handed over the large key. He was too surprised and dutiful to say much, but he was pleased. The vigils at the Folly since the murder had not been to his liking at all. Hanging about in the damp hollow, haunted by events, his imagination running riot and picturing a return of the maniac didn't suit his own busy nature. He wanted to be back on his normal routine on the beat, chucking his weight about when things weren't to his liking, digging his garden in his off-time, representing the majesty of the law in Carleton Unthank, and reading Carlyle's Cromwell's Letters and Speeches or Sherlock Holmes as the mood took him. He bade them both a deferential good-day and stumped away along Dan's Lane.

Left alone, Littlejohn and Cromwell lit their pipes and smiled with relief at one another.

"What now, sir?"

"Let's take a look round."

First they walked up Dan's Lane. It had a gentle upward incline all the way to the main road and, at the junction of the two, they were on higher ground than the Folly and could see the general lay-out of the district.

Facing Freake's, now lost again in its dark trees, they got a clear view of the buildings of Home Farm to their left. They walked a little way along the main highway to a large white gate at which terminated the long drive to the farm.

"Let's call on Bracknell's neighbours."

There could not have been a greater difference between Freake's and the next farm. This was a fine holding in a beautiful setting. The gentle undulating fields stretched, it seemed, for miles, some of them golden squares with the stubble of recent harvest, some already ploughed for the winter and showing their rich brown soil. The drive to the farm passed between pastures, the short grass of which was already beginning to glisten with the dampness of approaching night. At the end of the road, the farmhouse itself rose like a fortified place, set in a walled yard with its gaunt chimneys stark against the darkening sky.

In the courtyard a heavy, elderly man saw the visitors at the gate. He wore old tweeds and was examining the legs of a pony held by a groom. A younger man nearby was driving a cow and her calf to a water-trough. The rattle of cans, the sounds of activity in the dairy, and the steady hum of a milking-machine were going on around them. The older man handed the pony over and came to meet Littlejohn and Cromwell. He had a ruddy, old-fashioned, prosperous look. A broad red face, grey hair trimmed down to side-boards about his ears, slightly shifty blue eyes. His gait was a bit lumbering and he swung his arms rhythmically as he walked, as though ploughing his way across sticky ground.

"Good afternoon. What can I do for you?"

He spoke with a trace of the local sing-song, with a gut-tural ring when the words were resonant.

Littlejohn introduced himself and Cromwell.

"Ah ..."

The man seemed slow of thought and was turning-over cautiously in his mind the purposes of the visit.

"My name's Joseph Cropstone, I'm a J.P., and this is my farm. I'm going in for tea. Come and join me."

Having recited his credentials, he was now giving orders. They followed him through the side door, which stood open, and led into a vast room like the dining-hall of a small mon-astery. Plain white walls, red tiles on the floor, and a large table in the middle, covered with a white cloth. Windsor chairs, about a dozen in all, stood with their backs to two of the walls, and there was an armchair to match them at each end of the table. This was the kitchen where Cropstone pre-sided on working-days over the meals of his family and of the hands who slept in the farmhouse. It had a patriarchal look.

The farmer had been ready to sit down alone to the luxury of afternoon tea. The family and staff were about their business and would assemble for dinner later. His wife was, he explained, attending a meeting of the Women's Institute in Fenny Carleton—gone to town—and one of his daughters, a red-cheeked, striding Juno in riding-breeches and a canary pullover, brought a tray with extra cups for the visitors.

More introductions, some small-talk, and the girl left them to attend to her business. She was a qualified veterinary surgeon employed by the county.

"And now, sirs, what do you want from me? I'm sure I know nothing anybody else doesn't know about these shameful crimes in the village."

He wasn't much of a talker to strangers. Given a fellow farmer, he would drone away for hours about his business, his troubles, his ailments, and boast about his little personal adventures. But he was cautious and a bit sly when it came to police and crime.

"I'm not much of a one for discussing murders."

Outside, things seemed to get busier and busier. Men carrying churns, driving out cattle to pasture, wheeling out barrow-loads of manure as they cleaned-up the cowhouses, staggering under buckets of food to some pigs which were yelling their hungry heads off in unseen sties. Another girl, obviously the sister of the one they had met, carrying a bucket of eggs with one hand and an indignant broody hen with the other. Finally, a cowman started parading a monstrous bull round the farmyard...

"I thought you might give us some personal ideas about Bracknell. He was your nearest neighbour, wasn't he?"

Cropstone scratched his whiskers.

"Yes, him and Quarles were my nearest neighbours. Quarles has a holding called Turville's Ground, just off Dan's Lane, between Freake's and the main road. You won't see Turville's unless you look hard for it. It's hidden, like Quarles. Quarles is a secretive man."

Cromwell coughed. He wondered what Cropstone would say if he said, 'To hell with Quarles!' Littlejohn was asking about Bracknell, and here was the old boy yapping about somebody else.

"Bracknell's a distant cousin of the lord of the manor, Major Huncote, and he inherited Freake's Folly through his mother."

"He owned it?"

"Oh, yes. They say about a hundred and fifty years ago, perhaps more, one of the Huncotes built and gave it and the land round to his wife's father, who wasn't right in his head and who he refused to tolerate at the hall any longer. The land was carved out of the poorest acres of this farm. It's damp rushy ground and to have it cut out of the home farm and not to have rent to pay for it, must have pleased the ancestor of mine who was tenant at the time. Cropstones have farmed here for three hundred years as tenants till my day. I bought it when the old squire died and they had to sell land to meet death duties…"

He droned on and on in a monotone, like that of a milking-machine or the blow-fly which was buzzing round trying every window to get out of the place.

"And Bracknell inherited the Folly?"

"Yes. Old Freake's son came into it when his father died and if he hadn't fallen drunk off his horse and cracked his skull wide open, he'd have gambled it away by the way things were said to be going. It's been an unlucky spot and the locals give it a wide berth. Empty for years and two suicides there. Now, a murder…

"Bracknell inherited the property through his mother, as I said. She'd come into it through her father. She was a Freake and married a local farm labourer who emigrated to Australia. Their son, Samuel Bracknell, turned up later to claim it, and much good it's done him…"

The voice buzzed away. It had a soporific quality about it which dulled the senses. Littlejohn imagined the interview continuing until late in the night.

"What kind of a man was he? Did you ever visit one another?"

Cropstone gave him a sidelong look. He was, from all appearances and the way he spoke, a crafty man, who weighed each word carefully, and anxious that nothing he said should in any way implicate him.

"No, we weren't on neighbourly visiting terms. I never went there, except once when my cattle strayed on his land and I wanted to see him about the fencing. An ill-tempered fellow, he was. He'd have nothing to do with his distant relations, the Huncotes, and as for me, he kept me standing at the door in the rain and said I'd better fence against my own livestock straying. In my view, he didn't want visitors. He wished to be quiet and undisturbed for his own purposes."

"What purposes?"

Another sly look.

"Women. Bracknell was a ladies' man. One or two of the fair sex have been seen coming and going down Dan's Lane to the Folly."

He said it with relish and a lascivious smile and Littlejohn wouldn't have been surprised to hear that Cropstone was a philanderer, as well, when opportunity arose.

"Nobody has said anything to the police about this."

"Perhaps they haven't been asked."

"Is it well-known in the village?"

"I hardly think that's likely. Carryings-on of that sort are done in secret in a small community like this."

He sounded to speak from experience.

"Might I ask then, sir, how you came to know of them?"

"Me and my men are always about the fields, you know. They adjoin ours and in some of them we overlook Dan's Lane. Matter of fact, this is the only side that Freake's is visible from. The rest is either concealed by trees or there's no view on account of the hollow."

Littlejohn looked through the great window at the end of the room which gave a full view in the direction of Freake's Folly. He also noticed a case of binoculars standing on a chest of drawers nearby. From the room above the one in which they were sitting, the Folly would be wide open to anyone who cared to spy on it. And he was sure that Cropstone was a Peeping-Tom, who might even have taken his binoculars nearer the house in the wood than his upstairs windows.

"Were any particular women, women you can name, concerned in these affairs?"

Another pause.

"No. Those who saw them weren't near enough to recognise them."

The man knew more, but the blue eyes were hard and glassy, although his mouth was still grinning, exposing two even rows of false teeth. Cropstone wasn't going to be mixed up in any unsavoury business concerning the murdered man. In fact, he was getting uneasy lest further questions might be awkward. He began to gather the empty teacups and put them back on the tray as an indication that the session was over.

A little car was drawing-up in the yard and stopped at the side gate. A woman got out and walked slowly across the cobblestones. She wore tweeds and a soft felt hat, from beneath which wisps of grey hair strayed across her forehead. She had been very good-looking once, but now her fine grey eyes were dark-ringed and her clear complexion wore a shrivelled pallor which might have been due to anxiety or unhappiness. Cropstone introduced his visitors to his wife.

"They're here enquiring about our late neighbour, Bracknell. The local police have called-in Scotland Yard, you know."

She seemed tired and anxious to get indoors, so they bade her good-bye.

"She's been a bit under the weather of late. This murder so near our own place has upset everybody."

He took them to the gate of the courtyard and pointed out the short cut across the fields to Freake's.

"It's not been much used since the Folly was put up more than a hundred years ago, but before that it was a short cut from here to the town and led you to Dan's Lane. When they took the land for Freake's from this farm, they closed the road at one end. It's overgrown now and hardly visible, although they do say that from the air you can see it as plain as a pikestaff and it looks as if it was metalled."

They said good-bye to him and were sure he was glad to see the last of them. He returned to the house, now and then casting a glance over his shoulder on his way.

Littlejohn and Cromwell followed the old path Cropstone had indicated. It started in a pasture of short springy grass and then ran across the foot of a large field of stubble, the healthy soil of which crumbled and crunched beneath their feet as they walked. Finally, they reached an old gate, which they opened, and thence the very nature of the ground underfoot indicated they were in the few miserable barren acres which surrounded Freake's Folly. It was hard underfoot and untilled and, as they moved across it, deteriorated into swamp sprouting rank grass, thistles and rushes. The ditches were overgrown and must have repeatedly flooded the land in rainy weather. Soon, they entered the shadow of the trees surrounding the ruin and, in the light of the fading day, they seemed to be walking in the dusk.

They had been chatting almost merrily as they walked, but in the gloom of the woods, silence fell upon them and they grew busy finding their bearings. Suddenly they were in daylight again and the Folly stood right in front of them.

The first thing they noticed was a fine, thoroughbred mare, tied to a ring near the doorway. Then, the open door, a thread of smoke rising from one of the chimneys, and the sound of footsteps walking up and down across the bare floors.

Chapter III
The Intruders

Another Woman in riding kit! She must have overheard their footsteps entering the yard, for she appeared, flustered and a bit annoyed-looking, as though Littlejohn and Cromwell, and not she, were intruders. The mare whinnied to greet her.

A tall, very beautiful, well-built woman in her thirties. She was bare-headed and her short hair was crisp and almost artificially fair. High cheek-bones, blue eyes, and a haughty aquiline nose. She wore jodhpurs and a dramatic black jumper which accentuated her prominent breasts. She stood in the doorway aggressively waiting for them and giving them defiant looks. There was a key in the door.

"Good afternoon, madam."

Littlejohn raised his hat and smiled.

"What do you want?"

They might have been a couple of hawkers!

"I think I might be asking you the same question."

"More newspaper men from the looks of you."

She seemed more concerned with pulling-on her gloves than with the two officers and turned to untie the mare as she spoke.

"The police, madam..."

27

The hand holding the reins trembled for a second and then was firm again. She turned and looked them full in the face.

"I expected to find you here when I arrived, but as the place was locked-up, I took the key and went in."

"And lit the fire?"

The eyes were still defiant, but there was a touch of something different about the look. It might have been anxiety or even resignation.

"I called to pick up a book."

"And burned it?"

She flared-up this time.

"You are being insolent. I haven't to account to you for my movements like a suspect, I hope."

"You have entered private premises, madam, the scene of a crime and, therefore, under police jurisdiction."

"The key was on top of the lintel, its usual place. I let myself in."

"You must have been a regular caller here then during the lifetime of Mr. Bracknell."

"I refuse to discuss the matter with you. I didn't murder him and you can't question me like a criminal."

"I'm not treating you as a suspect. If you were a friend of Bracknell's, you might be able to help us. I'm asking for your co-operation, that's all."

Cromwell had meanwhile been in the living-room of the Folly and returned with the charred remnants of a book, which, judging from his blackened hands, he had extinguished with difficulty. About half of it was left and the title was still legible. *Mumphrey's Midshire Songs and Ballads.* He handed it to Littlejohn.

"Is this the book, madam?"

"Yes."

"You wanted it back lest someone should learn of your connection with the dead man?"

She laughed ironically.

"Whatever makes you think that?"

"You seem to have torn out the fly-leaf first and burned that before you set fire to the rest of the book. Perhaps it bore some intimate or affectionate dedication which might have ..."

"You're being stupid now. May I go?"

"You were very eager to burn the fly-leaf and the whole of the book for that matter. So eager that you couldn't wait until you got home to do it. I see there are notes in what is perhaps your handwriting on some of the pages. Did you think we might trace you by it?"

"If you've quite finished, I will go."

"First of all, I think you'd better answer one or two questions."

"I am suspected then? In that case, I shan't answer anything without a lawyer. And now ..."

She put her foot in the stirrup and quickly mounted. Littlejohn gently took hold of the bridle.

"I hope you don't propose to detain me by force. That would amount to assault, I think."

"Better leave your name, madam."

"Why?"

"I suppose it is Marcia Fitzpayne. It's on the title page, along with a dedication from the author."

"In that case ... Please unhand the bridle."

Littlejohn smiled again and did as he was asked. The woman rode away without looking back, a fine figure in the saddle.

"Well, well ... There goes a tartar, Cromwell. Bracknell seemed to have good taste in his women's appearance and style, if not their manners."

"There's nothing else in the ashes, sir. She seems to have burned some letters or another book, too. Why choose to do it here?"

Littlejohn entered the house again.

Cromwell had been poking among the burnt paper in the fireplace with a stick.

"It might have been a diary she burned and used pages from a book to make up a fire for the purpose. She's a cool one to come here and open-up as soon as the police-guard has gone. I'll bet Gullet's told all the town that his duties at the house are finished..."

"Psst..."

Cromwell hissed to warn the Superintendent. There was a sound of a motor coming down Dan's Lane and before they could even close the door, a newcomer arrived and parked her scooter in the yard.

Bracknell's liking for women must have been very catholic, if this was another of his lights of love.

A buxom country-girl, this time, with chubby apple cheeks, a little retroussé nose, firm flesh, and brawny arms and legs. She could hardly believe her eyes when she saw the open door. She called almost instinctively.

"Is anybody at home?"

It gave you the impression that she thought Bracknell had risen from the dead and installed himself in Freake's again!

"Yes. Come in."

She looked even more put-out at the strange voice, but she obeyed hesitantly and finally appeared in the doorway of the living-room, a bit like a chubby china doll, her eyes wide and her moist lips slightly apart. She was wearing an emerald green dress which was almost entirely concealed by a white overall like that of a dairy-maid. A roll of pink flesh, like a sausage, showed between the top of her black rubber boots and the hem of her frock.

Normally she would have entered with a sunny smile, no doubt, and Bracknell fascinated by her lack of subtlety and her red hair, might have greeted her with an embrace. Quite an armful, as Cromwell said later!

Now she was nonplussed.

"Have *you* called for a book, too?"

It was too ridiculous!

"Book? No."

"Why are you here, then, Miss...?"

"Miss Jolland. Lucy Jolland."

"Well, Miss Jolland? Did you leave something behind, too?"

"My driving-gloves."

Then she put her hand to her mouth as though to thrust back the words which had slipped out.

"Who are you? Are you from the auctioneer's?"

"Auctioneers? What makes you think that?"

"Gullet's saying that the police have finished here."

"I thought he might."

"I met him on the road and he said thank God his unpleasant task was finished, or something of the kind. He seemed to be telling everybody he met on the way to town."

She was leaning against the door and obviously feeling more at ease. Her smile was coming back.

"Dad said, as soon as the police got out, there'd be a sale by auction of all Mr. Bracknell's things. I thought I'd better get my gloves back. I left them one day by mistake."

"When were you last here, Miss Jolland?"

"The morning of the day Mr. Bracknell died. I called with the milk."

31

She'd called with the milk! And to see the innocent look in her round forget-me-not eyes, you'd have thought that was all there was to it.

"Mr. Bracknell was a friend of yours?"

"Yes."

Her lips trembled and suddenly, as though she'd turned on a tap, tears began to run down her chubby cheeks. They had to wait until she'd had her cry and then she wiped her eyes and sniffed.

"I'll just find my gloves and go, please."

"The police have taken them in Carleton, Miss Jolland."

"Police! Are you police?"

She gave Littlejohn an appealing look as though begging him to deny it. Perhaps her distress was showing her off to advantage, but now, with her lips closed and a frown which made her eyes less naïve, she might easily have turned the head of a lonely man like Bracknell. She must have been nineteen or twenty. Quite a change from the sophisticated and haughty Miss Fitzpayne.

"Did you meet Miss Fitzpayne on your way here?"

"Yes. She was riding home along the main road."

"Was she a friend of Mr. Bracknell's, too?"

The girl smiled to herself. There was something feline about it.

"She'd have liked to be. I think they were a bit friendly once. The way she threw herself at him was the talk of the town at one time."

It was obvious there had been rivalry between the pair of them at some stage or other, but Lucy was quite sure of her triumph. It shone from her face. Then a worried look again. "You don't think because I left my gloves, that I had anything to do with ... with ..."

"Of course we don't think you killed him. But if you took off your gloves and left them last time you were here, you could hardly have been simply leaving the milk on the doorstep and departing, could you? You must have been in the habit of staying for some time."

"Yes, I did. We used to talk together."

She watched Littlejohn closely to see what sort of impression her answer made on him.

"Was that all you did? Just talk."

Her face clouded, but not too much.

"What do you mean?"

"Did he use to make love to you, as well?"

"Sometimes he'd..."

Then she paused and changed her tack.

"He was always a perfect gentleman," she said in an artificial voice she might have used in the local dramatic society.

It was growing dark, but now that they'd got down to discussing Bracknell personally, the girl didn't seem disposed to go.

"What did you talk about, Miss Jolland?"

"The places he'd been to. You see, he'd travelled quite a lot..."

Cromwell had walked to the window and now began to whistle softly between his teeth ... *and tales of fair Kashmir*...

"What kind of a man was he?"

"Sam, you mean?"

"Yes. Did he call you Lucy?"

"We were good friends. I haven't got a photo of him, or I could have shown it to you..."

She didn't quite understand what Littlejohn was after. He probably knew much more about Sam's appearance from what he'd seen at the morgue, but that wasn't quite it...

"I mean, was he a recluse, a secretive man? Did he ever tell you about his past?"

"Oh, yes. Some people said he was a mystery. He didn't confide much in strangers, but he talked a lot to me. About his days in Australia...West Australia. He said he got a bit tired of roughing it and decided to come over here and see the old places his mother used to talk about. He liked it and, as he inherited Freake's Folly, he settled in."

"He was a bachelor, I believe."

"I never asked him. He never spoke of that part of his life. He never mentioned any women to me."

"Had he enemies, that you know of?"

"He never said anything about having any. I'm sure he'd have told me if he had. He was such a nice man..."

Another tear and another sniff or two.

"How often did you bring the milk?"

"Every day."

"Did you ever see anybody hanging about the place...? Anyone suspicious-looking?"

"No. It was always quiet here and he liked it that way. I got the impression that he didn't know many people around."

"How long did you stay when you came here with the milk?"

A pause as though she were going through it all again.

"Not more than twenty minutes or so. Sam was always ready for a chat. He must have been lonely and liked a bit of company. I didn't stay over-long. If my dad had got to know he'd have..."

"I'm sure he would," said Littlejohn finishing her train of thought. "Where do you live, Miss Jolland?"

"Pinder's Close Farm, just to the left out of Dan's Lane in the direction of the town. Dad farms there. We have a milk-round in the neighbourhood."

"And you called for the gloves, just in case the police found them and asked awkward questions?"

She looked surprised.

"I didn't think that at all. I'm the last person to wish to do any harm to a nice man like Sam..."

Her voice trembled again.

"I thought Gullet might show them to my dad, and then the fat would have been on the fire. Please don't mention them to dad, will you?"

"Is he a stern man?"

"Yes. He's a deacon of the Particular Baptist church in Fenny Carleton. He didn't like Sam Bracknell and said I wasn't to come here alone with the milk, and Charlie must deliver it. But Charlie knew Sam and I were friendly and he used to pretend to dad that he brought the milk, just so that I could ... well ... have a chat with Sam. He'd do anything for me, would Charlie. He often went delivering on his own and then met me later at the top of Dan's Lane."

"Most obliging. I'd like to meet Charlie."

"He might not like that. He's shy. And besides, dad might find out then about me meeting Sam and give Charlie the sack for helping me. I wouldn't want that to happen."

"You wouldn't?"

"No. No. Charlie wants to marry me, but can't pluck up courage to ask."

She giggled and sounded very pleased about it. Littlejohn felt he'd like to talk with the self-immolating Charlie, the man who to please his girl-friend, would even cover up her intrigues with another man!

"Wasn't Charlie jealous?"

"Why?"

"Going off and spending so much time every day with a man like Sam."

He almost said 'who was old enough to be your father.' but he left it at that.

"What type of a man was Bracknell? Well-mannered? Educated?"

"Awfully nice. He was very clever. He said he'd help me to be sophisticated like a city girl. He said he'd teach me French."

"Whatever for?"

She looked at him blankly. She couldn't understand anybody who lived in the country not wanting to be among the lights and pleasures of the city. They were things her father regarded as sinful. She had read about them in novelettes smuggled home and devoured in bed when the house was asleep and she could hear her father's snores shaking the place.

"Do you know Miss Fitzpayne?"

"Yes. She has a riding-school and lives in a flat in Carleton. They say she has money. She paints pictures, too, for a hobby. She'll never sell any pictures. She showed me some she'd done once. I didn't know which was the right end up of them."

"Was Mr. Bracknell friendly there, as well?"

"As I said before, she did most of the running. She came here sometimes on her horse. I used to laugh about her. Sam used to own a horse and she came to see about buying it. It was a good excuse."

"Any other women in the case?"

Her mouth tightened. It was almost too dark now to see it exactly, but he could feel it!

"I don't know what you mean. He wasn't that sort."

She was either very clever or very stupid!

"So you were the only one."

It was hardly put as a question, and she didn't answer it, except in a little self-satisfied giggle. Then, as she remembered Bracknell was dead, it ended in a sob.

"Pstt..."

Cromwell was signalling from the widow again.

Another!

This time it was a bicycle, with its lamp alight, trundling round the corner, carrying a woman of uncertain age, who dismounted, leant her machine against the front wall, and poked her head in at the front door.

"Are you there, Mr. Gullet?"

Littlejohn could feel the panic of Lucy Jolland.

"It's Miss Meynold from the Post Office. Don't let her see me here. It'll be the talk of the town..."

She said it in a hoarse whisper, approaching so close to Littlejohn's ear that he could smell the shampoo in her red hair.

He went to the front door.

"Gullet's left. Anything I can do for you, madam? I'm Superintendent Littlejohn."

"Oh...I thought Gullet was still here."

Another bouncing blonde, of forty more or less, but taller and more solidly built than Lucy. She wore tweeds and had excessively permed hair. She was breathing heavily and as she bent close to Littlejohn to make out who he was in the gloom of the doorway, he felt a waft of scented heat strike his face. She must have been pedalling hard.

"You gave me quite a shock, coming out like that, Superintendent."

Another giggler. Every sentence ended that way.

"Has it anything to do with the late Mr. Bracknell?"

"Yes. A letter came from Australia for him. It's like the others that came every month. He said they contained money. A cheque for some pension or other he drew."

"Have any other letters arrived since he died?"

"One or two. Circulars and such like."

She probably knew the contents of all the letters which passed through her hands.

"What did you do with the others, Miss...?"

"Miss Ethel Meynold. I'm postmistress at Carleton Unthank. I handed them over to the police."

"Have you this recent letter with you?"

"No. I left it at the office..."

She paused, embarrassed. Littlejohn wondered whether or not she was another after the key above the lintel, intent on making a search of the place now that Gullet had ceased to keep an eye on it.

"Do you think I might just come inside for a moment? Mr. Bracknell was an old friend of mine... He often called at the Post Office and we got on very well together. I would like to see the old place once again before it is sold up."

"It's rather too dark now to see much. Was there anything in particular...?"

He almost said, 'any letters, books, or gloves left behind?'

She was evasive, looked away, and hesitated.

Inside the house, Littlejohn could hear a door close. Lucy Jolland had evidently persuaded Cromwell to hide her somewhere. Then, Cromwell could be heard striking a match and the soft light from the paraffin lamp shone through the window.

"We're just going, but if you wish..."

He stood aside and let her enter.

She pretended to hesitate, but it was obvious that she was familiar with the place. Once inside the lighted

38

room, she quickly ran her eyes round, searching for something.

"Ah, there it is. It's mine. Mr. Bracknell borrowed it from me. He was interested in such things..."

In the middle of the mantelpiece was an old two-handled loving-cup in white china ornamented in pink and gilt, of the kind exchanged between lovers more than a century ago. It had apparently been specially made for some occasion, for two names had been written under the glaze in gilt. *William Meynold* and *Ruth Busby*, tied together by a gold lovers' knot.

"I wonder if I might take it back now. I only lent it to him."

As there wasn't another ornament in the room, it was rather clear that Bracknell hadn't much interest in such things. Probably Miss Meynold had made a sentimental gift of it to him. Now, she was after it again and perhaps had thought to persuade Gullet... Or even purloin it. Another initiate of the hidden key!

Littlejohn looked at her, as she reached to rescue her souvenir. If she hadn't been so inclined to coyness and overdoing her hairdressing, she'd have been very attractive to those who liked them bouncing. Her features were clearcut and handsome, she carried her weight gracefully and, in the light of the lamp, her eyes were almost green and might easily have fascinated a susceptible connoisseur like Bracknell.

"I'm afraid you'll have to leave it until the dead man's affairs have been gone into by his legal representatives, Miss Meynold."

"But it's *mine*."

She was getting angry.

"Nevertheless, I've no power to hand it over."

"Very well, then. But I think you're being very officious. I shall speak to Superintendent Herle about it."

"Do that, Miss Meynold. That will be best."

"Very good. I will go now. The letter is at the Post Office. I will hand it over to Superintendent Herle..."

She'd taken the huff.

"By the way," she said, as she wheeled out her bike. "I see that Lucy Jolland is somewhere about. That's her scooter, I'm sure."

She said it in ironic acid tones, as though suggesting that she had interrupted some illicit pleasures when she arrived on the scene.

"She called to ask about the milk bill and my colleague is dealing with it in another room."

The noise she made as she mounted gave him no doubts as to Miss Meynold's views on the matter.

"And now, you'd better be getting home, too, Miss Jolland," said Littlejohn a bit testily when he returned. "What will your father say about this long absence?"

"He thinks I'm still at the W.I. They're making jam today and I made an excuse for leaving."

She thanked them both for their courtesy and shook hands. She even blushed and giggled again as she did it, as though she wouldn't object to their kissing her goodbye.

"That's enough for one day," said Littlejohn after she'd chugged away.

They locked the door, pocketed the secret key, and made their way back along Dan's Lane to the road and the town.

There were lights in most of the cottages on the way. The little town ahead of them clustered round the church, with its square steeple still visible in the last of the daylight. Everything was very still and ominous. There wasn't a soul about. Carleton Unthank was again in its nightly grip of fear of the unknown killer and what was coming next.

CHAPTER IV

DEATH AT TURVILLE'S GROUND

A t half-past six in the morning there was excited knocking
on the door of Littlejohn's bedroom.

"Superintendent! Superintendent! It's Mr. Herle and he
wants you right away."

Littlejohn put on his dressing-gown and went outside.
Cromwell was already on the landing.

It was Bertha, the manageress of the *Huncote Arms*. She
must have been roused in a hurry, for she was wearing a fur
coat over her nightdress. She was as fresh as a daisy, however, although she hadn't had time to put on any make-up.
Russell, who was hanging about in nothing but his pyjamas,
looked awful. He'd been put to bed drunk, as usual, the
night before, his hair stood on end like a scrubbing-brush,
and his eyes were almost closed by large bags like balloons.

"What the hell's the matter at this time of the morning?"

Herle was in the dining-room stamping with impatience.

"I'm glad to see you, sir. There's been another development, another death ..."

There was a loud cry and a thud and Bertha fell in
the room in a dead faint. She'd been listening behind the
door and the news, coming on top of a sudden awakening,
had been too much for her. Russell, still in his pyjamas,

appeared and contemplated the body as though he couldn't believe his own eyes.

"Take her away and get out of this!" shouted Herle.

"How?"

Bertha was too big for him. He tried to take her under the arms and drag her out of the room. Then he had to give it up, shrugged his shoulders, and cast his bleary eyes on Herle as though expecting an act of violence. Cromwell helped him carry the limp body upstairs. They could hear them shuffling and bumping their way into the upper regions.

"Quarles, of Turville's Ground, has hanged himself."

It was such an anti-climax that Littlejohn was irritated. He was half-dressed, unwashed and unshaved, and here, apparently, was a development quite unconnected with him.

"What's that to do with the case we're on, Herle?"

"His wife arrived at the police station on an old bicycle at half-past five. Her husband had hanged himself over the cellar steps. We hurried back with her. The body was quite cold. Then she returned with us and came out with the queerest tale you can imagine. It seems..."

Herle was, as usual, driving him hard, and Littlejohn wasn't having any.

"Is she still there?"

"Yes. That's why I came for you. I want you to hear what she has to say, first-hand."

"Couldn't it have waited for another hour, or so, until we'd had time to get up, make ourselves fit to meet the public, and eat a bite of breakfast?"

"Well, I suppose it could. But time's precious and this affects the case very specially..."

"All the same, I'll go back for a wash and a shave, and then I'm going to have some breakfast. We'll both be down at the station in an hour."

Herle's turn now to look nettled.

"If that's the way you want it, sir ..."

"It is."

It took him quite a time to thaw out when, an hour later, Littlejohn and Cromwell met him again. He was sitting in an office which badly needed decorating. Heavy furniture must have been recently removed; there were two or three places on the walls where the paint hadn't faded owing to the protection of some large piece.

"Quarles farms Turville's Ground, as you no doubt have heard. His wife's in the other room and you can see her when you feel inclined ..."

He said it ironically, still nursing his grievance.

"They were a queer pair of birds. You can judge for yourself when you meet her. He was the same type. Thin, withered, stringy, mean ... The body's in the mortuary. You'll see it. They've been at Turville's about six years. Came from the eastern counties, near Norwich, I believe. Turville's is a small farm between Freake's and the road. Stands back from Dan's Lane, hidden from view by neglected bushes. Quarles encouraged the hedges to grow thick. He and his missus were a secretive couple. Never bothered with anybody except when it came to selling their stuff. They kept hens, a few cows, a market-garden, and a large orchard, and just scratched a living together. They had no friends and I don't know anybody who's ever been in their house. If you called you did your business at the door."

Herle was now in full spate. His eyes glowed with enthusiasm and he'd forgotten his huff at his previous treatment.

"We've had a bit of trouble a time or two with the pair of them. For instance, Quarles hated the Milk and the Egg Boards. He got so awkward about his bit of milk that the Board served a summons on him. He fired his shot-gun at the process-server and there looked like being a siege. However, Gullet managed to make him see sense... Then, when the apples were ripe and some of the roughs from the town raided his orchard, he loosed-off his gun at them, too. A good job he was a bad shot... That's the kind of man he was. A bit crazy."

Herle seemed to sense that Littlejohn was wondering what it was all about and when it was going to end.

"I'm only telling you this to give you some idea of the kind of people we're dealing with."

He rang a bell, and a heavy mournful constable entered and stood at attention.

"Bring in Mrs. Quarles now, Drayton, and be quick about it."

Drayton retired slowly without a word and the next thing was the sound of a thin, nagging voice, protesting in the lobby.

"I don't have to tell it all over again, do I? Because it's not good enough keeping me here all this time. The cows want milking, the hens feeding, and now that Quarles isn't there, it'll all fall on me. Besides, how do I know what the police will be doing while I'm away, wastin' my time with you lot? They'll be into everything and I wouldn't be surprised if there was things missin' when I get back..."

Drayton finally re-appeared making shovelling gestures to get the woman in the room. Once there, she spotted Herle and repeated all her complaint to him as well.

A small, scraggy, middle-aged woman with dishevelled grey hair, grimy lines of weariness and overwork on her face, and wearing an old coat and hat which must have served her for twenty years or more, judging from their style.

"Tell us what happened and then you can go."

"Do I have to go through it all again?"

"Yes. These two officers are on the case and are from London."

"Can't *you* tell 'em?"

Herle rose heavily, a look of exaggerated patience on his face.

"Look, Mrs. Quarles. You don't want to be here all day, do you? Well, tell us what happened and then we'll send you home in a police-car."

The woman was obviously completely bewildered and didn't know where to begin. Littlejohn drew up a chair.

"Sit down, Mrs. Quarles. I'm sorry to hear of the ordeal you've been through in the night. Just tell us briefly all about it."

"It wasn't much of an ordeal, as you call it. Quarles has tried to do away with himself a time or two before. Threw himself in Freake's Pond twice, but the water wasn't deep enough once, and the other time, he must have changed his mind. He came home wet through. Then he tried hanging himself twice, as well. The hook came out of the beam and he fell on his face at the first go; the other, I got to him before he passed-out and cut him down. He's managed it at last, now."

They felt that had he materialised then and there, she would have congratulated him on his final success!

"Not that he didn't have good reason for trying harder last night, with his brother lying dead under the manure-heap in the yard..."

Littlejohn leaned in her direction incredulously and Herle gave a triumphant nod of his head. That would teach them to insist on washing, shaving, and eating their break-fasts before listening to the night's sensations!

"We've found the body! It's the man who murdered the two girls. It was Quarles's brother who escaped from an asy-lum near Lincoln!"

Herle rattled it out with gusto. Mrs. Quarles took it all quite calmly, as though she was used to all her husband's mad antics.

"If you're going to tell 'im the rest, I'll be on my way."

She rose and pulled her old coat round her bony body.

"Here, wait a minute. Go on with what you were saying."

Littlejohn looked at the thin, tired face and the wild mad eyes of Mrs. Quarles. Her dirty little claws of hands moved convulsively as though she were taking hold of something from the thin air.

"Has she had any breakfast?"

"I had a boiled egg and some bread before I came to tell the police."

Littlejohn imagined her cutting the bread, boiling the egg, sitting down and eating them, perhaps even blowing on her tea to cool it, whilst her husband was swinging cold and dead over the cellar steps.

"Go on with your story then, please, Mrs. Quarles."

She gave him a bleak look and resumed in a shrill, dry monotone.

"It's been gettin' on Quarles's nerves more and more. Every now and then, he used to have one of his do's and it was then that he tried to do away with himself. But his brother comin' and Quarles strangling him ..."

"Did you see all this, Mrs. Quarles?"

"Of course. I wouldn't be able to tell you what happened if I hadn't been there, would I? His brother arrived one night. It was raining and he was wet-through. He'd not had a meal for two days and he'd been hidin' in Freake's Wood. He'd escaped from an asylum at Lincoln and he said he made straight for our place. We asked him why he hadn't come right away instead of hidin' ... Look! What about milking them cows ... ?"

46

"We've asked Mr. Cropstone to look after them for you. He's sent a man down."

"I shan't pay him. It's not my fault."

Herle shrugged his shoulders at some invisible person.

"We'll see you don't have to. Now, will you get on with the story? What was the date of your brother-in-law's arrival?"

"September 28th. I told you before. It was rent-day. That's why I remember it. He came in after dark, soaked to the skin. I got him an old jacket of Quarles's and as he was changin' it for his own, a hymn-book fell out of the pocket. What he'd taken it for, I'll never know. He was mad, you see..."

She said it in a kind of awe, as though he might have been a mystic or a magician.

"My husband picked it up and he knew straight away what it was. It was Nancy Tooley's. Her name was in the book. Albert... that's the name of Quarles's brother... said he'd picked it up on the road. But as he'd said when we asked him if he'd had any food, that all he'd had was a few scraps and that he'd lost an orange and a turnip that he'd pinched from behind a stall in Carleton open-market, we knew. The paper said they'd been found beside Marlene Turville's body. You see, Albert was put-away for killing a girl near his home in Norwich. He'd had these mad spells ever since his girl left him waiting at the church on their wedding-day and ran off with another man. Not that he wasn't odd before. All the Quarles family were mad. Their father died in the asylum. But when the spells came on Albert, he always went for young women."

"Your husband accused him of the crimes, Mrs. Quarles?"

"Yes. Quarles said he'd have to give himself up and go back to the asylum. Albert went off his head again and went for Quarles. He pulled a knife out of his pocket. Quarles held the hand with the knife and got Albert by the throat with the other. They went all over the place knocking things about. I'd a lot of tidying-up after it, I can tell you. The table overturned with eggs, butter and milk trampled all over the floor. I don't know which was the madder, Quarles or Albert. In the end, Albert got the knife free and, as I could see he was going to use it on Quarles, I hit Albert over the head with a bottle with a ship in it that we kept on the sideboard. He passed-out at that, but Quarles wouldn't stop shakin' him by the throat. Swearin' awful he was and froth on his lips. In the end, when I got him away, Albert was dead. When Quarles came to himself, we talked it over. We didn't want any bother with the police and, as it would all come out that Albert was Quarles's brother, we'd have to leave the district, even though Quarles would get off with self-defence. We didn't want the expense of another removal. So we buried his body under the manure in the yard. We put the knife and the hymn book with it."

"We found them. They're here."

Herle pointed to a side-table on which reposed the messy relics of the Carleton Unthank crimes.

Outside, it was raining and the woman opposite them, twiddling her thumbs, was staring at the drops running down the window-panes.

"Quarles got worse and worse after that. He kept thinking that Albert wasn't dead and was coming back after him from under the manure heap. Dead's dead, I told him, but he wouldn't listen. He seemed to be getting over it a bit, when Sam Bracknell was killed. That did it. 'What did I tell you?' he said to me. 'He's got out and killed Bracknell. It'll be me next.' You remember when you called, Mr. Herle, to ask if we'd seen anythin' the night Sam Bracknell was killed.

I said Quarles had gone to town. He hadn't. He was hiding in the loft. I daren't let you see him. I locked him in. He'd have said it was Albert who'd killed Bracknell and that would have made you suspect Quarles. I couldn't have him taken for a thing he hadn't done."

Herle looked round the room flabbergasted. He seemed to be trying to assure himself by recognising familiar things, that he wasn't dreaming it all.

"That's all?"

"Yes. Except that after that Quarles wouldn't stir a step without his gun. And he never went to bed again. He'd bolt and bar the door and sit staring with the gun between his knees till daybreak. Then, we'd milk the cows and do the other work and he'd never say a word. I went to bed and slept. You need your sleep when you've work to do and I did the most of it. Last night I left him as usual. When I got up at half-past four, there he was. I didn't need to cut him down. He was nearly cold. So I got out my bike ..."

She was as mad as a hatter, too. Living with the crazy Quarles, scraping, scheming, listening to his insane talk, subject to his violence and obscenity, she'd gone round the bend and even co-operated in his scheme to hide the body of the brother he'd killed. It was all part of the day's work in Turville's Ground.

The solemn Drayton appeared again and led out Mrs. Quarles.

"Come on, my old dear," he said. "Wait along o' me till the car arrives."

It was an ambulance to take her to the mental home at Fenny Carleton. As co-operative as she had been in her husband's crime, she allowed herself to be quietly led away.

The police-car took them down to Turville's Ground. Two constables and a couple of farm labourers had been busy there for hours. The bodies were under tarpaulins ready for removal to the morgue. The house was poverty-stricken, but neat and tidy. Mrs. Quarles had even washed-up the breakfast dishes before cycling off for the police.

Littlejohn wandered about the farmyard and then among the poorly-furnished rooms of the house, smoking his pipe, fascinated by the secret life lived here for so long by the two mad people who had finally reached the end of their tether and fallen into the pit. As he stood in the kitchen, he saw again the wild, fatal fight between the brothers, so suddenly ended by a blow from Mrs. Quarles with a ship in a bottle. The broken pieces of glass and the shattered model set in a stormy sea of coloured plaster were still on the sideboard, as though Mrs. Quarles had been loath to part with them.

The bedroom was the same. The high walnut bed had been made and the old-fashioned dressing-table had been polished. Old portraits of strange men and women hung on the walls and a few flyblown texts in Oxford frames expressed sentiments which now seemed pathetic.

Herle met them again at the front door, where he had been giving some final instructions. Scraggy chickens picked and scratched round their feet and one or two of them hesitantly entered the kitchen and ate morsels from the floor.

"It looks as if there was a streak of killing mania in Quarles as well as his brother. I wouldn't put it past him to have gone and murdered Bracknell after he'd killed and buried Albert. We'll have to question Mrs. Quarles again, if she's *compos mentis*. A reasonable theory would be, that Albert killed the two girls; his brother—his name's Oliver, by the way—kills Albert, buries him, and then goes off his head himself. Mrs. Quarles said as much, didn't she? It could be that Bracknell saw Albert on his way to Turville's, or he might even have seen them fighting. He asks Oliver about it when he sees him. So Oliver kills him for his own safety. Something on these lines, don't you think, sir?"

Herle looked quite pleased with himself.

Littlejohn knocked out his pipe against the door-jamb.

"Albert was dead long before Bracknell was killed. That eliminates Albert. Albert seemed to have a fancy for knives, not Oliver. You might ask Mrs. Quarles if she recognises the knife, or if Bracknell spoke to her husband after Albert's death, perhaps asking questions or threatening to tell the police."

"I did show her the knife that killed Bracknell, at the station. She said she'd never seen it in her life before. But that doesn't matter, does it? Quarles might have had it among his tools and she wouldn't know. She also said that they weren't on speaking terms with Bracknell, who'd never been near the place for months. But she might have been occupied elsewhere when Bracknell called and spoke to Quarles. That doesn't prove anything."

"You prefer to link all the crimes together, Herle. In other words, Oliver killed his brother, the murderer of the two girls, and then killed Bracknell who perhaps knew too much?"

"Yes. That seems a reasonable solution, eh?"

"No. I don't think Mrs. Quarles allowed Oliver out of her sight during the day. In fact, I'll bet the only time he was left alone was whilst she was snatching her sleep. She'd keep an eye on him to see that he didn't disturb his brother's body in the manure heap. Unless she's lying—and why should she with her husband dead? If Bracknell didn't call, why should Oliver kill Bracknell?"

"A homicidal maniac. It's in the family."

"But didn't his wife say Oliver wouldn't leave the place. He was, in his own tinpot way, seeing that the body stayed-put."

The ambulance had arrived to take away the corpses and the labourers were straightening the farmyard again and turning out the few thin cows into the pasture behind. One of them had unfastened the dog, a thin, docile little bitch, and was taking it home with him. The whole place was relapsing into silence and desolation.

"So, you don't think the case is finished, sir?"

"The murder of Samuel Bracknell needs further investigation. We can't leave it as it is."

"Why?"

"In my view, someone has used the homicidal killings as a shield for another crime. Bracknell was a dark horse. He might have been a blackmailer. Who knows? On the other hand, he was involved with, at least, three women. That might open up a whole swarm of motives; revenge, jealousy, lust, rage... The presence of what you might call a public murderer in the vicinity was just what someone wanted as a chance to kill Bracknell. We must go on with the Bracknell case."

"Very well, sir. I'm in your hands."

"Perhaps we'd better come back to Carleton Unthank with you, and take another look at the files. We might get a lead."

A Gas Board van was drawing-up at the gate. Two men climbed out intent on urgent business.

"Anybody at home?" asked the man who was obviously the senior of the two. He wore a bowler hat and carried an account book and a legal-looking document.

"No. Why?"

"We're here to take away the gas-stove. They've not kept up their instalments of the H.P. ..."

CHAPTER V
THE SOLE LEGATEE

Sitting at their lunch in the dining-room of the *Huncote Arms*, Littlejohn and Cromwell could see through the window all that was going on in the busy part of the town. They had spent most of the morning combing the files for fresh light on the case. It was a task which Littlejohn abhorred, but it pleased Herle and didn't do any harm.

Of one thing, however, Littlejohn was quite sure. Herle was afraid. So was everyone else in the town. The fact that Quarles's suicide had eliminated a mad murderer and solved two of his crimes, didn't make any difference. Herle and his fellow citizens were expecting another killing. And that, Littlejohn was convinced, was the cause of the local Superintendent's nervous, jumpy attitude and his eagerness to keep Littlejohn on the move.

It was just after one o'clock, it looked like rain, and the wind was blowing about the bits of paper littered here and there in the square in front of the hotel.

It had been the weekly cattle-market that morning and a small crowd of men, obviously farmers, the relics of the crowd which had, around eleven, almost filled the square, were gossiping in little groups. Most of them wore breeches and tweed jackets and some were already half-seas over. A man in a raincoat and soft felt hat was moving among them, talking to this one and that, adopting a jocular manner, but not getting very far. He was patently a plain-clothes detective, seeking news about Quarles and Bracknell. Now and then, one of the farmers would take a little interest and start a long rigmarole, which, judging from the expression of the detective, had nothing to do with the case. Finally, he left them alone, and they watched him disappear into the market-hall behind, where, presumably, he was going to continue his enquiries.

The dining-room was full of farmers. Men of the prosperous, more sophisticated type who'd got beyond eating their sandwiches in the main street. From time to time one or another of them cast sidelong glances at Littlejohn's table.

Bertha was supervising the luncheon. She had a black eye from a fall earlier in the day, but had contrived almost to paint it out with calamine lotion. A small boy in a soiled white jacket, who brought in the beer from the bar, entered with a note which Bertha snatched from him and took to Littlejohn. It was from Herle. The man couldn't leave them alone!

The Coroner, Mr. Sebastian Dommett, has arrived and would like to see you as soon as possible about the case. The doctor's report on Quarles is in, too.

Sebastian Dommett! It carried Littlejohn's mind back seven or eight years, when an unusual series of murders had brought the Midshire Coroner and Littlejohn rather unpleasantly together. Dommett, whatever he might now have become, in those days had been a tartar. His favourite daughter had eloped with a police constable and the very sight of a uniform had made him see red!

The coffee was poor and, to mend matters, a brewer's lorry drew up outside the window and two burly men started noisily rolling barrels of beer along the cobblestones and down a chute into the cellars. It seemed time to go and meet the Coroner.

When they arrived at the police station, it was to find Herle with a mass of books and papers, in fact, the files of the cases, spread all over the table. He seemed to be delivering a lecture to the Coroner and his men.

"Well?" said Herle to Littlejohn, in cheerful greetings as he entered.

"Very well, thank you. I hope you're the same."

Herle looked surprised and started to introduce Littlejohn and Cromwell all round.

The Coroner and two little men who were his clerks and, since he had been assaulted by a witness in a case ten years ago, his bodyguard as well. The police surgeon, fresh from examining Quarles and looking very pleased about it. The town clerk, to see that all the interests of the two Carletons were protected. Police constables Gullet and Drayton to add an official touch. And finally, Checkland, the mayor of the two Carletons, who was there for no apparent reason except that he was a pompous, self-opinionated man who was in at everything.

"We're going to my place for a cocktail when this conference is over. I hope you'll join us," said the mayor to the Scotland Yard men as soon as he was introduced.

Mr. Dommett hadn't changed much. The same Mephistophelian face and moustache, the same lean bitter manner, perhaps a little more bilious-looking...

"We've met before, Superintendent. The Newport pentagon case, eh...?"

Littlejohn even recollected the names he'd long ago given the two anonymous bodyguards, little men with bald heads, almost like a couple of twins. Tweedledee and

Tweedledum. Already Tweedledee was whispering in Mr. Dommett's ear. The Coroner indignantly dismissed him.

"I said Newport Pagnell... It was the case of the two old ladies and Superintendent Littlefield arrested a man with a club-foot... What was his name? Pilkington... that's it."

Littlejohn remembered neither the case nor the man with the infirmity. The mayor winked at him and so did Tweedledum. It was a good job he didn't wink back at the bodyguard for he was, it turned out, afflicted with a facial tic and was winking at everybody.

Littlejohn felt like throwing in his hand and returning to the Yard. A Coroner who'd apparently lost his memory, and imagined things. The mayor, bothering about his cocktail party instead of the inquest. A member of the Coroner's retinue winking all over the place. And now, Herle, surrounded by files and plans and looking very pleased with himself about something or other. He'd even had a drawing made of Turville's Ground and Freake's Folly and had spread out maps of the whole township and the roads leading in and out. The manure-heap at Turville's was ringed round in red. There were other diagrams, too, with red arrows on them, as though Herle had been able to trace the tracks of the murderer after he'd killed Sam Bracknell.

"Have you solved it?" asked Littlejohn. He couldn't help it!

The Coroner gave him a hostile look.

"In the present circumstances, Superintendent Littlefield, your jokes are not in very good taste."

Herle casually handed Littlejohn a sheet of paper. It was the police-surgeon's report. Albert Quarles had died of a fractured skull, not of strangulation! So, Mrs. Quarles had killed him with the ship in the bottle! No wonder Herle was smirking with self-satisfaction!

The sun was beginning to stream through the windows, a drover passed with a flock of sheep, and a disabled men's band came next, playing *The More we are Together*.

Mr. Dommett snatched a document from the hands of Tweedledum and read feverishly.

"So, it will be murder by the woman, suicide by the man, eh? The woman's gone to the asylum, I see. Will she be well enough to testify?"

"We hope so."

The surgeon spoke for the first time. He was a tall, heavy, ruddy man, who looked too important to hold much conversation with such a rickety-rackety crew.

"You hope so? What do you mean by that, Dr. Fotheringay?"

"The name's Fothergill. She's more composed now. In any case, she's signed a disposition."

"Why didn't you say so? Well, if that's all ..."

"We'll all go over for a drink," concluded the mayor, and they all streamed out.

The mayor was a large flabby man of around sixty. He had a rosy face of the type they seemed to breed in Carleton, a bald head with a faded fringe of fair hair circling it, and he wore a green tweed suit and brightly polished brown shoes.

He took Littlejohn by the arm familiarly.

"Have you found out anything, yet, Superintendent?"

"I can't say that I have, sir."

"Patience, then. Softee, softee, catchee monkey, eh?"

And he giggled to himself.

He owned a chain of grocer's shops in the district and was quite a personage locally. As they crossed the street to his house, he addressed himself to passers-by, who greeted him respectfully. He even enquired about their wives and children, as though, as principal citizen, it was his business.

"Excuse me ..."

He took the town clerk aside.

"That's Ashby. You might let him know we'll be along for some shooting next Wednesday ..."

"Certainly, Mr. Mayor ..."

The town clerk almost ran to convey the message.

"What do you think of the death of Samuel Bracknell, Mr. Mayor?"

"Eh?"

His Worship looked surprised at Littlejohn's question. The Superintendent repeated it.

Mr. Checkland hesitated and rubbed his chin.

"I haven't given the new situation much thought. Herle was telling us all when you came in that the case was completely changed. We'd all thought Bracknell was a victim of the maniac who stabbed the two girls. Now ..."

He shrugged his huge shoulders.

"You knew Bracknell?"

"A bit of a mystery man. I've seen him about the place. Distantly related to the Huncote family. Spent a long time abroad and then returned to sponge on his relatives here, I suppose."

"What did he live on?"

"What bit he'd accumulated abroad, I heard."

It was all in Herle's files, but it was a good topic of conversation and the Johnny-know-all mayor might reveal some odd scrap of information Herle had overlooked.

"Here we are ..."

The little party had crossed the road and were now waiting for Mr. Checkland to take them indoors.

The building in front of which the Coroner's party had gathered was quite unique in the neighbourhood and some good modern architect had evidently gone to town on it.

A large Georgian house, which, at some time or other, might have been a combined grocer's shop and living quarters. Now, it had a broad window on each side of an archway which led into a courtyard. The windows were decked-out to attract the wealthy and fastidious of the district. Continental delicacies, Italian warehouseman's goods, exotic Eastern dainties, appetising English cheeses, and bacon and hams. *Pâté de foie gras, pasta* in its many forms, Turkish delight, preserved ginger, wines of all kinds in one window, delicatessen in the other.

Two doors under the archway led to the separate departments. The atmosphere of the tunnel changed in flavour as the alternative doors opened and closed. Coffee, spices, vinegar and rum from one side; smoked bacon, cheese and butter from the other. From a third door farther along the passage emerged a smell of burnt toast. It led to a high-class café on the first floor.

The whole floor looked busy and prosperous. Assistants running here and there, a girl ceaselessly punching a cash-register and, in the delicatessen department, two men dismembering a side of bacon like high priests at sacrifice.

Over the archway, a sign in gilt old-English lettering.

Benj'n.
Checkland &
Son,
High Class
Grocers

"My late father and me," explained the mayor to Littlejohn, whom he saw examining the building. "When my son leaves college, he's joining the firm and the sign will be appropriate once again. Him and me. I'll be glad when he's finished at college. We've twelve branches in the county and I badly need a bit of help."

The archway led into a cobbled yard at the far side of which stood the mayor's house. A modern building on Georgian lines, with a walled garden at the back and, behind it, an open expanse of fields leading to the river.

Vans were loading and unloading in the yard and on either side were offices, warehouses and garages. A sign with an arrow pointing one way: *Administration Offices.* Another in the opposite direction: *Goods.*

From the front windows of his house, Mr. Checkland could see the whole of his domain. He also pointed out to Littlejohn the view through the archway from the court-yard: the town hall, itself, a Victorian monstrosity with Corinthian pillars and a wide stone staircase.

"Very handy, eh?"

As though he were going to remain mayor for ever!

The little party of officials slowly shuffled across the yard, not quite sure what all the fuss was about, but intent on being courteous to the principal citizen of the two Carletons.

In the hall of the house, Mrs. Checkland, in a dark silk dress, met the guests with sophisticated smiles and handshakes. A woman very different from her husband. As Cromwell later remarked to Littlejohn, she must have mar-ried Checkland for his money. There was very little else in common between them. She was tall, dark, grey-haired, and had refined aquiline features. She must have been beautiful in her prime. Evidently a woman of good taste and upbring-ing, too, who was treated with respect by the local guests who knew her. None of the familiarity and *bonhomie* with which her husband treated everybody. Even Mr. Dommett grew extremely polite, almost gallant. Someone later told

Littlejohn she was a member of the Huncote family. Not the Midshire branch, but a much more powerful one, the Trentshire Huncotes...

The entertaining rooms of the house were at the back facing the fields and the river.

"Bar on the left, gentlemen," said Mr. Checkland.

On the right they could see through the open door of the dining-room an exquisite Sheraton table and Hepplewhite chairs. Probably the choice of Mrs. Checkland, for the place they now entered was peculiar to Checkland himself. It was panelled in heavy mahogany and that was all there was nice about it.

"Bought the panels from an old Spanish battleship," he was telling Mr. Dommett, who, however was only interested in the bar.

A long counter, lighted by a string of coloured lamps which Mr. Checkland at once switched on. This vulgar illumination revealed rows of bottles of every conceivable drink. Modern tub-shaped chairs and little tables scattered about.

"Now, son, help serve some drinks."

Mr. Checkland addressed a young man of sixteen or so, who was standing by the window looking self-conscious, probably at his father's idea of entertainment. He resembled his mother, with hardly a solitary trace of the mayor himself. He seemed to know everyone except the two Scotland Yard men, to whom Checkland introduced him. A well-mannered, pleasant fellow, anxious to make them all feel at home, in spite of difficulties.

There were one or two others there waiting for them, too. A couple of magistrates, the judge of the county court, the borough treasurer... The little world of Carleton Unthank.

Everybody was talking at once. Mr. Dommett held a large glass of whisky and soda, and was addressing his hostess.

"I've been Coroner in this county for more than thirty years and this is the first time I ever heard of Turville's Ground. Who was Turville anyhow...?"

His face was flushed and he was showing his long teeth in what might have passed for a sociable smile.

Herle looked uneasy. He disapproved of wasting time with the case unsolved. He steered a slow course in Littlejohn's direction. He drank the last of his Dubonnet and put down his glass. Young Checkland immediately refilled it and handed it back to him. Finally, Herle spoke.

"There's something I wanted to show you. Not that it's much interest to the case, but..."

He took out an official-looking foolscap envelope bearing an Australian stamp and passed it to the Superintendent.

"Miss Meynold, the postmistress, handed it to me this morning. In the rush of the Quarles affair, I forgot all about it."

Littlejohn extracted the contents of the envelope. A letter from the Equitable Bank of Australia, Perth, enclosing a draft for fifty pounds. That was all.

"Where did Bracknell keep his local banking account? Had he one?"

"I don't know. We found nothing to guide us among his papers."

"We'd better enquire right away. It's not three o'clock yet."

"Let's ask Major Kite... He's manager of the Home Counties Bank here."

He indicated a tall lean man with a silver moustache, talking with Tweedledee and Tweedledum, who were treating him with deference. Major Kite, O.B.E., T.D., J.P., banker to the corporation of Carleton, was important enough to be invited to the mayor's party, although he'd arrived late and hadn't been introduced to Littlejohn in the scrimmage.

Kite proved to be a nice fellow. Modest and anxious to be helpful, he hadn't any idea where the murdered man had kept his account. His business, formerly that of Webb, Tribe and Gore, private bankers, was the most extensive in the district and he had to confess he didn't know the names of all his customers. He'd soon find out.

"Might I use your telephone, James?" he said to young Checkland.

"Not going to change the Bank Rate at this time in the afternoon, are you, Kite?" bellowed the mayor after him, and Tweedledum and Tweedledee choked over their drinks, until they caught Mr. Dommett's eye.

Kite was back.

"Yes. Bracknell kept his account with us. Sorry, we've so many, you see … My deputy, Mandeville … well … ahem …"

He almost said Mandeville ran the place!

"… Mandeville's been there all his life. Knows the business from A to Z."

Young Checkland re-filled his glass.

"Anything more I can do?"

"I think we'd perhaps better have a word with Mr. Mandeville."

"I've left him hanging-on the 'phone in case you … I'll tell him you're coming and to help you all you want. In confidence, of course. Strictest confidence …"

Littlejohn and Cromwell were glad to get away and, after apologising, they made off to the bank.

Cromwell, who hadn't said much since lunch, apologised.

"Sorry, sir. I don't seem to be much use on the case so far."

"You're keeping up my morale, old man. I'm glad to get away and make a start on our own."

It *was* a start, too!

Mr. Mandeville was a small, keen-looking man who occupied a dark office, in which a light burned all day, next to the sumptuous quarters of Major Kite. As the Major had already given full instructions about receiving Littlejohn affably and helpfully, he greeted his visitors with unusual cordiality, offered them cigarettes, and at once sent for the file and the account-sheets of the late Samuel Bracknell. Then he sat in his armchair and indicated that he was ready to be questioned.

"Did Bracknell keep much of an account with you, sir?"

"Not a very active one ..."

A careful glance through the account-sheets before him.

"But carrying a substantial balance. Over ten thousand pounds!"

Mr. Mandeville sat back and enjoyed Littlejohn's surprise.

"But I thought he came over here to settle in his inherited property because he wasn't doing very well in Australia."

"So did we, Superintendent, so did we. He's accumulated all this money since he arrived here. Let me see ... About four or five years ago. I could, in confidence, give you the details. They really ought not to be divulged without an order giving us the protection of the Court, but as this is a murder and we're anxious to put a stop to the reign of terror which has existed in Carleton for so long, I'm going to take the risk. In confidence, I said. I have your assurance ...?"

"Of course, sir."

Mr. Mandeville then began to go through the items to credit of the account. It wasn't very difficult. It had not been copiously used.

"He drew about ten pounds a week to live on. Then, of course, he'd a monthly cheque from the Equitable Bank of Australia. Fifty pounds monthly. I remember his telling me when he made his will, that it was some instalment or other. Capital someone was repaying him."

Littlejohn lit his pipe and puffed it thoughtfully.

"But that wouldn't account for the accumulation of such a substantial balance. The annuity wasn't enough to meet his regular monthly needs."

"No. The credit balance was mostly accumulated in cash. I've told them in the office to let me have the details. The account was started with a draft for £5,000 by an Australian bank in London. I remember Bracknell opening with us, and he told me at the time that the draft was for some property and other things he'd sold-off when he decided to come and settle in Carleton Unthank...Ah, here we are ..."

A clerk entered with some paying-in slips which he placed in front of the deputy-manager. Then after a keen glance at Littlejohn, in order that he might tell his fellow clerks in the office what the famous detective from London looked like, he quietly withdrew.

Mandeville was turning-over the slips.

"All in five-pound notes, over the past three years. Six payments, roughly at six-monthly intervals, as you'll see ..."

He passed the credits across to the Superintendent.

Five thousand pounds in regular instalments and, judging from the dates of the slips, another payment was about due.

"It might easily have been blackmail, Superintendent," said Mr. Mandeville. He spoke in a hushed tone, like one who stumbles across something horrible and most unusual.

"It certainly might."

Littlejohn handed back the slips.

"We might need to borrow those, sir."

"Of course. Let me know."

"Any chance of tracing the notes?"

"Not at all, Superintendent Littlejohn. We don't take records now of five-pound notes. In these days so many of them are used, we couldn't possibly..."

"I see. They'd all be put in circulation again?"

"Perhaps. The very soiled ones would be withdrawn, but even those we couldn't trace. I'm afraid we can give you no help whatever on that score."

"You mentioned Bracknell's making a will. Did he make it here?"

"Not exactly. You see, I happened to mention one day that if he ever thought of making a will, the bank would be very happy to act as his executor. We've a special department for such matters, you know. Bracknell didn't seem to have any relatives or close friends, and I suggested our services would be the very thing. He quite agreed."

Mandeville hesitated.

"This is a confidential matter, too. The will hasn't been proved yet and I really oughtn't to divulge... However, I'll take a chance. Confidentially, of course. Agreed?"

"Agreed."

"One of the local lawyers made the will. Incidentally, he tried to persuade Bracknell that his law firm would be much better than the bank as executors, but Bracknell was loyal to us. He brought in the will with the bank as executor."

"May I ask to whom he left his money? He'd no relatives, had he?"

"No. Confidentially, the lot goes to Miss Marcia Fitzpayne."

Chapter VI
A Present From Perth

"Of course, if you wish to, there's no earthly reason why you shouldn't tell her. None whatever. She'll inherit around ten thousand in cash and the property of Freake's Folly..."

Littlejohn was sitting in the office of Mr. Athelstan Lucas, the lawyer who had drawn-up Bracknell's will. Mandeville had given him his address. The first floor in a block of buildings facing the Corn Exchange.

Mr. Lucas, of Lucas, Freake, Son and Lucas was between seventy and eighty. A medium-built man who had been very dark before greyness attacked him. His hair was white and his eyebrows almost jet black, which made them look to be painted in. His striped grey trousers were braced too high and showed his thin ankles, which contrasted greatly with his paunchy figure and gave him an ill-balanced look.

The room had probably been the same for a century or more. An old table at which the lawyer was sitting in a large Victorian chair, upholstered in black worn leather held in place by studs like leather-covered shillings. Large japanned deed-boxes all over the place; documents yellow with age; law books, most of them out of date, in a heavy mahogany bookcase. Spy cartoons on the walls of judges and lawyers so ancient that nobody had ever heard of them.

Mr. Lucas earnestly assured Littlejohn that the Freake in the name of his firm had nothing whatever to do with the builder of the Folly.

"Our Freake was one of the Rutland Freakes. A much more stable and influential family."

When Littlejohn mentioned that Mr. Mandeville had suggested he should call, Mr. Lucas made gestures of distaste.

"It annoys me past telling the way these bankers nowadays poach upon the lawyers' preserves. Mandeville actually persuaded Bracknell to make the bank his trustee. What would Mandeville have said if I'd suggested Bracknell should open a banking account with our firm? Eh? What would he have said?"

Mr. Lucas had a long inquisitive nose, which he nervously tweaked from time to time as though he detested it. It was as flexible as India rubber and seemed a perpetual source of irritation to him.

"Marcia Fitzpayne inherits the lot. If you want to tell her so, I don't mind. She ought to have been told before, but you know what bankers are. Mandeville must have feared another will would turn up, in spite of the fact that the one in question was only recently made."

"Do you know Miss Fitzpayne, sir?"

Mr. Lucas pulled his nose again.

"Yes."

And then he smiled to himself, as though amused at his thoughts.

"Yes. There's no doubt about it, she was Bracknell's mistress."

"Is she a local woman?"

"No. Fitzpayne's a Leicestershire name. I believe she came from Market Harborough way. Been in Carleton five or six years. Opened a riding school here. Did very well, too. Attractive gel. Not out of the top drawer, though. Brought her mother with her when she came. Old lady died a year or two ago. Fat woman who looked like a charwoman, but who kept her daughter in order. No gallivantin' while the old lady was alive. She hadn't been dead a month before Marcia took up with Bracknell. Could have done better for herself. Still, there's no accounting for taste, is there? Wonder why they didn't marry if Bracknell was fond enough of her to leave her all he'd got. Perhaps he'd got a wife somewhere else. A dark horse, if you ask me."

Another tug at his nose.

"Does Miss Fitzpayne live in the town, sir?"

"Yes. Come to the window."

Mr. Lucas pointed a shaking finger at a row of neat Georgian houses flanking the Corn Exchange.

"See that row of property? The houses have been turned into flats. Marcia lives in the top flat in the last house. She stables her horses at an old farm on the Leicester Road, at the end of Horseferry Street. It was a farm till they sold the ground for building purposes. If she's not at home, you'll find her at the stables."

He looked slyly at Littlejohn and this time flattened his nose against his face with the back of his hand.

"Daresay you think I know a lot about her. I'm her lawyer when she needs one. Helped her buy the old stables. Saw quite a lot of her at one time ... Charming gel ..."

Cromwell had gone to the Post Office to send off a postcard to his eldest daughter to whom he wrote every day when away on a case. Littlejohn met him in the square.

"We're going to call on Marcia Fitzpayne. Old Lucas says we can divulge that Bracknell left her all he'd got. That is, if

69

she doesn't already know. Lucas is a queer fish. A funny nose that looks like a false one. I'll bet he's told her already. He thinks she's what is vulgarly called a tasty dish."

The front of the house where Marcia lived was gilded by the setting sun and from one of the windows a woman was shaking out a duster. She did it furtively, for such performances were prohibited by the stringent leases of the flats.

An old four-storied house with small brass plates and letterboxes fixed on the front door. Names like *Dr. Dalrymple* and *Colonel Flyte-Smythe*... Obviously a first-rate place. Marcia Fitzpayne lived on the top floor. Cromwell and Littlejohn climbed the stairs which were broad and fine for two floors and then thinned-out as they led from a landing up to what must, at one time, have been the servants' quarters.

"May we come in?" asked Littlejohn when Miss Fitzpayne answered his knock. She gave him a hostile look and seemed ready to slam the door.

"As I told you before, I had nothing whatever to do with Mr. Bracknell's death. I don't see why the police should keep pestering me."

"We haven't called to accuse you, Miss Fitzpayne. You may know something which will help us lay the murderer by the heels..."

"I know nothing."

"All the same, I'm sure you prefer us to talk in private, instead of here where everyone can hear us."

"Very well. Come in for a moment. I'm going out and have no time to spare."

She opened the door and admitted them.

It was an attic room and might have served well as a studio. The light entered through a skylight and fine dust danced in the rays of the late sunlight which was pouring in. There was a small table with some books on it, two easy chairs drawn up round a gas-fire, a miniature sideboard, and little else. A good carpet on the floor, and one or two of the pictures despised by Lucy Jolland and some photographs of horses in black frames on the walls. Two doors which might have led to a bedroom and the kitchen.

Miss Fitzpayne was definitely hostile. She was a fine-looking woman. Big and strong and strikingly fair. But now her sulky expression spoiled it all.

"We won't keep you, Miss Fitzpayne, but I wanted to ask you one or two personal questions about the late Samuel Bracknell. He was, I believe, a friend of yours."

Littlejohn kept his eyes on hers as he spoke and from the momentary flicker of anxiety in her look, he knew that she, too, was afraid. Like Herle, the mayor, Mr. Mandeville at the bank...in fact, like everybody who was intimately or remotely connected with the case.

"I'm sure I don't know what you mean."

"If you weren't his friend, why should he leave you all he possessed? Including Freake's Folly."

Instead of replying, she stretched out her hand to the telephone, which stood on the table beside the books.

"One minute, Miss Fitzpayne. Who are you going to call?"

"Mr. Lucas, my lawyer."

"Please don't. Mind you, you're free to ring him if you wish. You're even free to turn us out. But it will be better for everyone if you don't. We've just left Mr. Lucas."

"He had no right to discuss my affairs."

"He didn't. He simply told us the contents of Mr. Bracknell's will. They'll be in the newspapers in a day or two. Mr. Lucas is a model of discretion."

Now, she couldn't keep still. She walked from the telephone to the hearth and back. Littlejohn thought at first that she was preparing to show them the door. Or else, heap the pair of them with abuse. Finally, she sat down on a stool by the sideboard.

"Sit down, if you wish. I suppose this will be a long interview. I can see you think I committed the crime. I wanted Mr. Lucas here to advise me."

"You won't need him. You needn't answer a single question if you don't want to. I'd appreciate your help, however."

He passed across his cigarette case.

"Do you smoke? It might help you to relax."

She nodded, took a cigarette without a word, and Cromwell flicked his lighter and lit it for her.

"May we light our pipes, Miss Fitzpayne?"

"Of course, if you like. I thought this was a formal matter."

"Not at all. As I said, we need your help. Anything you say will be treated with discretion."

Littlejohn filled and lit his pipe as he spoke. Then he sat in one of the armchairs and passed his pouch to Cromwell, perched on the edge of the other chair.

Marcia Fitzpayne looked taut and anxious. She was wearing the same black jumper as when first they'd met her and she ran her finger round the high collar to ease it.

"Are you going to take all this down?"

She said it almost in a tone of appeal. She was thawing a little.

"No. It's unofficial."

"What do you want to know?"

"First of all, your visit to Freake's Folly on the first day we met you. You'd been burning something. Why, Miss Fitzpayne?"

She looked him straight in the eyes.

72

"There was nothing wrong in it. Mr. Bracknell and I had been friends. I'd written letters to him. I wanted them. I'd no wish for the police and the public to be poring over them. They were mine and I'd the right..."

"You knew where they were kept, then?"

"Yes. Among his books, Mr. Bracknell had a dummy one, a kind of box bound like a volume. The police hadn't found it and I took out the letters and burned them. There was a book, too, I once gave Mr. Bracknell. It was... well a book of poetry and certain passages were marked. I burned that, too... or half burned it. You took it before I'd finished."

She now seemed eager to make a clean breast of the whole affair. Her anger had gone. Her eyes were resigned and tired-looking, as though she'd reached the end of her tether.

"Were you and Mr. Bracknell engaged?"

"No."

"Just friends."

"That's all."

"Lovers?"

She didn't even flare up. She merely nodded her head.

"You may as well know it. Mr. Lucas hinted at it in an unpleasant sort of way when he told me about the will. And the whole town talks about it. There'll be more talk when the will becomes public. You can have the truth from me."

"Forgive me, but did he never mention marriage? You see, I want to know as much about Bracknell as I can. His background, his past life, his ways, his habits."

"He never mentioned it. He said I was his best friend. I don't think he was the marrying kind. Neither am I, for that matter. We both wanted to be free."

"You met socially in the town?"

73

"No. We met three years ago. He bought a horse. He'd done a lot of riding in Australia and was a good horseman. The one he bought didn't suit him. Not heavy enough. He advertised it and I went to Freake's to see it. I didn't buy it, but we became friendly. After that we went riding together often."

Littlejohn could imagine it. Marcia Fitzpayne and the susceptible, perhaps rather mysterious and considerably attractive Bracknell would soon be in the middle of an affair. But unlike the case of the little milk girl, Lucy Jolland, the attachment went deeper. Bracknell had left Marcia everything.

"He must have thought a lot of you, Miss Fitzpayne, to leave you all he had."

"He used to laugh about it. I thought it was just a joke. He'd say rather angrily, that if he'd his way, he'd make a lady of me instead of letting me run a riding-school and suffer the attentions of a lot of amorous clients...I thought it was banter. He had a jesting way with him. He was sometimes very bitter. I'd no idea..."

There was a look of genuine grief in her eyes now. Although she had not touched her hair, it had tumbled over her eyes and she thrust it back with an impatient gesture. She seemed somehow to have grown dishevelled, as though desperate and trying to escape from her thoughts.

"Did you know he had so much money, Miss Fitzpayne?"

"No. Honestly, I didn't. He used to complain about being hard-up. Again, in a kind of ironical funny way."

"He never spoke of his past life in Australia?"

"Oh, yes. He often talked of it. He'd farmed out there. I don't know whether or not he ever owned a farm, but he'd worked mostly among cattle and sheep. He used to compare the local stock with that of Australia."

"Where do you think he got his money from? I mean, he'd want ready money for his needs at Freake's Folly. Where did he get it?"

"He told me he'd an income from Australia. Every now and then, he'd get a bank draft... Quarterly, I think. He once said something about its being repayments of capital. He'd either sold a farm or a share in some ranch or other and the cheques were instalments from the buyer."

"Was he an extravagant man?"

"Not at all. He liked a drink, he had books sent from a London library. He was quite an educated man and liked reading. He was particularly interested in the history of these parts. He settled down here thoroughly. In fact, he loved the place and, although you might not think it, he loved Freake's, too. It is rather a ruin, I admit, but he once said if he'd the money he'd make it into a place to be proud of. He also said..."

She paused.

"No, I won't tell you that. It's nothing to do with the case."

"It may have. Please tell me."

"He said when he'd made it fit to live in, I could move in with him."

She must have been desperately fond of Bracknell, in spite of her case-hardening of pride, for now she was tugging at a small handkerchief she'd produced from somewhere and looked ready to burst into tears in it.

"Wouldn't you regard that as half-way to an offer to marry you?"

"I'm afraid we were both a little drunk at the time he said it. It was my birthday and he gave me a party at Freake's. Just the two of us. We had champagne, and well... Sam got a bit maudlin. He said he was tired of wandering and wanted to settle down, make Freake's a place to be proud of, and have me there with him. He was terribly proud of his family connections, particularly of the Huncote side. I do believe if he'd had enough money and could have bought back Huncote Hall from the county, who now run it as an old folk's home, he'd have done it and settled down there."

"So, he might have been keen on accumulating money to pay for re-building Freake's Folly."

"Quite. Only he hadn't any way of getting it, as far as I could see. He used to say he was broke. And yet..."

She looked anxiously at Littlejohn.

"And yet, Miss Fitzpayne, he had ten thousand pounds in the bank, which he's left to you along with Freake's Folly. It seems he might like to think of you moving-in there yourself, with money to make it a really nice home."

"Yes... I don't know where he got it all."

"He brought half of it from Australia, I gather. He must have sold his interests out there, perhaps for a cash-down payment and the rest in instalments. Had he many friends locally, do you know?"

"I don't think so. He'd a few acquaintances in the town. He did his own shopping and came in two or three times a week. He used to call here for lunch sometimes; others he'd dine at one of the hotels and have a drink after with the regulars."

"Any particular hotel?"

"He didn't care for the *Huncote Arms*. He said you paid too much for style. He used to go across to the *Barley Mow*, just past the Corn Exchange on the other side of the square from here. If I was out, I'd leave a note and he'd come inside and make himself comfortable till I got back."

"What did he do with the rest of his time?"

"Reading, riding... he kept his horse at my stables... doing odd jobs about Freake's, loafing... He was like a retired man, if you understand what I mean. He used to get his own wood from the spinney at the Folly, which went with the property. He liked cutting down trees, chopping them up, and hacking out dead wood in the copses. In fact, he was in love with Freake's. It meant so much to him."

"He liked pottering about the town, too?"

"Yes. Antique shops fascinated him and he liked buying-in his own food. We often had an evening meal together at Freake's and he used to be proud of the food he produced. Cold chickens, salads, *foie gras,* Melton pies, cheeses of all kinds ... And always a good bottle of wine ..."

She was lost in reminiscences and glad to turn over the old days again.

"We'd some good times together."

She looked at Littlejohn and her look softened.

"Please forgive me. I know you'll not be interested in my memories, especially of the things we ate. And I want to apologise for the rude way I treated you when first we met. I was annoyed at strangers milling around the place Sam loved so much and I ... I ..."

"You were grieving for him?"

"Yes."

Tears began to run down her cheeks, large ones like pearls, and she didn't seem to care and let them drop from her chin and vanish in the wool of her jumper.

"I'm sorry ..."

"Don't mind us, Miss Fitzpayne. It will do you good to have a cry and tell someone about things."

Littlejohn gave her another cigarette and lit it for her.

"And finally, Miss Fitzpayne, have you any idea why Bracknell was killed? Had he any enemies? People who might have wanted him out of the way?"

"But I thought he was murdered by a madman, the maniac who killed the two girls earlier in the year..."

"You haven't seen the papers, yet, or heard the latest news?"

She looked astonished.

"No. What has happened? There hasn't been another murder? Not another, surely?"

"No. You know the Quarleses of Turville's Ground...?"

"Yes. Sam hated them. They used to be always sneaking around peeping over the hedges and even dodging Sam, as though he might steal their money or something... What's happened to them?"

"Quarles hanged himself last night and his wife is in the asylum. It seems that the homicidal maniac who killed the two girls was Quarles's brother, who turned-up at Turville's after the crimes and asked for shelter. After a quarrel with his brother the madman attacked him, and Mrs. Quarles killed him and they buried him under the manure heap. That was before Bracknell's death. So, it looks as if Sam Bracknell's murder had nothing to do with the other two, but the real murderer might have used them as cover for it..."

"Oh... How horrible..."

She raised her hands to her face in alarm.

"So it may have been somebody in the town?"

"Easily. That's why I want to know had Bracknell any enemies."

"Then..."

Her eyes opened wide and she impulsively rose and searched in one of the drawers of the sideboard and took a small object from it which she passed to Littlejohn.

It was a red plastic ball-pointed fountain-pen, the writing end of which emerged when you pressed a button at the bottom. Quite a common object. This, however, was an advertisement. Along the barrel was the name of the firm who had given it. *Fowler's Universal Stores, Perth, W. Australia.*

"What is this, Miss Fitzpayne?"

"When I knelt to light the fire on the day you caught me there, I found it. It had rolled to the brick kerb round the fireplace and lodged between it and the hearthrug. It puzzled me, because you'll see it's an old one and well used. It didn't belong to Sam."

"How do you know?"

"I'd surely have seen it before. In the time we were together, I knew everything there was in the place. Even down to his socks, which I sometimes darned for him. The police must have overlooked it when they searched the house. But it wasn't Sam's."

"Are you sure? This is most important."

"He was never a man for hoarding useless things. He had one pen, that style, which wrote black, whereas that is blue. I never saw him write anything in blue ink and I knew most of the writing he did. He'd one pen. He threw them away as they gave out. And he'd a pencil... an imitation gold one which somebody gave him. That was all. That pen wasn't his, I'm sure."

"Why didn't you turn it in to the police, Miss Fitzpayne?"

"I slipped it instinctively in my pocket at the time. Then, I got so angry about the police, including you, Superintendent, tramping all over the place, that I just couldn't bear to call on any of you and give it up. Besides, I never thought it might be a clue. With a maniac... well... clues don't seem to matter... Or so I thought."

"It might have been dropped there before or after the crime, then?"

"I suppose so. I think before, or at the time of the crime. Because, you see, I was the first to enter the house after the police guard was removed. I met Gullet at the end of Dan's Lane and he was a bit talkative and said he was glad the job of guarding the house was over. You had said it was no longer necessary. So, I went to Freake's, found it deserted, and burned my letters. I took the key from over the door lintel. May I please have the key? After all, the Folly will soon be mine and I promise not to go again till you say I may."

"That's all right, Miss Fitzpayne. But it appears, if what you say is true, that the pen wasn't Bracknell's, as if someone from Australia, or at least, connected with it, was down at the Folly around the time of the crime. We'd better look into that..."

"I don't think there's much more I can tell you, but please come again if there's anything I can do."

She shook hands with them both. Her eyes were still red and she looked forlorn.

Outside, the Corn Exchange clock was striking six as they left, and a man in uniform emerged from the town hall, solemnly rang twelve strokes on a bell hanging above the ancient butter market, and marched away. It was the curfew which had been sounded unbrokenly in Carleton Unthank since 1087.

Chapter VII
His Worship the Mayor

"Everything all right, sir?"

Russell, the landlord asked it after every course. "Yes, thanks. All very nice."

Littlejohn and Cromwell were dining in the room marked, for some extraordinary reason, *salle à manger*. Russell was said to have worked in France at a fashionable restaurant on the Riviera, and he thought the label added tone to the hotel.

The place was almost full. It was market-day and many in the neighbourhood took it as a half-holiday. In addition to the couples dotted here and there under little shaded lamps, there was a long table at which the Carleton Law Society was holding its annual dinner, and another which held the remnants of a wedding-party. The latter had been functioning since four o'clock, the happy pair had already left for a secret destination, and the rest were noisily rejoicing.

Mr. Russell was officially keeping an eye on things, although, as usual, Bertha was doing the work. A squad of bald-headed extra waiters had been signed on and looked like a crowd of brothers; well-on in years, resembling the priests in a sacred procession. The youngest among them,

Herbert, the regular waiter of the *Arms,* was looking as black as thunder. He had been prevented from going to see his girl, for it was normally his day off, and, had he not valued his job, would have assaulted the hired *maître d'hôtel,* who kept picking on him and ordering him about.

Littlejohn and Cromwell were enjoying the doubtful privilege of being honoured with the same menu as the Law Society; turtle soup, sole Mornay, roast duck, and ice cream. Cromwell was disgusted. It was the same fare, albeit much inferior, as that served the week before at the dinner of the Scotland Yard Male Voice Choir, of which he was an enthusiastic bass member.

Littlejohn pointed out Mr. Lucas among the members of the legal party.

"No wonder he's pulling his nose," said Cromwell. "This duck tastes as if it was cooked yesterday and warmed-up."

"Everything all right?"

Mr. Russell poured out their coffee himself.

"The speeches'll be starting in a few minutes. I'd stay and listen, if I was you. Lucas is proposing the toast of the guests. That'll be good..."

Telephone, somewhere in the hall. Bertha hurried in. It was for Littlejohn.

"The mayor is asking if you would care to call and have a drink with him after dinner. He seemed quite surprised when I told him you'd almost finished. We started half an hour earlier to-night on account of the Law Society dinner. He's at home and said would you go there as soon as you liked."

"Thank you, Bertha."

"Sorry, old man. The invitation doesn't seem to include you. I won't be late and we can have a drink together before bed..."

"I don't mind, sir. I'll find the bar where the locals and farmers gather and see if there's any talk about the murders. It may lead to something. I must say it's not fair of the mayor. He doesn't seem to think you're entitled to any leisure."

It had been a busy day, starting with Herle knocking them up about Quarles's suicide and ending just before dinner with a lot of enquiries about the mysterious man from Australia who'd dropped his pen at Freake's Folly.

Herle had been surprised when Littlejohn arrived at the police station with the new clue which Marcia Fitzpayne had produced. And when the Scotland Yard man had left, he'd given his subordinates, who were supposed to have searched the Folly, a very bad-tempered ticking-off.

First, a message through Scotland Yard to the Australian police at Perth, asking them to find out from the Perth office of the Equitable Bank of Australia exactly by whom the regular payments had been made to Samuel Bracknell's account in Carlton Unthank.

Then, another request for full particulars of the sender of such remittances, if it happened to be an individual and not a firm of lawyers or bankers. Was he still in Perth? If not, had he set out for England ... and when? Then, a description of him and the reason for his trip.

Finally, a request for as much information as possible about Bracknell during his life in Australia.

"You don't mean to say that somebody's come all the way from Australia to murder Bracknell," said Herle, when it had all been attended to. "Why didn't he come earlier instead of waiting all that time? In any event, there's nobody from Australia been seen around Carleton lately."

"Perhaps you'll enquire if anybody passed through. He may have been in a car and stopped for petrol or to ask the way. The garages and the constables may know something."

And now the mayor...

"Everything all right?" asked Russell as the two detectives rose to go. He was anxious that the Law Society should notice that he had, for the present, a famous detective staying with him.

There was hardly a soul to be seen as Littlejohn crossed the square on his way to the mayor's house. It was like a zone of silence. Fear was still abroad in Carleton Unthank. In spite of the fact that news had got about that the maniac was dead, people wondered who'd be the next. Most of them stayed indoors. In the older thickly-populated parts of the town near the river, which flowed behind the Corn Exchange, some young people were abroad and shouting out of bravado, but the square was completely deserted and Littlejohn's footsteps echoed as he made his way. A policeman at the corner of the High Street looked at him closely as he passed under a lamp, and then drew himself up rigidly with a brisk salute, his hand trembling stiffly with enthusiasm.

"Good night, sir."

"Good night."

Checkland and Son's shop was closed but there were lights on in the café upstairs, where, judging from the noises coming through an open window, they were still washing-up. There was a light under the archway and another over the doors of the mayor's house. When Littlejohn rang the bell, Mr. Checkland himself appeared. He was breathing heavily as though he'd just run up and down stairs or else hurried at top speed to answer the doorbell.

"Come in, Superintendent. I'd have sent the car for you, but it's only a cock-stride away, isn't it? Come in. Hang up your hat and coat... or give them to me."

He was most affable and breathed a blast of whisky over Littlejohn as he took his hat. Through the tall window at the end of the corridor they could see the string of lights which illuminated the promenade along the riverside.

A maid, tying on her apron, emerged from her quarters at the far end of the passage.

"I'm sorry, sir. I didn't hear the bell."

"That's all right, Maudie. Has Mrs. Checkland gone to bed, yet?"

"No sir. She's in the library. It's a bit early..."

As though to confirm it, a clock in the hall struck eight.

"Let's go up, Littlejohn."

Mrs. Checkland looked more refined than ever, sitting there, a book on her lap, under a standard-lamp, which threw into relief her striking profile and the calm poise of her manner. Checkland himself looked hot and flustered at the arrival of Littlejohn. He was anxious to show-off his position and authority in the town and was doing it so thoroughly that he was sweating with the effort.

"Have you finished your work?"

"Yes, my dear. I've been at it an hour and I've had enough. I asked the Superintendent to come over for a drink and a talk."

She rose and shook hands.

"Not another murder, I hope."

Checkland didn't allow Littlejohn to reply.

"No, no," he said roughly, and then toned-down. "He's on his own and there's nothing much to do except go to the pictures after dark here. I thought he might like a change. That's all there is to it."

She said she hoped that Littlejohn would soon solve his case and then bade them both goodnight. The closing of the heavy door seemed to shut them out of the world. For a moment there was no sound but the ticking of the clock and the cheerful noise of the fire burning in the open grate.

"Draw up a chair, Superintendent. I always think there's nothing better than a real fire. They can all have their gas and electricity who like. Give me some good logs for comfort..."

He threw on a couple of large ones to emphasise it.

"Whisky, gin, beer?"

The mayor passed his large strong hand, like a celebrant blessing the wine, over a number of bottles set-out on a table.

"Whisky, please."

The library was cosy, smallish and in modern style. Light walnut panelling, ornamental ceiling, and a lustre chandelier. The name of the room justified simply by two closed bookcases with glass-panelled doors, behind which were assembled on shelves a conglomeration of books of all shapes and sizes, many of them complete editions of English novels. The rest was a glorified office, with a desk, chairs, cabinets and a table in unpolished mahogany. Here was luxury and good taste and it looked as if Mrs. Checkland had again had a hand in it.

The mayor was offering Littlejohn a cigar from a box.

"Help yourself, Superintendent. Take one or two with you. Nothing like a good cigar after a good meal. I hope you're comfortable at the *Arms*."

"Doing very nicely, thanks, Mr. Mayor. Do you mind if I smoke my pipe?"

"Certainly. Tobacco in the blue jar on the table..."

There seemed to be everything!

"Your good health, Superintendent..."

They were settled in front of the fire and Checkland cleared his throat.

"We've always been surrounded by a crowd when we've met before, Littlejohn. I thought I'd like you to come across for a quiet little chat about things. I've lived here all my life and perhaps I might be able to help you a bit about local matters..."

The smooth, ruddy face wrinkled into a smile and the small cloudy blue eyes seemed to sink in their sockets. Mr. Checkland thrust his big cigar aggressively back in his mouth and spoke round it.

"...How's the case going on? Have you any ideas, yet? Any nearer a solution?"

The mayor said it casually, too casually, and Littlejohn knew at once why he was there. He'd been 'sent-for,' politely, of course, to bring Mr. Checkland up to date. In other words, the mayor wanted his reports straight from the horse's mouth, not through the intermediary of Herle.

"We've not got very far, yet, sir. Of course, the Quarles affair has simplified matters, by accounting for two of the crimes, but, as far as Bracknell's concerned, we aren't much nearer."

"No clues?"

"Nothing."

"H'm."

It was a snort composed of half question and half surprise. As though Mr. Checkland only half believed Littlejohn. He leaned forward in his chair and spoke earnestly.

"I hope you aren't going to be long in clearing-up the affair. This series of crimes has shaken the town very badly. The place is dead now after dark. It's like it was during the war. As soon as night fell you didn't know what was in store. It's bad for trade, especially the licensed houses and the cinemas and such. I've no authority over the police and hence I wouldn't presume to order you about, but as mayor of the town, I represent the people and I do hope..."

"But surely, Mr. Mayor, confidence will return now the homicidal maniac is dead. In a day or two, the people will be about again. Bracknell's case isn't one of a series. Everybody knows that."

The mayor plunged about impatiently in his huge armchair.

"All the same, there's a murderer at large and it's got everybody on the jump."

He took a good drink from his glass and gave Littlejohn a reproachful look. The mayor, too, was afraid. He was struggling to keep calm and polite about it all, which was something new for a man accustomed to bully his subordinates.

"Did you know much about Bracknell, Mr. Checkland?"

"Not much. He came here, let me see ... four or five years ago. He'd inherited Freake's Folly. It was a ruin. He made quite a reasonable place out of part of it. Or so they tell me. I was never there. He was born in Australia, I gather, and inherited the property through his mother, who was a member of the Huncote family. The Huncotes were big county people here at one time. Now, they've left the hall and let it to the county council for an old folk's home. Major Huncote lives in the south of France. He's lord of the manor, officially, but he's a bad chest and is out of England most of the time. When he's here, he occupies the dower-house, in the grounds. He's away at present."

"Did you ever meet Bracknell, sir?"

"Of course, I did. He lunched at the *Barley Mow* two or three times a week. I go there sometimes myself. We used to pass the time of day. He also did some of his shopping at my shops. I didn't like the fellow. Most unsociable, and he had an impertinent, often sarcastic way with him. As though he looked down on most of the rest of the world because he fancied himself as local gentry. When all the time, his mother married a farm labourer. There are still Bracknells related to Samuel living in Fenny Carleton, and they're not much to speak of. He never associated with them, either."

Mr. Checkland was annoyed at the very memory of Bracknell's lack of respect for His Worship. He made a disgusted gesture, quarrelled with his cigar, and flung it in the fire.

"Have you got a list of suspects?"

What a question! The mayor must have noticed Littlejohn's surprise, and he was as surprised himself when the Superintendent pulled a used envelope from his pocket and consulted it.

"Is *that* your list?"

"No; it's just a few notes I scribbled. Here's one. Ladies' man, with a question-mark. *Was* Bracknell a petticoat-chaser, Mr. Checkland? And might his death not have been a crime of passion?"

There was nothing on the envelope but the address, but Littlejohn was determined to give Mr. Checkland his money's worth. Already the mayor was interested. He cut himself a new cigar and lit it.

"More whisky?"

He was smiling again and poured out two good helpings.

"I wouldn't be a bit surprised if that were the case. He was good-looking, well set-up, single fellow. The kind of chap who takes the eye of a certain type of woman..."

"Such as...?"

The mayor looked surprised again.

"You remember, sir, you offered to help me on the strength of your local knowledge."

"Yes, but affairs of the kind you're thinking about are usually kept in the dark, aren't they? Discreet, that's the word... Discreet..."

He repeated it to himself, quite pleased with it.

GEORGE BELLAIRS

"Do you know Marcia Fitzpayne, sir?"

The mayor's eyes narrowed, as though he half suspected Littlejohn of trying to catch him out.

"Yes, I do. She runs a riding-school just outside the town. What's she got to do with it?"

"Isn't it true that there's talk around the town about the relations of Bracknell with Miss Fitzpayne?"

The mayor removed his cigar and looked hard at the white ash. Then he took a gulp of his whisky and spoke as he swallowed it. "Listen, Littlejohn..."

And then he had to stop to assimilate the rest of his drink.

"Listen. I don't deal in gossip and scandal..."

He weighed his words pompously and paused now and then.

"Nobody can accuse me of scandalmongering. I deal in facts. It's necessary that I should do so. I'm head of the local bench and mayor of the town. I've my integrity to consider."

"It doesn't seem that this *is* gossip, sir. Bracknell's will hasn't been proved, yet, but I believe he's left all he has to Miss Fitzpayne..."

The mayor's face was a study. He was obviously annoyed that someone hadn't told him about it.

"Who told you that?"

"Mr. Lucas, the lawyer."

"He'd no right... Well, if it helps you with the case, I don't begrudge you the information. It's no business of mine. Lucas always was an indiscreet gasbag."

"It's about the only piece of substantial information we've obtained about Bracknell's affairs since we began to investigate them. That, and the fact that he had some business connections with Australia."

The mayor thumbed his broad chin.

"Yes. And it gives us a suspect. I don't know how much Bracknell was worth. I wouldn't say very much. But he owned the Folly. If the Fitzpayne girl knew about the will, she might... Well, she's not much money of her own, I can tell you that. I own the property on the right of the Corn Exchange and she's a tenant in one of the flats there. She's been behind with her rent quite a bit from time to time. She's invested all her money in her riding-school and I've no doubt borrowed for it, as well. If she'd set herself up in a flower-shop or something where her good looks would have attracted custom, she'd have done far better. Have you met her?"

"Yes. She came down to Freake's Folly when we were there looking it over."

"Taking a look at her inheritance, eh? She's quite a good-looking girl."

His face wore the same kind of mysterious, lecherous smirk as that of Lucas when Marcia Fitzpayne had been discussed. Checkland rose and re-filled the glasses. The window at the end of the room looked full across the river. The curtains had not been drawn and lights were visible along the river promenade and beyond.

"A nice outlook from your window, Your Worship."

"Yes, isn't it? I don't like to draw the curtains. It's so pleasant looking out at all the lights and the river, there, and on the extreme right, you can see the square and the Corn Exchange. We floodlight the Corn Exchange at times. It looks very fine..."

He handed Littlejohn his drink and stood over him. Then he touched him on the arm.

"I'm sorry if I've seemed a bit bad-tempered tonight. It's these damned crimes have got on my nerves. There are heavy public responsibilities on my shoulders. I've my duty to the public as mayor, you know. No hard feelings."

"Of course not, sir. I appreciate your position. It's good of you to give me so much of your time."

"I haven't been much help. You see, if we knew that Bracknell had any enemies in the town, it would be easier. But nobody knows anything about him intimately. He was a bit of a mystery."

"There is, of course, his past life, sir. Perhaps he made enemies during his spell in Australia. Could it be that some visitor from over the water called on him, quarrelled with him, and killed him? I wonder."

The mayor looked upset. His large hands began to tremble.

"You don't mean to say that there's some stranger at large in the town, a newcomer who murdered Bracknell? That complicates the issue, by jove! The man might be any-where. He might be on his way back to Australia now that he's done what he came for. It gives one quite a turn to think how easy it is for a murderer to get away. Here's a man from anywhere in Australia, calls here, kills one of our people, and then vanishes into the blue. Just like that..."

He snapped his fingers. "It makes one..."

"I only made the suggestion, sir. I didn't say we'd any reason for thinking it actually happened."

"I do hope you're not long in getting a lead, Littlejohn. As I said, it makes things bad in the community."

Littlejohn rose.

"Another glass of whisky, Superintendent? Then, I'll drive you back to the *Huncote Arms.*"

"It's very kind of you, sir, but I'd rather walk. It'll give me a breath of fresh air before bed."

"All right. It'll be no trouble, you know..."

They descended the stairs and the mayor helped Littlejohn into his coat and handed him his hat.

The clock in the hall chimed and struck ten, and halfway through the strokes the telephone bell rang in the library above.

"I'll see you to the door and then answer it, Littlejohn. They ring me up at all hours of the day and night..."

The front door closed and Littlejohn found himself in the courtyard of the buildings again. The lamps were still on over the front door and in the passage which led to the street. It was a fine night and the moon kept appearing and vanishing behind scudding clouds.

Littlejohn walked briskly with his hands in his pockets, smoking his pipe. Turning the corner into the square, he saw the light go off in the passage leading to Checkland's house. The mayor was shutting up shop for the night. Beyond the Corn Exchange the building in which Marcia Fitzpayne lived was illuminated from top to bottom and two cars stood at the front door. Perhaps there was a party on...

The windows of the *Huncote Arms* were still fully lit-up on the ground floor. Littlejohn pushed open the door. The place was quiet. All the parties ended, all the guests apparently in bed.

Russell was in the office and rushed out as soon as he saw Littlejohn. He was half drunk.

"We've been trying to get you, Super. I just rang up the mayor's where they said you'd gone, but Mr. Checkland said you were on your way back, so I said I'd let you know when you got here. I didn't tell the mayor. It didn't seem right till I'd told you..."

Russell's breath smelled of brandy and he'd a job to sort out the words as they came to his tongue.

"What is it, Mr. Russell...?"

But before Russel could reply, the answer came from the void. A journalist staying at the hotel was apparently in trouble with the other end and raised his voice in the phone box until it rang round the hall.

"Death and Fear are abroad again to-night in the little town of Carleton Unthank... Have you got that?... Right... *The mysterious murderer has struck again. This time it is the beautiful young horsewoman, Marcia Fitzpayne*... No, no... Not Dispain... Fitz... F-I-T-Z ..."

Chapter VIII

A Stranger in the Town

"If she hadn't happened to leave the milk on the stove in the kitchen and it boiled over and smelled the place out, we might not have found her for days..."

The little, short-sighted man who looked after the flats and lived with his wife in an attic at the top, repeated his tale to every newcomer.

Cromwell had arrived on the scene at ten o'clock.

"We've been hunting all over the place for you and the Superintendent..."

Herle was there already and greeted Cromwell with reproachful discourtesy. He seemed to think that the two Scotland Yard men should be at the stand-to and ready for any emergency, day or night.

"You didn't look very far. I was in the public bar all night, after Superintendent Littlejohn left to see the mayor. That would be around eight o'clock."

"I sent across as soon as the crime was reported, and Russell said you'd both gone out and he didn't know where."

"If Russell hadn't put his head in the bar at just before ten, I'd still have been there. He seemed surprised to see me. I've left a message asking the Superintendent to come across as soon as he turns in. He'd just left the mayor's when we telephoned."

"Well, this is a pretty kettle of fish. Another murder now."

"If she hadn't happened to leave the milk on the stove ..."

The caretaker was busy telling it all to a reporter who had just arrived.

Herle didn't look at his best. He seemed to be starting with a cold and sneezed now and then. Every time he sneezed, he squinted horribly.

"The crime must have occurred about eight o'clock. The doctor says between seven and eight, he'd put it. But this boiling milk episode Chettle, the caretaker, keeps talking about, puts the time near eight. She must have been getting ready to make some coffee and had put the milk in a pan over a low light on the electric stove. It boiled over and began to stink the place out. Chettle came down, couldn't get any answer, so let himself in with his pass-key ..."

"If I hadn't, it might have been days before we found 'er."

"I was at the office and Chettle rang up right away. That would be just about eight-fifteen. So there wasn't much time wasted. We couldn't get in touch with you."

He sneezed again. "I've got a cold. It's through messing about at Turville's so long ..."

Herle spoke monotonously, like someone in a daze. He seemed more anxious to get his grievances off his chest than to show Cromwell the body.

It was then that Littlejohn entered and he had to be told the story all over again.

"Come in. We've been trying to get you for hours ..."

Herle's eyes were glassy and his nose was red.

"I've told them not to touch anything until you arrived."

Chettle told him about the milk.

"We've had to move the body, of course. The doctor's been and gone, and our men took photographs, which you can see as soon as they're developed."

They had marked the carpet in chalk where the body had been found, half way across the hearthrug.

"She'd been stabbed with her own bread-knife."

The body was laid in one corner under a sheet to await the ambulance. Littlejohn gently raised the cover and looked at the still face. There was no trace of horror on it. The eyes were closed and the colour had remained. Marcia Fitzpayne might have been asleep.

"The wound?"

"Through the heart from the back. Whoever did it must have come upon her from behind, the surgeon says. She was dead before she knew what was happening. A dirty business and I'd have said if the maniac hadn't been dead already, it was another of his crimes. It looks very much as if we've another homicidal lunatic at large among us..."

Herle blew his nose noisily. It gave you the impression that he was weeping about it all.

"You've questioned the other tenants?"

"Yes. They were both in. A doctor on the ground floor, who was busy writing; and a colonel in the room below this, who was looking at the television programme, which was a noisy one, according to what the doctor says. He could hear it in the flat below. So, you see, nobody heard anything."

"And the caretaker?"

Chettle answered for himself.

"I saw nobody. Missus an' me was lookin' in at the telly. It was the milk boilin' over...Awful. I thought the place was on fire. Soon as I opened the door, I saw 'er. Lyin' half on the rug there, flat on 'er face. Knife stickin' out of 'er back. I didn't touch anythin'. I shouts up to the missus and tells 'er to 'phone for the police and I stayed 'ere to see that it wasn't disturbed. I done right, didn't I?"

"Quite right, Mr. Chettle."

"Where is Mrs. Chettle?"

"She's up in our flat. She went up to get a cup o' tea, It give 'er quite a turn. Shall I shout up for 'er?"

"No. I'll just take a turn round the place and call and see her on the way."

The ambulance had drawn up outside and a small crowd had gathered round the main door. They could hear voices, the opening of the ambulance, and then heavy footsteps manoeuvring a stretcher up the stairs.

Littlejohn strolled round the flat, opening the inner doors, turning over the books and magazines scattered about. One door led into a kitchenette. It was tidy, with a small table with a red plastic top, a little refrigerator, a stainless steel sink, and the electric stove which was the centre of Chettle's dramatic monologue. The top was still swimming in burnt milk. On the table, the cup and coffee-pot with which Marcia had presumably been concerned when the murderer disturbed her. Another room; this time the bedroom. The usual furniture, rather in miniature, to fit in. A door led into a bathroom, if such it could be called. There was no bath. Just a shower in a surround of primrose-coloured tiles, a washbowl and a pedestal. There wasn't room to whip a cat round in the place.

"They've moved the body now…"

Herle was anxious to hear what Littlejohn thought of it all. He trailed about after the Superintendent like an apprentice picking up tips of technique.

There seemed much more room now the body had gone. Littlejohn noticed the meal half ready on the little table in the living-room. A half loaf, a bread board, a plate with some cheese on it...

"Mrs. Chettle recognised the knife. It was Marcia Fitzpayne's own bread-knife. It's here ..."

He had kept it back for Littlejohn to see. A long, bright, steel blade and a wooden handle. The kind you can buy any day for bread or carving fowl. There was coagulated blood on the blade.

"No fingerprints. There never are in this case."

"You'll be going through her papers?"

"We've already done it. Roughly, of course. So far, there's not a thing of interest. They're all in the top drawer of the sideboard if you want to examine them yourself."

"I won't bother just now, thanks."

Littlejohn strolled on the landing. There were no other flats on it. At the end, facing the staircase, another door. It was fastened by a spring lock.

"Fire escape," explained Chettle, who was following him.

"It's always locked?"

"Yes. It was locked when this happened. In case of need, it can be opened from the inside by the spring lock. I showed it to the police and they tried it. They searched round for fingerprints and took photos."

He opened the door. Outside, a wooden staircase led downwards into the blackness of a yard or entry below. In the distance, the string of lamps on the river waterfront were still alight.

"And that's the way up to your flat?"

It was another narrow staircase to a couple of attics with a landing outside. Light streamed from one of the open doorways. Littlejohn climbed up. The room was clean and threadbare and a small fire burned in an old iron grate. The walls were covered with old fashioned imitation marble wallpaper, once cream and now beige from age. A woman dressed in a sombre frock and with bedraggled grey hair was sitting at a table illuminated by a cheap lamp, drinking from a cup and blowing on its contents to cool them. Littlejohn stood for a moment looking at her. She raised her eyes and met his, all the time calmly drinking. The rest of the room was in the shade. Quietness, a kind of syrupy silence, filled the place as the woman enjoyed her drink.

At first, Littlejohn thought he had met her before, but then he realised that she was of the usual type which repeats itself so often among charwomen, caretakers and modest seamstresses. Small, thin, undernourished, doing her best to be cheerful and bear-up under life's shabby treatment. Like many of her kind, too, she wore a frock too large for her and outsize shoes. Someone else's cast-offs in all probability.

"Mrs. Chettle?"

"Yes. Am I wanted again? I'm not feeling so well after all this. It's turned me up proper. It's time all this killin' was stopped. You don't know who's goin' to be the next."

She took another swig of tea. Of uncertain age, perhaps between sixty and seventy. You never know with her type. She was dried-up and her thin grey hair showed the scalp almost bald in parts.

"I'm from the police. I don't want to upset you, but you can perhaps help us."

"Yes, you're the London man, aren't you? I see your picture in the paper this mornin'. And now there's been two more murders. Quarles and Miss Fitzpayne ... Nice, was Miss Fitzpayne, although there were some didn't think so. I'm broad-minded myself and take people as I find 'em. She was always good to me."

Littlejohn sat astride the other chair at the table.

"How long have you been looking after these flats, Mrs. Chettle?"

"Two years last December, when they was ready and first let."

"Miss Fitzpayne lived here ever since they were made?"

"Yes."

Mrs. Chettle got up, poured out a second cup of tea, and handed it to Littlejohn. It was hot and almost black.

"If you're anything like me, you'll need a cup. I don't mind a burglary. We've had two in the flats since we came here. But when it comes to murder, I draw the line. Sugar?"

She scooped two large spoonfuls in Littlejohn's cup.

"You do the cleaning of the flats?"

"Yes. The two lower ones I do every day. Nice gentlemen, they are, too. Miss Fitzpayne's is a little 'un compared with theirs. I did for 'er two mornings a week."

"Your husband helps you?"

"He hasn't worked for years. His back's bad. Now and then, when he's better side out, he might do an odd job or two about the place. But it's nice to have him around..."

There was no irony in her voice. She included Chettle and his bad back in her philosophy of life and was content merely with his protection, for what it was worth.

"You were in when my colleague and I called late in the afternoon?"

"Yes. I was havin' a cup of tea when I heard you. She didn't want to let you in at first, did she? She's been a bit under the weather of late. I don't blame 'er. Her boy-friend, if you can call 'im such at his age, was murdered the other week. Wonder if it's the same one as has done for 'er, too."

She brooded over it cheerfully as though she'd come upon a profound truth.

"Bracknell, you mean?"

"Yes. He used to come to see 'er two or three times a week. I think they was carryin'-on, but it was no business of mine. I've enough keepin' the place clean, without inter- ferin' with the morals of the tenants."

She said it all without indignation or resentment.

"Any other callers?"

"Now and then. Travellers and the like. Oh, I know what you mean. No. Nothin' o' that sort. Not that I see anyhow. I'd say she was true to poor Mr. Bracknell. Why they didn't get married was beyond me. Silly keepin' two places goin' when they could have lived together for the price of one, you might say."

"You went downstairs to the flat when your husband found the body. Did you notice anything peculiar?"

"Such as ... ?"

"Anything unusual, disturbed, out of its place?"

"No. The milk was burnin'. I went in the kitchen and moved it off the 'ot-plate of the stove, while me 'usband was seein' if she was alive. I could 'ave told him she wasn't with- out even touchin' 'er."

"You didn't hear anyone about below just before the crime was committed?"

"No. We was sittin' listenin' to the telly..."

She pointed to a small set in one corner of the little room.

"We 'ire it and if you haven't got one yet, I can recom- mend you to 'ire one."

"Thanks. I'll bear it in mind. Let us get this in order. You were watching the telly when you smelled the burning milk. Your husband went down to investigate, entered Miss Fitzpayne's flat with his pass-key, found her dead, and called for you..."

"That's right. I went down, saw to the milk, we tele- phoned the police, and then we jest waited."

"You didn't send for the neighbours?"

"What good would that do? She was dead. They couldn't bring 'er back to life again, even if one of 'em is a doctor, could they? The doctor's a specialist on people as has gone off their heads. Much good he'd 'ave been. No, we jest waited."

"You touched nothing?"

"I'm sure we didn't. Only the pan on the stove and me 'usband felt Miss Fitzpayne's pulse to see if she was dead. Not that 'e knew where 'er pulse was, but he was always one for bein' a bit clever. He'd read somethin' about pulses in the paper. She's dead, I sez to 'im, pulse or no pulse. You can see she is, I says. And she was."

"I suppose you tidied the drawers in the rooms when you cleaned up...?"

"Yes."

For the first time she gave him a suspicious look. His tact in testing her inquisitiveness was wasted.

"You knew what was in all the drawers?"

"Yes. After tidyin' 'em for nearly three years. I'm not a busy interferin' sort, but you can't 'elp noticin' ..."

"Any letters?"

"No. She never seemed to get much in the way of letters. A bill or two in connection with 'er horses, circulars and leaflets, electricity accounts. She'd some nice clothes, too. Always kept 'erself well dressed and neat. Liked the best of everythin'. Not many, but good, includin' underwear. All of the best."

Mrs. Chettle fascinated Littlejohn. Downstairs, he could hear them coming and going. Chettle had gone out for a drink with a reporter who said he had a bottle in his hotel bedroom. Herle was pacing up and down, sneezing and blowing his nose, impatiently waiting for Littlejohn.

Cromwell, whose footsteps were recognisable on the stairs, was presumably calling on the two other tenants, for the colonel on the first floor, evidently an elderly man who spoke with a plum in his mouth, was politely inviting him in. The Superintendent felt that his interview with Mrs. Chettle would be of much more use.

"Have you any idea who might have killed Miss Fitzpayne?"

"I haven't. I'd have told you before if I 'ad. Drink up your tea and I'll pour you some more."

She swung her legs, which didn't touch the floor, from her chair, poured more boiling water on the tea in the pot, and then gave him another black brew.

"Had she any relatives?"

"Not that I'd know. Her mother died about two years since. Then Miss Fitzpayne moved in here. That's all I ever heard of."

"Her rent? Did she pay you or your husband?"

"No. Greenways, the agents, look after the flats, pay me and me 'usband, and collect the rents for Mr. Checkland, who owns the flats."

"Does Mr. Checkland ever come round here?"

"Not been since they was tenanted. Leaves it all to the agents."

"She paid her rent regularly?"

"Yes, I believe so. They all do. If they didn't we'd soon be hearin' from Greenways. They're a hard lot."

"Try to throw your mind back over the past week or two, Mrs. Chettle. Did anyone out of the ordinary call?"

She sat silent, sipping and blowing on her tea, showing no signs of mental exertion or concentration.

"Yes," she said at last. "The man from Australier..."

"Who was he?"

"He called after Mr. Bracknell. It was this way, you see. He'd been down to Freake's Folly and found Mr. Bracknell out. He said he'd passed somebody on the lane, Dan's Lane that 'ud be, who said he should try 'ere. He was offen here when not at home. Which was jest a bit o' spite, if you ask me. You'd think he never went out of Freake's except to come 'ere. Which wasn't true. You're not drinkin' your tea..."

Littlejohn hastily drained his cup and had it filled again.

"Did he give any name?"

"No. 'e was very chary, like, and in a hurry. He kept lookin' down the stairs, too, as if he didn't want to be seen. He'd come in a car. I looked out of the landin' winder when he'd gone and saw him drive off. I told 'im there was neither of 'em in and he might find Mr. Bracknell in the town, perhaps shoppin', if he cared to look around. But he never. He went off in the direction of Freake's again, as though intendin' to wait till Mr. Bracknell got back."

"You said he was Australian ... Did he tell you?"

"No. But he spoke like one. Or that's what Chettle sez to me after he'd gone. Chettle was sittin' up here with the door open all the time."

"Had Mr. Chettle been in Australia, then?"

"No, but 'e was with the Anzacs in the first war. In the Middle East, he was, alongside 'em. He knew a lot of 'em. That's where he got his back. In the Middle East in the war."

By the tone of her voice, it might have been the V.C.

"And he recognised his voice?"

"When I got back 'ere, I sez to Chettle, 'He sounded like a Cockney, or somethin'.' 'Get away, missus,' sez Chettle. 'Cockney, me foot! He's Australian.' An' Chettle ought to know, oughtn't he?"

"What kind of a fellow was he?"

"Between fifty and sixty... Not quite as tall as you, sir. Nor as broad. Grey 'air. Blue eyes, because I noticed they was the colour of the tie 'e was wearin'."

"Excellent. You're quite a good witness, Mrs. Chettle. Anything else?"

She was enjoying herself now. She put her elbows on the table and her chin in her hands and smiled a tired smile.

"Grey suit... sort o' flannel..."

"His face? Did he wear glasses?"

"No. Let me see... Wait a minute..."

She closed her eyes and began to talk.

"His nose looked as if it had been broke. It was jest a bit on one side. Plenty of hair; not bald at all. Thickish lips and a square chin with a thing like a dimple in the middle. Heavy dark eyebrows, which made 'is eyes look bluer. That's all..." She opened her eyes again and looked dreamy until she shook herself and had a good drink of tea.

Littlejohn had taken it all down on the back of an old envelope.

"Excellent! That's a great help, Mrs. Chettle."

But she hadn't finished.

"A funny ear. You know the sort boxers an' wrestlers get through havin' 'em twisted or hit..."

"A cauliflower ear! Which side?"

"Let me see. Left... Left, that's it."

Littlejohn put his pen and paper away.

"And now, Mrs. Chettle, will you kindly tell me how you come to give me such a good description? It's almost photographic."

She hesitated.

"It's no business of yours... But as you've treated me like a proper gentleman, I'll tell you, if you won't say anything to anybody else. It's all over an' done with and I've been punished for me sins..."

By the way she looked at him, he knew.

"You've been in prison?"

There was no shame or fear in her face and she gave him a straight look. He couldn't imagine what she was thinking. Her tired face was perfectly tranquil.

"Yes. I was took for fortune-tellin'. When I was a young girl me father found out I'd got what he used ter call *the faculty*. I was mediumistic, you see. We went on the halls in a show where he asked me questions and I answered them. Questions from the audience. You know the kind of thing, sir. We were called Mademoiselle Lemont and Partner. My father used to make me work all the hours God sent, practi- cin', memorisin', learnin' the tricks and clues he'd give me for the answers. One thing he made me learn was memori- sin' faces..."

"What part of the show did that come in?"

"Before my act started, I'd look in the audience from behind the curtain and memorise faces. Then, when the turn came on, I'd be able to say—I was blindfolded, remem- ber—'the man on the tenth row with a broken nose, grey hair, a cauliflower ear, a blue tie, a dark suit...' And he'd know who I meant. I'd then tell 'im that he was goin' to win at the races... or somethin' such. It pleased people and, likely as not, if they didn't win, they'd never see us on the stage again or else be sporty and admit they'd been had for a mug. They hadn't paid me anything, so couldn't complain. After father died, I set up fortune-tellin'. That was where the police got me. I'm a bit out of practice now, not havin' done anything at it since I came out after two months gaol. You'd better not tell Chettle, though. He knows nothin' about that part in my past. It'll give him money-makin' ideas and I'll get no peace till I start again."

Littlejohn thanked her and said it was time for him to go.

"You've been a great help, Mrs. Chettle."

He put a pound note on the table.

"You shouldn't have bothered, sir. It's been a pleasure to 'elp you. I hope somethin' comes of it."

The money vanished by a feat of prestidigitation. Chettle would never hear of it.

Below, he could hear the door of the bottom flat close after Cromwell had thanked the doctor. Chettle and the reporter were returning. Chettle was talkative and stumbled as he climbed the stairs.

"To think that all this commotion was started by the milk boilin' over. If I hadn't smelled it, you might not have found her yet..."

Herle was waiting. He'd been through all the drawers again.

"Not a thing. Not a clue. It's another mystery."

Littlejohn gave him the minute description of the Australian visitor who'd impressed Mrs. Chettle.

"Please have this circulated at once to all police stations, ask them to detain a man answering to the details and, if possible, bring him here for questioning. It's urgent and vital."

"But where did you get this, sir? It's so detailed that the man might have given us a photograph, or else been on the spot as you wrote down the particulars."

"Mrs. Chettle described him."

Herle's face was a study.

"It's incredible. I'll bet she's bluffing us."

"All the same, I wouldn't risk it. That mental picture tallies with the man who might have followed Bracknell from

Australia, perhaps the one who's been blackmailed and come over here to put an end to it, once and for all. The man who left his pen on the floor of Freake's Folly."

Outside, the town was quiet. The clouds had gathered, the moon had gone, and it had started to rain. Puddles of water reflected the street lamps and here and there a belated car slid past, lit up a stretch of shining asphalt, and then vanished, as though in a hurry to get away from the town where murder couldn't be stopped.

Littlejohn and Cromwell turned up the collars of their coats and crossed to their hotel. They were both wondering whether or not the stranger was sleeping somewhere nearby, or skulking not far from his latest crime, or else hurling hither and thither in his hired car, trying to evade the men who were hunting him down.

CHAPTER IX
THE MAN WITH ALL THE
ANSWERS

"What's this, Herbert?"

Littlejohn and Cromwell were sitting down to breakfast in the *'salle à manger'* of the hotel.

Saturday morning. It was the beginning of one of those rare, fine autumn days which remind you of the past summer and revive the holiday feeling all too briefly. The sun was shining and the sky, swept clean by a light wind of the clouds of the night before, looked to have been shampooed. One after another, private motor-coaches and the road-cars of the transport company filled-up with crowds off to Northampton, where Carleton Athletic were playing away. Men wearing scarves and rosettes blazing with the colours of the local team scampered noisily about the square, waving rattles, and one of them was wearing a striped bowler hat and was ringing a bell under a striped umbrella.

Along the front of the Corn Exchange the stalls for the weekly open market had been erected. The stallholders were shouting their wares—vegetables, fruit, cheese, eggs, and a conglomeration of eatables and lengths of cloth of all kinds. Women were jostling for bargains. The scent of fruit, vegetables and cheese filled the air and even entered the hotel.

On Littlejohn's plate was a visiting-card.

Cuthbert
Blower,
Mus.Bac.,
F.R.C.O.
Church of St.
Peter,
Carleton
Unthank.

Herbert paused in his languid labours. He wore a white coat a size too big for him. He had not yet fully mastered the delicate art of balancing a tray of crockery and food. He slowly lowered his burden on a convenient table, as though to speak with it held aloft would precipitate its contents all over the place. Then, he reverently bent his head over Littlejohn, who caught a scented whiff of cheap brilliantine mixed with the stale cigarette smoke on Herbert's breath.

"Mr. Blower was 'ere at h'eight-thirty, sir," he said in what he thought was an educated voice. The aged head-waiter of the *Huncote Arms* was training him in the profession and Herbert was determined to get on. "He h'asked me to give you that card, sir. There's a message wrote on the back..."

I have something urgent to communicate. Could you see me at the church at 10.00 *a.m. today?—C.B.*

The writing was so small and spidery that Littlejohn needed his glasses to make it out.

The Church of St. Peter was almost as large as a cathedral and the upper-ten of Carleton Unthank lived in a close which surrounded it. The incumbent was a suffragan bishop and the organist a man distinguished in execution and composition. When Littlejohn and Cromwell arrived at the church, he was playing *Blower in B.*

The notes of the full organ surged and bounced around the vast building, out of the door, and into the main street like a river in flood. As you entered the church, it was like swimming against a mighty tide of Blower. It was exactly ten by the great clock, the chimes of which were swamped by the organ. Mr. Blower was obviously 'playing-in' the detectives to keep their appointment.

Littlejohn, bewildered by the weight of the diapasons, looked round the church for the keyboard. The organ pipes were set all over the place and the notes came like shots fired from an ambush. There was no sign of the manipulator of this mighty machine. But, Littlejohn grew aware that he was being watched by a single eye reflected in a mirror to the right of the chancel. This solitary unblinking stare was fixed upon him, like that all-seeing eye of God which heads the membership certificates of certain secret societies. The Superintendent nodded at it convivially. The organ ceased and the music seemed to roar out of the building into the street, leaving an almost unbearable silence behind. Mr. Blower appeared.

He was a small, frail man, which made his mastery of the tremendous instrument all the more surprising. His head was almost completely bald except for a fringe of pepper-coloured hair, he wore lozenge-shaped spectacles in gold frames in front of his peering eyes, and his face was shrivelled like a walnut. He was bad on his feet as he walked, presumably from over-much trampling of the organ pedals. Before he could speak to the newcomers, a huge woman, like a featherbed, rose from the choir, seized him like a child taking up a favourite doll, and kissed him.

"Splendid, my love ..."

And turning to Cromwell, whom she seemed to claim as a kindred and sympathetic spirit, she informed him that he had just heard the first performance of another new Blower.

The organist obviously enjoyed the embrace and the congratulations. Later, the two detectives were informed that Mrs. Blower, née Huncote-Smythe, had claimed Cuthbert for her own from early days, much against the wishes of her family. It had been a *cause célèbre* and a *grande passion*, although to see them together, you would never have believed it.

"Come home as soon as you have transacted your business, my love. And don't forget to put on your muffler. It's cold outside."

With that parting shot, she left them together, released a large boxer dog, which had been tied-up in the north porch and was still howling at *Blower in B*, and crossed the close to toast the muffins.

"Thank you for calling, Superintendent."

A most kindly, quiet and cultured voice, almost apologetic.

"I asked you to be good enough to meet me here because I am not on speaking terms with the local police. Last winter when I gave my services at a charity concert and parked my car outside the Public Hall, Herle and his far-from-merry men had me fined two pounds for being on the wrong side. After that, I washed my hands of them."

He washed his hands in thin air to show how he did it and then drew mysteriously near to Littlejohn and whispered to him.

"Come this way, sir ..."

He led them a flat-footed way to a spiral staircase behind the keyboards, climbed it nimbly, and they followed.

It ended in a loft which, before electric power had been added to the instrument, had been the eyrie of the man who manipulated the bellows. The long pump-handle projected still, in case of emergencies, which were frequent in winter. At times the power consumed by the chilly people of the district attenuated that of the organ to a degree which made manual help necessary to cope with the might of Mr. Blower's compositions.

The organist switched on a light, revealing a dusty room, with a floor of bare boards. Two tumbledown chairs and a large outcast pew were all the furnishings. Mr. Blower pointed to the floor, which was littered with crumbs and a crust of bread.

"Mice?" said Cromwell.

"Certainly not! I don't allow mice about my organ."

He then indicated the old pew, across the seat of which was stretched a long, ecclesiastical-looking red cushion headed by two old hassocks.

"Last night, there was an intruder in the church. He ate and slept here, gentlemen."

Mr. Blower said it with a convulsive dramatic gesture and stood with his head on one side awaiting what Littlejohn had to say.

"It certainly looks like an improvised bed, sir. But are you sure it was used last night, and by an intruder?"

"Of course, I am. I was in this loft late last night. There was nobody here then. Nor was there a hassock and a long cushion. Nor any bread-crumbs. Someone must have hidden in church until the verger locked-up. He closed the place as I left. I had been busy on my new *Blower in B.*"

"Is this a place where anybody accidentally locked-in might sleep?"

"Yes. It is more comfortable here than anywhere else. It is warm, because there are no draughts, as in the nave or vestries."

"It also has the advantage of being quiet. I suppose anybody sleeping in the anterooms or body of the church on the ground floor might be easily discovered by someone entering and finding him asleep the morning after."

"Yes. This place is out of the way. Furthermore, hidden here you could hear the ascending footsteps of whoever climbed the spiral staircase, which, as you will have observed, is made of metal, and rings under the feet."

"And why did you send for us, sir? I'm here on the murder investigation, you know."

Mr. Blower nodded vigorously.

"That's why. I heard of last night's murder. I could not conceive the murderer calling at a local hotel or at any nearby town or village and asking for a bed for the night. He'd either to flee far away, or sleep where he could, in hiding. So, he chose the church."

"The murder was committed around eight o'clock, sir."

"I was here until almost eleven, trying out my new composition, which I shall play tomorrow at evening service."

Littlejohn was quite aware that under the noise of *Blower in B* a herd of cattle could have entered the church and gone out again without being heard!

Mr. Blower started to titter.

"Excuse me, Superintendent. I was just struck by a strange thought. Suppose the murderer takes up successive lodgings night after night in all the town churches. There are fourteen of them, including the Catholic one and the Pentecostal Wrestlers. The Wrestlers have only a harmonium, but the rest have organs and organ-lofts. I've played on them all and some of them are diabolical. It amused me to think of Herle having to post a constable on duty at every organ. If by any chance the policeman were a musical one, he could at least amuse himself on the keyboard..."

"I'd better report this, sir. There may be useful finger-prints left around."

"What you do is your own business, Superintendent. I certainly will have nothing to do with Herle. You can take it that nothing here has been touched or moved. I realised that you would wish it that way the moment I found there had been intruders."

"It may have been quite a harmless person..."

"Come, come, Superintendent. I'm surprised at you. An innocent man wouldn't have sought out such a dusty secret spot as this. He'd have slept in the vestry or the choir chang-ing-room. Our intruder wanted to hide and also wished to be comfortable. He hauled up the hassocks and the long cushion from the choir."

"And nobody saw any trespasser enter or leave?"

"I really couldn't say, Superintendent. Perhaps if Herle's bobbies ask all round the close, someone may be able to help them. Have you any idea whom you are seeking? Have you a description of the murderer?"

"Yes, a rough one."

"Very good, then. I suggest you start at once. The man might have been seen in the precincts late last evening."

"It was dark, sir."

"All the same, it's worth trying, I would think. Will that be all?"

"I think so, sir. I'm very much obliged to you for notify-ing us. May we lock this loft until the local police arrive."

"Yes. I have the key. And now, I must be off. My wife will be wondering where I am. She'll think I have perhaps been assassinated, too."

Herle was furious when Littlejohn called to tell him about the matter at St. Peter's.

"The little squirt!"

But the police hunted all day for clues and fingerprints and found nothing. Herle didn't take Blower's joke about keeping vigils in all the churches kindly, either.

"We'll search them all by day and have them locked up at night. The old fool's lost his wits. I never did like Blower. He thinks too much of himself. Him and his bloomin' organ."

"All the same, it is obvious there's a stranger in Carleton, someone connected with the death of Marcia Fitzpayne. We have a rough description of him and we know, according to Mrs. Chettle, that he is likely to be an Australian. I take it your men are combing the town for him, Herle?"

Herle smiled with satisfaction.

"They've been out and about at all the hotels and likely places all night. The answer is a lemon. A complete blank. So far, nobody seems to have seen him."

"Precisely. He spent the night in St. Peter's Church. We said he might have arrived here in a hired car. Has any such car been picked up yet?"

"Our men are on it. The garages weren't open all night. If he left it at any of those in town or round about, it should have been reported by now. He may have come by train."

"If he's trying to get about unseen, he's probably travelling by road..."

Telephone. Herle snatched up the instrument impatiently.

"Yes?"

A farmer on the outskirts of the town had found an abandoned car in a spinney on his land adjoining the main road. He described it and the licence on the windscreen. Obviously a hired one from London.

"If he's ditched the car, he's probably still in town, sir. And if he's in town, my men will get him. They're combing the place."

Littlejohn stood silently puffing his pipe.

"If you'd abandoned a car, Herle, and knew the stations and all the town were being watched, what would you do?"

"I don't know... I'd either disguise myself or get among a crowd if I wanted to get away."

"Exactly. You might even muffle yourself in a scarf of the colours of the local football team, mix among the followers of Carleton Athletic, go to Northampton, and sneak away from there."

"By Gad! That might be it."

Herle shouted for Drayton, his factotum, loud enough to be heard for miles. Drayton appeared at his usual pace.

"What time did the main rush of football fans go to Northampton, Drayton?"

"Kick-off's at two. Some went first-thing for a day out. They'd go on the ten o'clock. There were specials, for football crowds only, at eleven and eleven thirty. Those are road company buses. There's some charabancs, too. Private, like. Book in advance. They've been gone a good half-hour."

"It takes roughly an hour to Northampton, doesn't it?"

"That's right. Ten minutes short of an hour..."

Drayton recited his piece in a dull monotonous voice, scrupulously correct, standing at attention.

"Get me Northampton police on the phone then, and look slippy."

Drayton ponderously left the room and could be heard reciting instructions to someone in charge of the switchboard.

In five minutes Northampton had been asked to keep an eye on all vehicles arriving at their bus stations and to detain any stranger answering to the description of the man detailed by Mrs. Chettle.

"What a hope! Like looking for a needle in a haystack! He might have got away on the buses which have already reached Northampton, he might not have gone that way at all, he might have got off half-way there ... He might be anywhere now."

But Herle was wrong. The net had been cast by the Carleton and the Northampton police over the whole countryside between the two towns. A man wearing a Carleton Athletic scarf had left a 'bus at Brixworth, saying he wasn't feeling well and had decided not to go on to Northampton. A policeman at Brixworth had seen him get off the bus half an hour before the call went out. Some good local staff work had resulted in Brixworth police finding the man quietly sitting on the station waiting for a connection to London. A police car was bringing him to Carleton Unthank and would be there very soon.

Two policemen from Brixworth were not long in arriving with the man from Australia. The spokesman of the two reported that their captive had seemed to relish being brought back to Carleton.

"We didn't need to handcuff him ..."

Littlejohn laughed.

"A good job you didn't. We've nothing to charge him with yet, except leaving someone else's car dumped in a wood."

"But I thought it was murder ..."

"We're in no position to charge him with anything yet. He's just an important witness. Bring him in, please."

The newcomer was calm, even smiling, as though glad to meet the police.

"Who is in charge?" he asked, looking round at the three officers and the group of constables.

Herle shrugged his shoulders. He felt he could very well have managed the affair himself, but Littlejohn was his superior.

"Superintendent Littlejohn."

"Thank you. I was surprised when the police arrested me..."

Herle was furious.

"You've not been arrested yet. You've been brought back here for questioning. If you wish a charge to be made, you may have one. Being on enclosed premises..."

"You mean St. Peter's Church...?"

The man was unperturbed. He laughed outright.

"The church was open. I took a look round, and fell asleep in the quietness of the organ loft..."

"After eating your supper and making yourself a comfortable bed with the church cushions?"

The man tallied with Mrs. Chettle's description. He spoke with an Australian accent and was tall and well-built. He still wore his blue tie, which matched his eyes, and there was the cauliflower left ear, the good head of grey hair, and the bushy eyebrows. His well-cut grey suit bore the traces of his night out.

"Your name?"

"Walter Upshott."

"You are Australian?"

"By adoption. I emigrated there years ago."

"Where did you live in Australia, Mr. Upshott?"

"Perth."

The man was still smiling. He answered Littlejohn's questions without hesitation.

"Were you born in England?"

"Yes. In Carleton Unthank..."

If he'd said he was born on the moon, it couldn't have startled them more, and Upshott enjoyed the sensation he'd created.

Littlejohn nodded. A gentle trickle of smoke rose from his pipe. "When did you emigrate to Australia?"

"Eighteen years ago. I lost my job, so I thought I'd try my luck abroad."

"And you've done well?"

"Not bad. I'm a farmer."

"And what made you return here? Homesickness?"

Upshott grinned again, baring his clean strong teeth. Now and then, Littlejohn came across men in a case who understood him thoroughly, never missed a humorous or ironical quip, never misunderstood the implications of a question. Upshott was one of them.

"Call it that if you like, Superintendent. Let's say I wanted to see the old places. I'd earned a holiday, I took it, spent a few days in London, and then came here to see if it had changed much."

"So you passed the nights exploring it in the darkness, and disappeared during the daytime?"

"Not particularly. I took a quick look around and then decided I'd had enough ..."

"Instead of finding an hotel and sleeping there, you went to St. Peter's instead."

"I was locked in. I went there after dark. It was lit up. I had a look round, listened to a man playing the organ, and when it came time to go, I found I couldn't get out. I didn't want to break out and damage the place. It has some happy memories for me. So I made myself comfortable in the organ loft. It was the cosiest spot. I've been used to rough-ing it out in Australia. It was like the Ritz up there when I think of some of the places I've slept in."

Although he was still smiling, there was something intense, serious, watchful in the look he gave Littlejohn now and then. He was full of self-confidence and replied to the questions amiably and politely.

"Why did you abandon your hired car and try to make a break in a football coach?"

"I didn't. I just wanted to see the Northampton match. I used to follow the local team when I was a boy. If you wonder why I got off the bus, I was faint. I hadn't had a proper meal after my night in the church. That's all."

"You were found sitting on Brixworth station after enquiring for the London train."

"It was quiet. I bought some sandwiches and went there to eat them. I asked a porter if trains for London went from Brixworth. I was being matey. I didn't buy a ticket."

He'd an answer for everything. And the way he said it was persuasive and prompt. He seemed to wonder what all the fuss was about.

"Do you know many people in Carleton? Any of your old friends left?"

"One or two. I've seen a few familiar faces about. I didn't speak to any of them."

"Why? I'd have thought a re-union would have pleased you after coming all that way."

"We've all changed. It's nice to see the old places, such as are left. But when you seek out old acquaintances after so long, it's unpleasant. You find those life hasn't treated well eyeing you up and down almost jealously and showing all the signs of defeat and disillusionment. Those who've got on look you up and down just the same, sizing you up and comparing your progress with theirs, and looking self-satisfied with themselves, with all the bloom of their young days worn thin through self-satisfaction and greed. It's not worth doing it. It leaves you sad and upset."

"So you kept out of their way. Did you know the mayor of Carleton?"

"Who's he?"

"Mr. Checkland."

"Ben Checkland? Sure I do. We went to the same school. Carleton Grammar. So Ben's mayor, is he?"

"Yes. I think you might like to meet him. It's a wonder he isn't here if he's heard we've made some progress in the murder case ..."

The smile vanished and the face grew serious.

"What's that? Murder case? Look here, Superintendent, I don't mind suffering all this rigmarole for sleeping in a church or behaving a bit queerly when I visit my home-town, but I draw the line at murder. What's all this about?"

"Where were you on the night of September 29th, Mr. Upshott?"

Upshott gave him a quick look.

"Where were *you*?"

He smiled blandly at Littlejohn.

"I'm not being impertinent. But can you tell me, just in a moment, where you were at a certain time on a certain day?"

"You were here in Carleton Unthank?"

"Wait a minute. Was that the night of the crime? I wasn't here, that's definite. Come to think of it, I was in London. I only spent one night here, last night, in church. I slept at the Piccadilly Hotel on the 29th. I'm sure the staff would confirm it. Of course, if you're going to suggest that I shinned down a water-pipe after I'd retired to bed, hurried here, and killed somebody, I'm sunk. Nobody can give a proper alibi in a case like that. But I do assure you, I've nothing to do with murder here."

"You knew Samuel Bracknell?"

"Ah, now we're coming to it, Superintendent. Yes, I did. So that's it. Sam's murder. I read about it in the paper and I was damned sorry. Sam was a decent chap. The last man I'd think of killing."

"And yet, you pretended you knew nothing about a local murder. You knew all the time the police were hunting for his murderer."

"I knew he'd been murdered, but it just slipped my memory..."

"Did it? I'm surprised. There was another murder last night. Whilst you were in church, or supposed to be, Miss Marcia Fitzpayne was stabbed to death. Did you know her?"

"Fitzpayne? No."

"She knew you, I believe. You called at her place once, but found she wasn't in. I think you were out hunting for Bracknell."

"Oh ... Fitzpayne. Was that her name?"

"You asked the caretaker of the flats she lived in for her, and you gave her name."

"It had slipped my memory."

"Again?"

Upshott was still polite and smiling.

"Yes, again. She was of no account to me. A farmer near Bracknell's place mentioned that Sam might be at her flat and gave me the name and address. When I found he wasn't there, I forgot all about it. It's quite a natural thing to do. She was of no importance."

"When was that?"

"The afternoon of September 29th."

"You're quick to remember it."

"Four days after I arrived at London airport. Easy."

"You saw Bracknell then?"

"Yes. After I left Miss Fitzpayne's I tried Bracknell's again. He'd just got in. I had tea with him and a talk, and left for London about seven in the evening."

"You were friends?"

"We knew one another in Perth for years. Sam ran a farm not far out of town. We met once in a pub and got talking. It turned out he'd roots in Carleton. We became friends."

"Did Bracknell express any fears to you when you were with him. Any fears of someone who might be out to kill him?"

"No. Not a thing. Why should anybody want to kill Sam Bracknell?"

"He might have been indulging in a little blackmail."

Upshott laughed loudly.

"Sam! A blackmailer!! Come off it. Sam was the straightest man I ever came across."

Judging from Herle's expression, he was almost ready to tear his hair. Here was a suspicious character, a so-called friend of Bracknell's, who knew Marcia Fitzpayne, whatever he said, and yet he'd answers for everything. And he hadn't an alibi for anything either. He wondered when Littlejohn was going to charge him on suspicion.

"Didn't Bracknell mention Marcia Fitzpayne?"

"He might have done. He did talk about women at one time in the conversation. He was rather fond of them. He mentioned one or two. But their names went in at one ear and out of the other. I wasn't interested in women I'd never met."

"So you've told us. Is that your property?"

Littlejohn passed the pen with the Perth advertisement to Upshott.

"Where did you find this? I thought it had gone for good. Not that it's worth much, but it's useful."

"It was found on the floor of Bracknell's house."

"I must have dropped it when I was there. May I keep it?"

"Not just now, Mr. Upshott."

"A vital clue...?"

"Call it such if you wish."

Herle was busy telephoning. He was ringing up Mr. Checkland's house. His voice softened, it was almost mellifluous as he addressed whoever was at the other end.

"Could I speak to His Worship the Mayor, Mrs Checkland...?"

Herle's look of distress as he listened to the reply was comic.

"Accident...? Indeed... I'm sorry, very sorry. Please convey my regrets and my sympathy, Mayoress. Last night...? How did it happen...?"

More information, whilst Herle clucked and tut-tutted down the mouthpiece. Finally he hung-up, very gently, as though he might disturb the sufferer at the other end.

"The mayor can't come. He's in bed. After you left last night, Superintendent, it seems someone telephoned you, and the mayor, knowing you'd hardly have reached the street, hurried after you to tell you to take the call. Someone had left a packing-case lying about and he fell over it. A pretty heavy fall. Shook him up, and he's got a black eye. He'll be out tomorrow, his wife says."

Upshott laughed loudly again.

"A black eye! That'll upset his mayoral dignity a bit."

Herle didn't like it.

"Upshott, your jokes are out of place at present. Please behave properly..."

"I'm sorry. It was the black eye tickled me. I wonder if Mr. Checkland's changed since we were young fellows together. He was solemn and slim then. He's probably still solemn, but he was the type who'd grow fat with prosperity..."

He turned to Littlejohn.

"Well, Superintendent, will that be all? Do I spend the night in a cell instead of a church, this time?"

"No, Mr. Upshott. But you'll remain in Carleton Unthank until we say you can go. There are some comfortable hotels here. No doubt you'll know them. Which shall it be?"

"If you put it that way, the *Barley Mow*. I always liked the old *Barley Mow*."

"Very well. And please don't try to leave town. I have your word?"

"Of course, if you say so. But don't keep me here long. I've lost all interest in Carleton nowadays."

"You'd better collect your hired car. The local police have brought it here. Don't try to make off in it, or we'll have to bring you back."

"As if I would!"

"Very well. You may go, for the present, Mr. Upshott."

Upshott bade them all a polite good-bye and went away very casually.

Herle's face was a study.

"Do we put a man on to tail him?"

"I don't think he'll run for it, but it might be as well. Your man can report what Upshott does with himself in his spare time."

"Don't you think it would have been better to arrest him?"

"On what charge? We've not a trace of a case for holding him for murder. Sleeping in a church doesn't merit our detaining him. No, he's better loose."

"Why?"

"A sprat to catch a mackerel."

Herle still didn't understand and thought Littlejohn was talking in riddles to cover up his own incompetence.

CHAPTER X
THE TRIBULATIONS OF
MR. CHECKLAND

L ate on Saturday afternoon, news arrived from Scotland Yard about Bracknell's affairs in Australia. There was nothing sensational about them.

The Equitable Bank of Australia, Perth, gave the information that the monthly remittances covered interest and repayments of a mortgage taken by Bracknell from the purchaser of his property. There had been a payment down of £5,000 and the rest had been the subject of arrangements for gradual liquidation by instalments. As regards Bracknell's life in Australia, this seemed quite unspectacular, too. His former lawyer and the bank again had briefly stated that he had farmed and prospered there, accumulated considerable capital in his farm, and seemed settled and content. Then, suddenly, he had evinced a passion for visiting England, where he stated he had landed property in the Midlands. He was uncertain when he left whether or not he would remain in England and had made all arrangements for the disposal of his Australian farm in the event of his deciding not to return. He had left Australia in the autumn of 1954 and almost as soon as he arrived in England had instructed his lawyers to put his farm up for sale and remit the proceeds to him at Carleton Unthank. Bracknell, during the whole time the informants had known him, had led an industrious quiet life and he had been well thought of by all who knew him.

And that was that. Nothing helpful in the case at all.

Herle, who gave Littlejohn the telegram at the police station, was obviously out of patience. Everything in connection with the investigation of the murders seemed to have come to a full stop. All the theories about Bracknell's murder had petered out. There wasn't even a theory at all about the death of Marcia Fitzpayne. Littlejohn persisted they hadn't any grounds for accusing Upshott of the crimes. And now, the plain-clothes officer who was keeping an eye on Upshott, had reported that the Australian was calmly eating afternoon tea in the lounge of the *Barley Mow*, had made friends with a couple of good-looking ladies also staying there, and was thoroughly enjoying himself. Tonight, there would probably be another killing. Herle couldn't contain himself.

"Where do we go from here?" he said hotly.

"I'm just going over to see the mayor. I owe it to him."

Littlejohn slowly rose to his feet as he said it.

"Whatever for? He's indisposed."

"It was partly my fault. He was chasing after me to bring me back to the telephone when he came a cropper. It's the least I can do to call and ask how he is and, in a way, apologise for the trouble I've caused him."

"You know your own business best, sir. You might offer him my condolences, as well, and tell him I'll call myself when I'm not so busy."

Herle, with a pained expression on his face, bent and hauled a pile of files from the floor behind his desk, and placed them in front of himself. It was a gesture of impatient dismissal.

The maid answered the door to the two detectives and at once took them to a small morning-room at the back of the house, overlooking the same view of the river and the country beyond as the one above it in which Mr. Checkland had received Littlejohn when last he called. Mrs. Checkland and her son were there and had just finished tea.

"It's most kind of you to call, Superintendent. We've just finished tea. I'll ring for some more ..."

It was said in the form of a question. Mother and son were uneasy, as though expecting the visit to be more than a purely formal one. When Littlejohn declined, they seemed relieved for some reason.

Mrs. Checkland was wearing a plain expensive black gown relieved at the neck and cuffs by white lace. She was still handsome and vigorous in middle-age and must have been beautiful in her youth. When Littlejohn had met her for the first time earlier in the week, she had been gracious and poised. Now she was nervous and tense. Her son was the same.

James Checkland bore a striking resemblance to his mother and had the same dark eyes, regular aquiline features, and signs of good breeding. Difficult to think of him as Checkland's son, too, and his successor to a string of prosperous, high-class grocery shops all over the county. According to local talk, he had just finished at public school and was now about to enter the family business. James did not look too happy about it. There was a trace of suppressed anger about his reception of the two detectives, as though he wondered what they were intruding about.

"If you'd care to see Mr. Checkland, I think it would please him for you to go up and talk to him for a minute or two. We are worried about him. His heart isn't too good and he's had a bad shaking. He fell in the courtyard in front of the house last night after you called, Superintendent. In fact he was hurrying after you to tell you a telephone call had come through for you, when he fell over a packing-case. It seems he'd put out the lights in front as you left and was sure he could find his way after you in the dark..."

Young Checkland gave Littlejohn another reproachful look. It seemed to explain the doubtful reception Littlejohn and Cromwell had been given. Littlejohn was being held responsible for the mayor's tumble. After all, the telephone call had been for him.

"My husband managed to get up and return to the library where he took some whisky and tried to compose himself. When, however, he began to feel faint, he called for me and I found him in rather a sorry state. I'd to send for the doctor, who put him to bed. Of course, Mr. Checkland won't stay in bed. You'll find him in front of the fire."

"Shall we go?"

James Checkland seemed in a hurry to be rid of them.

When his son opened the library door and revealed His Worship the Mayor sitting in a high-backed chair in front of a large fire of logs, Littlejohn paused in surprise.

Mr. Checkland resembled a boxer who had been knocked out in a heavyweight contest the night before. He was wearing a red foulard dressing-gown and was slumped in his seat, a glass of whisky at his elbow, casting a melancholy look in the fire. He turned to greet the newcomers. He had a black eye, his upper lip was swollen, and there was a large bruise on his forehead. He must have tangled very thoroughly with the offending packing-case.

The two detectives were so stupified at the sight that a minute passed before Littlejohn could express his condolences.

132

"Superintendent Littlejohn and Sergeant Cromwell to see you, sir. Mother said they might have a minute with you."

"I'm glad to see them, son. Come in, gentlemen. James, pour them out a drink."

Young Checkland did this as quickly as possible and then seemed glad to leave the three of them together.

Mr. Checkland was breathing heavily. His usual high colour had been diluted and his hands trembled on the arms of his chair.

"It's good of you to call, Littlejohn. I can't get out and I suppose you've come to report how things are getting along. Any nearer solving the case ... ? Or should I say cases? They've told me about the shocking affair of the Fitzpayne girl. Where's it all going to end?"

For a sick man, the mayor wasn't doing very badly. His swollen lip made it a bit difficult for him to articulate, but he still had plenty to say if only he could get it all out.

"We didn't call to trouble you with the cases, sir. I came to ask how you are and to apologise for being the indirect cause of your accident."

The mayor took a gulp of his drink, swallowed hard, and shook his head.

"Don't mention it. How were you to know I'd meet with a packing-case half-way down the yard? Some fool cleared off and left it there. My son says when he finds out who did it, he'll sack the fellow right away. But it won't get as far as that. Anybody can make a mistake. I ought to have switched the light on before I came after you."

The mayor had his dentures out, too, but didn't seem very embarrassed by it. The arrival of the police had livened him up and he prattled away as though he'd forgotten his misfortunes.

"It must have been a nasty fall, sir?"

"It was. I caught the packing-case with my shins, tumbled in it, and fell with my face on one of the edges. I thought I'd killed myself. I felt bad, I can tell you."

He took another good swig of his whisky. If he'd been drinking so steadily all day, it was no wonder he was garrulous.

"Anything fresh?"

He looked anxiously at Littlejohn with his one good eye. The other was half closed and the pupil kept turning upwards to the ceiling, like that of an ecstatic saint, and showing nothing but the white.

"We've put our hands on the stranger in the town everybody seems to have been talking about. A man on holiday from Australia..."

Mr. Checkland's excitement was such that he turned in his chair to hear more of what Littlejohn had to say. His bruises must have suffered thereby, for he then groaned and sank back on his cushions like one defeated.

"What happened? Tell me."

The mayor drank deeply and coughed because his throat revolted at the weight of fluid. Each cough was accompanied or mixed up with more groans as his injuries tormented him.

"He told us nothing. A man who left for Australia long ago and had an itch to return to his birthplace, Carleton Unthank. He was not impressed by what he found here. He seems to have visited the places of long ago in secret, sometimes by night, and to have kept himself aloof by day because he didn't care to meet old friends. His attitude towards the effects of time on human beings is, to say the least of it, cynical."

"Damn his impudence! What's he called?"

"Upshott."

"Never heard of him."

And that, coming from so prominent a citizen as Mr. Checkland, seemed all there was to say about him.

Littlejohn went on to tell the mayor about Upshott's being found half-way to the Northampton football match and how he was instructed to remain within call until the police gave him a release.

"I'd have thought you'd have arrested him. A fellow like that. He might have been up to anything. Suspicious, I'd call him. Very suspicious. He might even be the murderer."

"He visited Bracknell on the afternoon of his death..."

"What did I tell you!"

Mr. Checkland was so excited that this time he forgot his wounds and waved his arms about freely.

"We've no proof of his association with the crime. He also knew Marcia Fitzpayne... The same applies there. We could only arrest him for being on enclosed premises. He slept in St. Peter's church last night."

"He must be a heathen... a hooligan. Yes, a hooligan. Nobody with any decency would do such a thing."

"We allowed him on a kind of parole to stay at the *Barley Mow* and we have a detective keeping on his track. He won't get far."

"What kind of a feller is he? A roughneck?"

"Far from it, sir. He's very gentlemanly and polite. He seems anxious to help all he can."

"All the same, he ought to be under lock and key. Meanwhile, who was he and what did he do before he left Carleton?"

"He says he was a clerk in a company long defunct and left for Australia to better himself."

Mr. Checkland relaxed with another cry of distress and looked sourly in the fire.

"I hope we don't have another crime tonight, Littlejohn. It's getting very serious, you know, all this murdering."

Mr. Checkland gently touched his eyes and his lip to test their condition.

"It'll not be long before I'm out and about again. I'd like to see this imposter from Australia. That's what he probably is. An imposter."

He turned his eyes, one bright from his drinking, the other half-closed and glaucous, appealingly on Littlejohn.

"And you've no theories, no suspects yet?"

"No, sir."

"Pity. You've my sympathy. It must be a hard job with no clues to go on and half the town yapping like dogs for an arrest."

Mr. Checkland took up a box of cigars from the table beside him, offered them round, and then tried to light one himself. The task was too much for his damaged mouth and he finally flung the cigar back in the box in disgust.

"Have you got a cigarette, Superintendent? There are some in the desk there, but I can't get up ..."

Littlejohn gave him one and lit it. Such a small object thrust in the mayor's large face and deformed mouth looked out of place. It was difficult to decide whether the situation was tragic or comic.

Littlejohn and Cromwell had already been there more than fifteen minutes and the Superintendent expected at any time that young Checkland or his mother would arrive to terminate the interview, in view of the state of the mayor's health. However, nobody came and he seemed loath to part with them.

"Have you any idea why the Fitzpayne woman was killed?"

Mr. Checkland seemed to want to plough the same furrows over and over again.

"No, sir. Unless, of course, Bracknell shared some secret with her which whoever killed him was afraid might come to light. She and Bracknell were very intimate, you know."

Littlejohn looked uneasily at his watch. If one of the family was not coming to terminate the interview, then they would have to leave without them. The mayor, Mrs. Checkland had said, was unfit for a long visit.

"Well, sir, we've taken up far too much of your time. You have orders to rest, Mrs. Checkland tells me."

The mayor elevated the white of his ill-treated eye to the ceiling and then turned the other on Littlejohn.

"Just have another drink for the road. Your visit's done me a world of good. I'm normally a very busy man, and forced inactivity bores me. Help yourselves and get me another cigarette from the box in the top drawer of the desk."

Littlejohn obeyed, mixed three more glasses of whisky and soda, and lit their three cigarettes. The mayor, a habitual cigar-smoker, puffed hard at his cigarette and disposed of it in half the time of the others.

"You knew Bracknell, sir? I think you mentioned it when first we met."

Mr. Checkland looked meditatively in the fire.

"I didn't *know* him very well. He didn't mix, you know. I believe he was a customer in the shop, and, well, people talk. There's not much goes on in Carleton that I don't hear about. News travels fast in these small communities."

"What kind of a man was he?"

"I'd call him a bit of a roughneck..."

It seemed to be Mr. Checkland's favourite term for a certain type.

"A roughneck...A bit of a backwoodsman, if you get what I mean. When you saw him about town, he looked as if he'd come up from the back of beyond. I guess he continued down at Freake's the type of life he'd lived in Australia."

"Was he much of a drinker?"

"I don't know. He might have indulged in it at home. All I can say is, he never misbehaved in the town. Otherwise he'd have been before the Bench, of which I'm chairman..."

"Women?"

"Well, as you know, he was very friendly with the Fitzpayne girl who owned a riding-school. It was common knowledge."

"I was thinking of others. He didn't seem satisfied with one woman. He was friendly with several more, to say the least of it."

"Was he, indeed...?"

The mayor smiled, and combined with his black eye and his damaged lip, it twisted his face into a diabolical grin.

"...I'm not surprised. He looked the sort. And, in that case, you might have another motive. Did one of them kill him out of jealousy, or self-defence, or even anger? Who *were* the women?"

Mr. Checkland licked his swollen lip and gently touched his bad eye to confirm that they were improving under treatment.

"Where's my wife or Maudie? I expected them up before this. I've to have my medicine and have my eye and lip painted with the stuff the doctor gave me."

"I'll ring the bell, sir..."

Littlejohn rose and was crossing to the push-button at the side of the fireplace.

"Don't, Littlejohn. If we get them up, they'll break up our little chat just when it's interesting. On second thoughts, perhaps Cromwell wouldn't mind passing the bottle and spoon from the table in the window there, and bring the green one labelled poison, and I'll paint my bruises myself."

Cromwell not only went for the stuff, but measured out a dose, gave it to the mayor, and then, after soaking a wad of cotton-wool with some liquid from the poison bottle, he gently dabbed the eye and the lips. After all, he trained the members of the Shepherd Market Lads' Club in first-aid...

"Thank you...Now what were you saying about these other women, Littlejohn?"

The mayor was so eager to hear it, that he protruded his tongue to lick his lips, suddenly remembered that Cromwell had smeared them with poison, and drew it in again.

"When we first arrived and were examining Freake's Folly, three women arrived. Marcia Fitzpayne to rescue some letters, which she'd already burned when we caught her. After she'd left, a young girl of about eighteen arrived. Lucy Jolland..."

"Jolland! My God, Littlejohn, you've got a motive *there* if her father got to know about any jiggery-pokery between Bracknell and his daughter! He's a very straight-laced man with a devil of a temper. He was in court once for assaulting a drover who was ill-treating a beast in the cattle-market. When Jolland interfered, the man got rough, Jolland replied in kind, and half-killed him. What was Lucy after? She'd always seemed a nice kid to me. A good-looking girl, who Bracknell might have made a pass at, however..."

"She'd been in the habit of calling with the milk, had left her gloves, and came whilst we were there to retrieve them. When I asked her a few questions, she seemed a bit embarrassed by too much insistence on her relations with Bracknell."

It was painful to see the mayor trying to indulge in ribald laughter, yet restrained by his injuries. He roared with mirth, screwed up his face, winced, then roared with pain.

"Damn this blasted mouth! I can't laugh. But to think of Lucy saying she delivered the milk! What a tale!"

"She seemed honest enough about it. She's either very naïve or much deeper than she seems."

"Probably a deep one. I don't need to tell you that all women are deeper than they seem..."

He gave them a bitter, twisted look and took a good drink.

"Who's the other?"

"The postmistress..."

"What! Miss Meynold... Ethel... I'm not surprised. She's very anxious not to die in a state of single blessedness. She chases the eligibles like mad. But chastely, Superintendent, chastely. There won't be any illicit amours where Ethel's concerned."

"I'm sure there won't, sir."

"Anybody else?"

The mayor was enjoying himself. He indicated in gleeful pantomime that Cromwell might refill the glasses again. Cromwell replied by negative gestures.

"No. But Mr. Cropstone, Bracknell's neighbour on the home farm, seemed to know a lot about him. He said he'd seen women frequently on the way to Freake's Folly."

Mr. Checkland growled.

"Cropstone *would*. He's perhaps jealous. Added to that, he resented Bracknell's taking over Freake's and living so near the home farm where he could overlook Cropstone, who liked overlooking everybody else, but didn't like them to return the compliment. He's not blameless where women go. He's got a very fine woman for a wife, but he's caused her a lot of unhappiness with his philandering. Is that all?"

"Yes."

Checkland gave a disappointed grunt. He seemed to expect some big name to enter into the affair and make it spectacular. Instead ... A mere milk-girl and the postmistress!

"You'd better be sure of your ground about Lucy Jolland before you tackle her or her father about the murder, you know. As I said, Jolland's quite a man to reckon with, Littlejohn."

"I've completely ignored that angle, sir. In the first place, Lucy said her father didn't know she was friendly with Bracknell. He didn't even know she went regularly to Freake's Folly. I believed her. Besides, if what you say is true, Jolland was more likely to go after Bracknell explosively with a shot-gun after putting Lucy across his knee and giving her a good spanking. It would have been a dramatic situation, instead of one of a knife in the back in the night. Don't you agree?"

"I must confess I do. That's right."

Mr. Checkland nodded wisely and then winced, for he'd a crick in the neck as well.

"And that's all ..."

"That's all, sir. I'm sure none of the women committed the murder. The blow was too savage and deep for any one of them to inflict ..."

"Don't you believe it, Littlejohn. An angry woman's capable of anything a mere man can do."

The mayor gave a grumpy nod and slid down among his cushions with a long, ostentatious sigh.

"I'm fed up with this. Whatever they say, I'm going out tomorrow."

Littlejohn and Cromwell rose.

"We must be going, sir. We've talked too long and you must feel quite exhausted."

"On the contrary, it's done me good. Come again as soon as you like. You can ring the bell, please, and Maudie'll let you out."

Maudie answered in a flutter.

"Sorry, sir, about the medicine. I'd quite forgot it. I'll give it you now."

Mr. Checkland was the sick man again. He looked sorry for himself and gave the maid a reproachful look.

"I had to ask Cromwell to give it to me. And the lotion, too. He painted my eye and mouth with it."

"I'm sorry, sir."

"No need to be. It wasn't your job to do it. Mrs. Checkland's been doing it. Where is she?"

"She went out, sir, with Mr. James."

"Where?"

"I don't know, sir."

Checkland scrambled to his feet in his anger, his damaged lips quivering, his black-eye twitching.

"Why didn't they tell me they were going out? This is the limit! Me ill and confined to my room and they off gallivantin' without so much as a word of warning. When did they go?"

"Soon after the gentlemen called. There was a telephone call for madam. After that, she ordered the car and her and Mr. James went off together..."

"But why?...Why did they go off without a word to me? They've never done that before. Not even when I was well. What's been going on in this house...?"

Checkland gasped, pawed the air, and then sank exhausted in his chair. They gave him brandy this time, but he seemed to ail little except violent temper, frustration, and the ill effects of self-pity.

"I'm sorry, Littlejohn. Shouldn't have lost my temper. But you'll admit it's a queer trick to walk out on me, and me in my present state, and not even leave a message."

"Perhaps they've just gone a brief errand and didn't wish to disturb you, sir."

"I hope you're right."

They left him still browbeating Maudie and trying to get out of her where his family had gone.

A policeman was standing in the entry which led into the street.

"Superintendent Herle would like to see you as soon as possible, sir..."

Herle was waiting for them with a grim expression on his face.

"I didn't want to disturb you during your visit to the mayor," he said acidly. "There was enough trouble last time His Worship took a phone call for you, sir. But five minutes ago, the man detailed to watch Upshott reported that he'd bolted from the *Barley Mow*. I thought he might."

"Did your man get after him?"

"No. He dodged him. I've men out combing the town. Like hunting for the proverbial needle again. We ought to have found some excuse for putting him in the cells. I was never in favour..."

"Never mind that now, Herle. What happened?"

"Upshott went in the lounge of the hotel for afternoon tea. Our man was there having tea as well and keeping an eye on him..."

Littlejohn could see it all. Upshott was no fool. He'd be well aware what the constabulary-looking man, awkwardly eating cake and drinking tea, was about.

"First he went in the hall and telephoned someone. Our man kept him in view. Upshott was very casual and returned to the two ladies whose acquaintance he'd made at the hotel, and went on with his tea. Then he took out his case, found only one cigarette apparently, and told the ladies he was going in the bar for more..."

"And your man fell for it?"

"How the hell was he to know! He's not a trained sleuth like your Scotland Yard men. Upshott just walked out of the side door of the hotel and vanished. Our man said he was at the door almost immediately after Upshott, who must have ordered a car or something when he telephoned. Anyhow, he's gone. He's given us the slip as I said he would."

Littlejohn was slowly filling his pipe, which seemed to annoy Herle all the more. There was a large notice over the fireplace. *No Smoking.*

"How long ago was this?"

"Twenty minutes, or so. Our man couldn't phone right away. He was after Upshott."

"What kind of a car does Mrs. Checkland drive?"

"It's a Daimler. She doesn't drive. She has a chauffeur. I don't see what that has to do with it."

"Let's just try a hunch. You have some squad-cars on the roads?"

"Yes. Four. One patrolling each of the main highways."

"Send out a call and ask if they've seen Mrs. Checkland's car."

Herle shrugged his shoulders. He couldn't understand Littlejohn at all. And what the mayor would say about it, he couldn't even guess.

"Very well."

Herle rang the bell for Drayton, who didn't reply.

"Drayton! DRAYTON!!"

Heavy feet.

"Yes, sir."

"Why the hell don't you answer the bell!"

The squad cars were contacted.

Number 3, stationed on the Leicester Road, had not only seen Mrs. Checkland's car; he knew where it was at present.

"I passed the *Marquis of Granby*...you know the place...only a couple of minutes ago. The mayoress's car was standing in the car park there..."

Herle looked dumbfounded.

"That doesn't say we'll find Upshott..."

But there was a strange light in his eyes. He cast a sidelong look at Littlejohn as he put on his official cap. It was the first admiring glance he'd yet bestowed upon the Superintendent.

Littlejohn was slowly lighting his pipe.

CHAPTER XI
AT THE *MARQUIS OF GRANBY*

There were about ten houses in the hamlet of Fixby, strung along the road in a kind of high street. There was nobody about but at some of the windows of the cottages the curtains trembled and behind, in the gloom of the interior, the faces of curious old women were visible staring out.

The village inn stood in the middle of the cluster of houses. The present proprietor had taken advantage of its situation on the main Leicester road and converted it into a roadhouse.

The Marquis of Granby
Restaurant — Lunches — Dinners
Fine Cuisine Choice Wines
Your Host: *J. Vivian Wheeler.*

And the figure of a chef pointing the way to the front door.

A car park and two petrol pumps in front. Behind, a stretch of country, with cattle placidly chewing and watching passers-by, and a couple of horses cantering round and round.

The police car drew up in front of the hotel.

"That's Mrs. Checkland's car," said Herle as the three of them climbed out. Young Checkland was sitting at the wheel and when he saw the new arrivals, made as if to leave the car and warn his mother.

"Stay where you are, Mr. James," said Herle.

"But..."

"I said, stay where you are."

The youth was still young enough to obey a firm order and remained where he was with an ill grace, his glance moving from the police to the window of the front room of the hotel.

Everything was quiet. It was too early for dinner and the afternoon teas had been cleared away. Sounds of preparation for the next meal came from the kitchens behind. There were a few drinkers in the cocktail bar to the left.

The old character of the place had been spoiled. Modern tinted lighting, contemporary vivid decorations, red rubber flooring and chromium and formica bars. Mr. J. Vivian Wheeler emerged rubbing his hands. He stopped his washing gestures when he recognised Herle.

"How-de-ye-do, Superintendent. Nothing wrong, I hope."

A middle-sized, swarthy man, with dark bloodshot eyes and a large handlebar moustache. He oozed shifty self-confidence.

"No, Mr. Wheeler. Is Mrs. Checkland here?"

"Yes. She's in the private room. There's a gentleman with her."

Wheeler's poached eyes lit up dimly.

"We'll go in."

"Shall I tell them you're here?"

"No."

"May I serve you with drinks while you're there?"

"No. Please don't let us detain you. We'll look after ourselves."

"Nothing wrong, I hope."

"You said that before, Mr. Wheeler, and I said there wasn't."

Herle's bad manners had their origins in something unpleasant in the past. A matter of drinking after hours, and another about cruelty to a dog. Wheeler shrugged his shoulders and sidled off.

The place was hot and had an unhealthy atmosphere, as though shady goings-on were frequent there. There was a smell of sage and onion stuffing preparing for the chickens for dinner.

Littlejohn, whose head almost touched the ceiling of the passage, could see the door of the private room indicated by Wheeler, at the far end of the dim corridor. Without saying anything more, he walked to it and opened it. Mrs. Checkland and Upshott were inside, sitting quietly at a table, with glasses of what appeared to be gin-and-tonic half-full in front of them. There was a log fire burning at one end of the room in a large old fireplace.

It all looked very nice and peaceful. No dramatic scenes, no compromising situations. Just the pair of them calmly talking over their drinks. The room, apparently set aside for small private parties, held half a dozen small round tables of light oak, with chairs to match. A sideboard, a clock, a carpet on the floor, and old coaching prints on the walls.

Littlejohn strolled to the fire and stretched out his hands to the flames. He kicked a pile of ash lying in the hot embers under the large logs.

"Been burning something?"

Upshott rose hastily and, for a minute, lost his temper.

"What the hell's it got to do with you what we've been doing? Am I a criminal that the blasted police must be following me all over the countryside prying into my affairs? I managed to shake off that flatfoot you put on my heels, and now the whole force is here..."

Before Littlejohn could reply, Mrs. Checkland laid a hand on Upshott's arm.

"Don't, Walter. You'll only upset yourself. It's natural that they should try to find you if you gave their man the slip."

She spoke to him like an old friend.

"Was your name Walter Upshott when you were here years ago?"

Littlejohn's voice had a chuckle in it, as though he found the situation humorous.

Upshott had cooled down. His anger had vanished at a word from Mrs. Checkland, whose tranquil dignity dominated the whole situation.

"I left my old surname behind when I went abroad. I shook it off with the dust of Carleton Unthank. It's quite legitimate. I did it by deed-poll."

"What was it before you changed it?"

"Mason. Walter Mason."

"I see. What made you give us the slip and telephone Mrs. Checkland to meet you here?"

"I knew her in the old days. She was the only one worth renewing an acquaintance with. As I couldn't meet her in the town without causing a local uproar, I phoned and asked her to see me here."

The couple smiled at each other as though completely in accord. Mrs. Checkland was pale and her face drawn. She was obviously keeping calm under considerable strain. Now and then her eyes strayed to where the car was parked outside the hotel. Littlejohn admired her perfect control of herself and all the evidence of good breeding she manifested. For the existence she led—the tolerance of the bumptious ill-bred mayor, her duties as the great lady of a small conservative community, the cares of family life—she was wonderfully preserved and dignified. Littlejohn had a feeling that if he could penetrate her shield of invulnerability, she might help him in the present case. But that would be difficult. Her *sang-froid* was not only her own protection, but that of her companion as well. Without her, Upshott might easily break down.

Upshott emptied his glass. Littlejohn noticed that he was wearing light chamois-leather gloves. The idea of paying for his drinks had evidently struck him and he removed that on his left hand, but not that on the right.

"Please remove the other glove, Mr. Upshott."

The man looked surprised and then made a clicking noise with his tongue against his teeth, either in disgust... or it may have been in admiration.

"I've got to hand it to you, Superintendent Littlejohn..."

Herle's mouth sagged. He wondered what Littlejohn was at. Cromwell, in the background, seemed to be enjoying himself.

Littlejohn and Upshott looked each other straight in the eyes. It seemed, for a moment, like a battle of wills. Then Upshott slowly took off the glove. His knuckles were covered with sticking-plaster, as though he'd barked them on something.

"Well?"

Upshott smiled again. Even Mrs. Checkland was puzzled and waited for what he had to say.

"Just a scratch. I had to change the wheel of the car the other day and I caught them on the jack as I let it down..."

"I see."

Again the two men looked each other in the eyes.

"And that is all you and Mrs. Checkland met for? Just to renew an old friendship and talk about old times?"

"What else? You didn't find us doing anything but chatting peacefully together. The meeting's over now. I can go—when you fellows will allow me—knowing I've done my duty by my oldest friend."

"Your oldest...?"

"We went to school together. At the age of seven, we met at a little private school in Carleton Unthank. Then she left for Cheltenham. I went to the local grammar school."

"Oh!"

"Oh, what? Don't you believe me?"

"Of course. The 'Oh!' was just a polite acknowledgment of the information."

As in every other aspect of the case, a heavy inertia was falling over the situation. Plenty of talk, but little of any use.

"May I ask if you were sweethearts once upon a time?"

It sounded impertinent, but Littlejohn had to ask it. Neither Mrs. Checkland nor Upshott was moved by it. It was obvious that she still held their emotions in check and, as far as Upshott was concerned, she gave the lead.

"Yes," he said. "You're right, Superintendent. It passed ... It passed, like all the other pleasant things of life. She chose Checkland and I decided to try my luck elsewhere."

"You left Carleton because of that?"

"Really, Littlejohn. Really. Are you aware the lady is present. Do you want to know all my secrets? Well ... Perhaps it will please you to learn that I left Carleton exactly for that reason. I've never married ..."

He got no further. The door was thrust roughly open and the huge tormented form of Mr. Checkland appeared.

He was livid with rage and almost unrecognisable. He was palpitating with fury. His black eye and twisted lip added to the ugliness of his appearance. His fists closed and opened as though he were ready to pounce on Upshott and beat him up.

"What's going on here? What's Mason doing here? And my wife...?"

Mr. Checkland's eyes moved from one group to another. As he spoke, his speech grew thicker and then he began to choke. He tottered to a chair and sat down heavily, fighting for breath.

"You know Mason, Mr. Mayor?"

"Of course I do. He's a native of Carleton who left years ago..."

"His other name is Upshott. The man I mentioned to you earlier this afternoon. He's over from Australia."

The mayor was still recovering his breath.

"Shall I get some brandy, Checkland?"

Upshott made for the door.

"Stay where you are. I wouldn't accept brandy from you, you scoundrel, if I were dying. What do you mean being here with my wife?"

Mrs. Checkland and Upshott seemed to hang on every word spoken by the mayor. And Mr. Checkland, having uttered his own maledictions, now seemed unable to find further speech.

Littlejohn became aware that they were all afraid. Afraid of the same thing? Or each with his own fear? He did not know. He turned to the three of them.

"We are not concerned with your private family affairs, gentlemen...and you, too, Mrs. Checkland. Unless they affect the murders we are investigating. If they do, it is your duty to tell us at once what you know. Has any of you anything to say to me?"

The mayor looked steadily at his large hands, which were now spread on the table before him. Upshott lowered his head and was silent. Mrs. Checkland, her fine eyes bright as with fever, looked first at one and then the other of the two men.

There was dead silence in the room. Outside strings of cars moved at high speed along the main road in both directions. Dusk was falling and fresh arrivals were now appearing in the car park. Young Checkland was still sitting in the car, hunched up, bored with the delay.

Then, Mrs. Checkland doubled up in her chair and fainted. Upshott bent and gently raised her. The mayor was on his feet, pawing at Upshott's shoulder.

"Leave her alone. Don't touch her, you scoundrel. Leave her ... or ..."

"Or what?" said Herle, finding tongue at last.

The mayor said nothing more.

Cromwell ran into the bar and brought back brandy and a bottle of sal volatile. Soon the odours of alcohol and ammonia mingled with the stuffy air of the room.

Mrs. Checkland slowly opened her eyes, glanced around fearfully, and sobbed.

Littlejohn bent gently over her.

"I'm sorry. Are you fit to walk to the car, madam? We'd better get you home."

"I'll be all right now. I apologise for making a fuss. I feel much better."

Cromwell and the mayor, who insisted, helped Mrs Checkland to her car.

"What's the matter, mother?"

Young James stared at her in anxious anger.

"What have you been doing to her?"

He glared at the circle of men who followed in procession.

"Nothing, my dear. It's all right. The air in the room was stuffy and I felt a bit faint."

Still glaring venomously around, James made his mother comfortable and started the engine.

Parked beside his wife's car was the mayor's transport. A delivery van marked *Benj'n. Checkland & Son, Grocers, etc., Carleton Unthank*. In his haste, Mr. Checkland had taken the first available vehicle. The driver was in his seat, his eyes wide at the sight of so many police and the spectacular exit of the party. The mayor, who missed nothing, saw the look of busybody eagerness on the man's face.

"Remember, Headley, not a word about this. It's as much as your job's worth ... Remember ..."

"I'm discreet, sir. I won't say anything. You know that."

"You'd better be discreet this time ... I'm getting in with you again ..."

He scrambled in the seat beside the driver. He was obviously so annoyed with his wife that he couldn't bear to travel home with her in comfort. She called to him anxiously.

"Don't go back in that thing, Ben. Come with us ..."

Mr. Checkland pursed his damaged mouth in a stubborn fit of sulks.

"I'll go the way I want, the way I came, seeing that you sneaked off in the car without telling me. Get going, Headley."

Upshott, who had travelled out with Mrs. Checkland after meeting her at the side door of the *Barley Mow*, was embarrassed now. His good humour had gone and he looked ready to start walking back to town rather than cause more trouble with the mayor.

"You'd better come with us ..."

Littlejohn indicated the police car. It was a tight squeeze, but they managed.

"And don't leave town again, Mr. Upshott, on any pretext whatever. Otherwise, I shall arrest you."

Upshott looked up sharply.

"What's the charge?"

"You'll be detained on suspicion. I have your word you won't leave town?"

"Yes."

"And you still won't tell me anything you know about the murders of Bracknell and Miss Fitzpayne?"

"I don't know anything about either of them. Why should I?"

Littlejohn shrugged.

They drove to town and dropped Upshott at the hotel door. The Checkland vehicles had vanished from sight on their way home.

At the police station again, Herle hung up his hat and mopped his forehead with a gesture of despair.

"Do you think we'll ever find out the truth about the murders?"

"I'm sure of it, Herle."

"I doubt it. Nobody seems to know anything. But you surely don't think the mayor or his wife is involved?"

"I don't know. Bracknell came from Australia. So does Upshott. Upshott, as Mason, knew Checkland well, from all accounts, before he emigrated. And, he seems to have been on more than good terms with the mayoress. Judging from the way they behaved towards each other, and the *tête à tête* at the *Marquis of Granby*, they were childhood sweethearts. Upshott left Carleton when Mrs. Checkland chose the mayor instead of himself. He's still unmarried. Sort that out, if you can, Herle."

"I said I didn't think we'd ever get to the bottom of it. We can't take two people like Mr. and Mrs. Checkland and shake some truth out of them. We can't even do it with a nonentity like Upshott. We're stumped."

"We've got to find out more about Upshott, in the days when he lived here and was known as Walter Mason. Where did he work? What was his job? Why did he leave?"

"We could ask him."

"I prefer to find out another way. Any suggestions, Herle?"

"The *Carleton Gazette* might have something about it on the old files. We know the approximate date he left Carleton. It would be when Checkland got married. Upshott said he left when it happened."

"The local newspaper won't get below the surface. It might just say he's left for Australia. Think again. What about some old employees of Checklands? Is there anybody in the office or the shop who could tell us about the mayor's marriage, romance, or whatever you care to call it?"

"There's old Nicholson, the accountant in Checkland's office. He's getting on for seventy and has been with the firm since he left school. But he won't be at business, now. It's Saturday and he'll have left early. He's a late stayer most nights, but not on Saturday."

"Where does he live?"

"Off the Northampton Road... Wait a minute..."

Herle fumbled with the telephone directory.

"Here he is. Montrose, Hinkley Avenue... Telephone Carleton 5463."

"Will you ring him and find out if he can see us?"

No sooner said than done. Nicholson was entertaining friends, but would come down to the police station right away, if necessary. It was difficult to convince him that the Checkland shops and offices were intact, that Mr. Checkland hadn't had a turn for the worse, that none of the employees of the firm had been misbehaving. Finally, he said he'd come immediately.

For one who had been subservient to a bully like Checkland all his life, Mr. Jeremiah Nicholson was wonderfully active and cheerful. This was due to the happiness of his domestic life. He had four daughters, who had married and, in turn, produced eleven grandchildren. His wife, too, was a woman with a whimsical sense of humour, in which, during her conversations in private with her husband, Mr. Checkland was the principal comic turn. Mr. Nicholson, who always felt a twinge of fear whenever the boss entered the office, who spoke softly and walked about on tiptoe if Mr. Checkland was about, who entered the mayor's private office crabwise to take his orders, would, when he arrived home and described the humiliations and cares of the busy day, be quickly reduced to laughter when his wife imitated the manner of Mr. Checkland in his daily role as heavy villain.

"I've met you before, Mr. Cromwell," he immediately said to the sergeant on being introduced. "Cleethorpes, 1955."

Cromwell, who had never been to Cleethorpes in his life, politely denied the meeting.

"*The Good Companions* boarding house ... Come, my dear fellow, you must remember ..."

And when Cromwell regretfully said he didn't, Mr. Nicholson cast upon him a reproachful glance which accused the sergeant of lying.

"Please sit down, Mr. Nicholson," said Littlejohn, and the little accountant obeyed like a man used to doing as he was told. He had a large bald head on a small, slender body, bright dark eyes, and a long inquisitive nose. He was obviously dressed in his best as becomes a man entertaining friends at home.

"Do you smoke, Mr. Nicholson?"

"One cigar every evening after my meal. I gave up the rest years ago."

"In that case, sir, I hope you'll enjoy this one..."

Littlejohn presented him with a choice specimen pressed upon him during one of his previous visits to the mayor. It was in an aluminium case and resembled a small bomb.

"Now," said Littlejohn, after Mr. Nicholson had carefully cut and lighted his cigar, "I wonder if you could give me some past history in connection with the Checkland family..."

Mr. Nicholson sat suddenly upright on his chair, his cigar held between thumb and forefinger.

"I'm sorry, Superintendent, but mine is a confidential job. I could not possibly commit a breach of trust, even for the police."

His mouth tightened as though he were prepared to undergo untold tortures rather than divulge anything whatsoever about his work.

"Don't be disturbed, sir. This is a matter with which Mr. Checkland has entrusted us. We shall ask for no financial details of the firm. Just past history."

"That's better."

Mr. Nicholson began to enjoy his cigar again.

"How long have you been with them?"

"Fifty-two years. They gave me a gold watch on my fiftieth anniversary. I was there in the time of old Mr. Benjamin, and, although *his* father, Mr. Theodore, was then alive, he'd had a stroke and took little interest in affairs."

"And I suppose now, you are the man who makes the wheels go round?"

Mr. Nicholson smiled benignly.

"Financially, yes."

"Have you known Mrs. Checkland all her life, too?"

"Yes. I remember her as a little girl in pigtails. She was a Miss Eileen Huncote, a member of a well-known county family. Mr. Benjamin...I mean the present Mr. Benjamin...was fond of her right from being a boy. But he was shy in those days. I don't recollect his ever having any other girl. We were surprised, however, when she married him. As I said, Mr. Ben was shy and let the other men take possession. Then, suddenly, their engagement was announced, they were married, and they seem happy together."

Mr. Nicholson's eyes strayed questioningly in Cromwell's direction, as though he hoped the sergeant would sooner or later remember Cleethorpes and confess to their previous encounter.

"Did you ever know a Mr. Walter Mason, sir?"

The old man raised astonished eyes.

"Did Mr. Checkland tell you about him?"

"Yes. Was he a relative?"

"It used to be said he was a second cousin or something, but that made no difference to his status in the firm. He was one of the under-cashiers, one of my subordinates. He left the firm to go abroad...let me see...it must be fifteen or sixteen years ago. He was rather wild in those days."

"In what way?"

"He spent a lot more than he earned. He got among the wrong set; betting, girls, fast cars...It could only have one end. And yet, he was a charming man. Good manners and respect for his elders. And a way with the ladies. They ran after him in dozens."

Now Mr. Nicholson was beginning to look cautious and to choose his words carefully as he spoke. Littlejohn had to tread warily.

"You say Mr. Mason was under-cashier. What kind of a job was that?"

"As you know, we have many branches up and down the county. A lot of business is done and a lot of cash accumulated after the banks close at three o'clock. Normally, such cash would be paid into a local bank next morning and would arrive for credit at our bank in Carleton Unthank the day after that. I will be quite candid, Superintendent. In those days Checkland and Son hadn't much ready money. They were borrowing heavily from the bank for expansion. Mr. Benjamin calculated that if he had a man to collect the cash which was received after the banks had closed and pay it in at Carleton next morning, he would save a day in bank transit and the interest saved would well pay for the collection. Mr. Mason did the collecting. He also went round to branches weekly and paid wages."

"I see. There was trouble?"

"I don't know that I ought to talk about it, without Mr. Benjamin's personal consent. It would be a breach of trust."

Mr. Nicholson's smile had vanished and beads of sweat glittered on his bald head.

Littlejohn was very serious, too.

"I'm sorry, Mr. Nicholson, but I must insist. You see, this may have something to do with the recent murders in Carleton..."

The old man's eyebrows shot up and he began to look afraid.

"If you don't tell us now what we wish to know, here and in confidence, it will have to be later when you will be questioned in the presence of Mr. Checkland. It would be very unpleasant."

"Oh dear. Well, I'd better tell you, although I beg you not to... It's very awkward. You see, there was a shortage in the cash. Mr. Mason was found to have appropriated over a thousand pounds over a period of time. He'd hidden the difference in the books, but was laid-up with an attack of 'flu and couldn't get to the office for some days. It was discovered in his absence, by me. I reported it, of course. I was relieved when the matter was hushed-up and Mr. Mason allowed to leave the country and begin afresh in Australia."

"I suppose you and Mr. Benjamin were the only ones who knew about these thefts."

"Yes. Mr. Mason signed a full confession and Mr. Benjamin told me he'd overlook it, if Mr. Mason left the country."

"And he did."

"Oh, yes. Right away."

"Was Mr. Benjamin married then?"

"No. Why?"

"But he married soon afterwards?"

"Yes. I remember it because my daughter, Barbara, was married two days before."

"One other question, Mr. Nicholson, and then we won't detain you any longer. Was Mr. Mason a friend of Mrs. Checkland, then Miss Huncote, at the time he was obliged to leave for Australia."

"Why, yes. I was very surprised when the defalcations came to light. I thought Mason had quietened down. You see, he and Miss Huncote appeared to be going steadily together, as the saying is, and an engagement was expected, in spite of the fact that she was quite above his class. They seemed very much in love. It was said she married Mr. Benjamin on the rebound after Mason fled. However, she did far better for herself. Mr. Benjamin is a steady man. Quite unlike Mason and much more worthy of a fine woman like Mrs. Checkland."

"Thank you very much, Mr. Nicholson. We'll treat your information with great discretion. I'm sorry we had to disturb your Saturday evening's pleasure."

"Don't mention it, Superintendent. Glad to have been of help."

He shook hands all round, his eyes, as he said good-bye to Cromwell, expressive of the one word "Cleethorpes." But Cromwell sadly shook his head and Mr. Nicholson left him in a hurry.

Chapter XII
The End of his Tether

After Mr. Nicholson had left them, Littlejohn almost wished he'd detained him longer, or, perhaps that he would return with something more to say. It was like the end of a party where the cheerful guests have gone, leaving behind a wreckage of dirty dishes to be washed-up, the reek of brandy and cigars, the paper hats of revelry. Boredom was setting in.

Outside, it was quite dark and it was beginning to drizzle. The street lamps, visible through the windows of Herle's office, were surrounded by aureoles of milky mist. The footsteps of passers-by sounded now and then, and a car or two rushed past as if eager to get to their destinations and deposit their contents indoors. All the shops were closed, and opposite, Checkland's Stores was in darkness. The tunnel and the doorway of the house beyond were illuminated by their hanging lamps. Although it was Saturday, nobody seemed tempted to walk the streets. Even the gangs of boys and girls who roamed about singing and cat-calling on fine nights were silent.

The depressing weight of ennui descended on Littlejohn, and, judging from the melancholy look on his face, Cromwell was feeling the same. Herle was an unsociable man with little in the way of cheerful small-talk and his expression was one of faint disapproval. He thought Littlejohn either knew something and wasn't going to let him into the secret, or else that he knew nothing at all and that all his investigations hitherto had ended in total failure.

"I think we'll get back to the *Arms* and see what they have for dinner..."

That was all there was to do. The cinema, the bar of one of the local hotels, a walk in the dismal streets, or an hour in the *salle à manger* of the *Huncote Arms,* where, the waiter had warned them beforehand, they were going to be very busy tonight.

"It's Saturday. We'll be rushed off our feet..."

"Would you care to join us at the *Arms* for a meal, Herle?"

But, no. Even that didn't raise a gratified smile from the dour Superintendent. He merely sighed and looked pained.

"I promised my wife I'd be home for seven. It's half-past now and I've a good hour's routine work to do yet... A policeman's work is never done."

They might have been a pair of casual visitors taking a look over the police-station, instead of colleagues trying to help him! Fundamentally, Herle thought he could manage the case far better himself and he was hoping to show everybody what he was made of before much longer. Even he, however, didn't know where to start. A pall of desolate inertia had fallen upon the murder cases. They'd interviewed everybody concerned. Result, a blank. They'd worked *ad nauseam* on the scenes of the crimes. Nothing. They'd spun theories and followed leads. Confusion and dead ends...

Littlejohn was just stretching his hand for his hat and coat from the bentwood hat stand, when he paused.

Scuttering feet from across the way, a muffled echoing ring as they passed through the tunnel under Checkland's property, and then young James became visible running for all he was worth in the direction of the police station. A minute more and he was in the room, panting, wild-eyed, unable to speak until he'd pulled himself together. He wore no hat or coat and was in his house slippers.

"Come over right away. Father's shot himself!"

Herle almost collapsed, too. He rose and held on his desk for support.

"The mayor! Why...?"

"Never mind why or where. Come right away."

And with that, James Checkland turned and ran out of the place again. His pattering feet rang on the pavement and then through the tunnel, and died away.

As the three police officers reached the door, a car, obviously a doctor's and driven at breakneck speed, appeared, braked noisily in front of the passage, and then ran straight through it and to Checkland's house.

The mayor had shot himself in his study. Stretched full-length across the carpet in front of his desk, he looked enormous. A service revolver lay just out of reach of the large outstretched hand, as though it had fallen from Checkland's grasp as he collapsed.

But, as the three officers entered, the sight before them froze them to the spot. Mr. Checkland wasn't dead. His hands, spread ahead of him on the carpet, his feet, shod also in red leather house-slippers, moved convulsively, like those of a bird, winged by a shot, dying open-eyed and wondering why.

The doctor was already on his knees beside the body.

"James... Get an ambulance quickly. He's not dead. There may be a chance to save him, yet. Get along quickly and 'phone Carleton 3131. Tell them to hurry..."

Then he muttered to himself, "God knows where they'll find Lapage on a Saturday night. He'll be out somewhere..."

165

He sounded annoyed that the mayor should choose, of all nights, the one on which the brain surgeon would be hard to locate.

The doctor filled a syringe, gave the injured man an injection, and then gently turned him over. The eyes were open and terribly alive. Checkland looked straight up to the ceiling with a fixed, puzzled expression, as though struggling dimly in the shadows to make out what it was all about.

The doctor made a noise like a humourless chuckle.

"Good job he didn't know much about anatomy, *or* firing a gun. The bullet seems to have gone in and out along the top of the skull. It must be somewhere in the room ... The walls or the ceiling ... It's passed through ..."

He sounded to be talking to himself, or maybe, lecturing a ghostly crowd of medical students, and as he chatted, he worked, applying gauze and a bandage to the two wounds, feeling Checkland's pulse intermittently, testing eyes, limbs, reflexes, to make sure of the victim's condition.

"He should pull through with a bit of luck."

A small, broad, dapper man, calm, skilled and patient. His busy hands moved rapidly here and there and as Checkland lapsed into unconsciousness, he gently settled his body in comfort.

"Where the hell's that ambulance?"

As if in answer to his question, two men appeared carrying a stretcher. Mr. Checkland was borne off to the local infirmary.

Only then did the rest of them become really aware of Mrs. Checkland's presence in the room. She had remained calm, unweeping, motionless, staring at the body as though she couldn't understand what it was all about.

"We'll let you know how things go. No use your coming now, Mrs. Checkland. As soon as Lapage has operated, we'll send for you. Keep cheerful. I think it will be all right..."

The doctor was off and they could hear his car roaring away under the tunnel and the noise dying in the distance.

Littlejohn was the first to speak.

"Please sit down, Mrs. Checkland..."

He pulled up one of the large armchairs and gently led her to it. Then he rang the bell.

Maudie, the elderly maid, appeared. She had been sent below because her hysterical behaviour in an emergency had been a menace. She was still sobbing in her handkerchief and her eyes were swollen with tears and hardly visible.

"Please pull yourself together, Maudie. This is no time for a scene. Your mistress needs some tea. Please see to it right away."

A firm hand did Maudie a lot of good. She almost ran to do the job.

Herle looked awkward.

"I'm very sorry about all this, Mrs Checkland. Do you think...?"

The mayoress hadn't spoken. She sat with her head resting against the wing of the chair, her eyes closed, her hand before them.

Littlejohn glanced at Cromwell and gently and almost imperceptibly nodded his head in the direction of Herle. The sergeant and Littlejohn had been together for so long that Cromwell could usually interpret his chief's wishes without a word being spoken.

"Would you like us to leave the two of you together for a little while?" said Cromwell. "We could go and wait at the police station until we're needed."

Herle's eyes almost emerged from his head and rolled down his cheeks. They were actually dismissing him from the scene of one of his own cases!

"I think it would be better. The three of us will only confuse Mrs. Checkland and she's obviously in no state to be questioned for a little while. When she's had a cup of tea, she'll perhaps feel better. It's very good of you to offer to leave the mayoress in peace for a bit, Herle ..."

Cromwell was leading Herle away. The local Superintendent was in a confused state. First the mayor shooting himself. Then, he wasn't dead. Then Littlejohn was talking about Herle himself offering to leave the field ... He allowed himself to be tactfully steered off.

"I'm very sorry, Mrs. Checkland ... As the doctor said, everything's going to be all right ... If you need me, I'm just over the way ..."

"Thank you very much indeed, Mr. Herle. It's most kind of you. I will never forget your sympathy and help ..."

Mrs. Checkland opened her eyes and gave him a faint smile as she said it. It did Herle a lot of good.

James had gone with his father in the ambulance. Mrs. Checkland and Littlejohn were alone.

All the lights were on; about eight of them all over the place. Littlejohn had always seen the room dimly lighted and cosy from the large standard lamp over the desk. Now, it seemed stark, cold and severe. The dark curtains were drawn in front of the windows and the large fire of logs which Mr. Checkland liked so well, was burning busily. Littlejohn rose and switched off all the lights except the table-lamp on the desk.

"That is better, Superintendent."

She still seemed dazed, but was wonderfully self-possessed.

"Did *you* find him, madam?"

"I was dressing in my own room when the shot was fired. I hurried down at once."

"There was nobody else in the room?"

"No. James was upstairs changing for the evening. He was going to a birthday party."

"Did Mr. Checkland speak to you?"

"No. He was lying on the floor when I entered. I called for James and sent for the doctor. James came for you."

She was still calm, almost friendly now, as though it gave her confidence to have the massive, kindly man, seated opposite in another winged armchair, to talk to.

Maudie brought the tea and poured out two cups.

"Would you be wantin' the brandy, madam?"

"No, thank you, Maudie. That will be all. Unless the Superintendent would...?"

"No thank you, Mrs. Checkland."

Sitting there drinking their tea, they might have been old friends. The colour was returning to the mayoress's cheeks and she was obviously anxious now to take Littlejohn into her confidence.

"I heard him pacing up and down after he got home. He was very angry with me for going out to meet Mr. ... Mr. Mason without telling him. Mr. Checkland is an impulsive man, quick to anger, but very soon himself again and very kind, too."

Littlejohn nodded.

"Smoke your pipe, if you wish, Superintendent. Perhaps I may have a cigarette at the same time..."

He passed her his case and lit her cigarette. Then he filled and began to smoke his pipe. He did it all quietly, without a word. Then:

"Do you feel able to answer one or two questions, madam? It would help us greatly if you could."

"Yes, I'll try."

"You may find them rather painful and personal."

"I'll try to answer."

"Why did your husband wish to take his own life?"

A spasm of pain shot across her face and she slowly laid down her cup on the desk at her elbow, as though she were afraid of dropping it.

"Recent events seem to have got on top of him. He hasn't slept properly since the murder of Bracknell. I've heard him pacing up and down in this room until almost dawn sometimes. When he stays up late working, he sleeps in his dressing-room rather than disturb me when he retires. He has slept there since the murder at Freake's Folly. He has been getting up for sleeping tablets every night and then, when he's fallen asleep, he's talked to himself and seemed distressed. He said it was the business of the town which troubled him."

"What do you think was on his mind, Mrs. Checkland?"

She hesitated as though deciding whether or not to confide in him.

"There are so many things. Myself, for one thing ..."

"You, madam?"

"Yes."

Her voice changed and she was deeply moved. She seemed to have difficulty in setting her thoughts in order.

"Perhaps this isn't the time, Mrs. Checkland. I'm sorry to trouble you just after such a great shock. I'll call again in a day or two."

She made a gesture with her graceful, well-kept hand, as though to dismiss his arguments.

"No. Now is the time. Let this opportunity pass and it may never return. It's a strange thing, Superintendent, but you seem to be the only person I can confide in. James is too young and would not understand me at all. I have no intimate friends left. They have all died or gone. Even my own husband...I could never...I have not been the wife I ought to have been. You understand? You are a far-seeing man of the world and I have no doubt that during your stay here, you have learned very much about us all. What can you tell me? It will ease my own problem of just what to say, if you tell me what you know."

"That you loved Walter Mason when you were young and intended to marry him? That he turned dishonest and had to flee the country, and that you married Mr. Checkland...?"

"He has been a good husband to me. And I haven't deserved it."

"Because you didn't love him when you married him? That is no sin, Mrs. Checkland. It is a commonplace of marriage. How many people, men and women alike, never get the one they consider their ideal partner, the one they love first and best. It's human to be content with second-best then..."

It sounded a bit trite, but he was trying to comfort her. And as he spoke, he felt gratitude rise in him for his own happy marriage and the way it had influenced his life.

"Walter Mason was a cashier in Mr. Checkland's office. He was wrong in his books. It was obvious...I wouldn't try to hide it...that he'd stolen money to pay his debts. Mr. Checkland said unless he left the country and started a new life elsewhere, he would turn him over to the police. Walter had to go. Two or three times afterwards in the course of the years, he wrote to my husband asking to be allowed to return. Mr. Checkland always told me. 'Do you want him back?' he would say and would show me his reply. It was always a telegram with the same brief message, *Return and be Arrested.* As soon as Walter was away, Mr. Checkland proposed to me and insisted on our immediate marriage. It was as though he feared Walter would return willy-nilly and carry me off. A fortnight after Walter left, we were engaged. I was afraid at the time that if I didn't do as he wished, Mr. Checkland would have Walter arrested and brought back for prosecution. My parents, too, pressed for the marriage. They said it would steady me. They had been against my attachment to Walter and my father threatened to disinherit me ..."

She spoke in a slow, detached voice, as though telling someone else's story.

"Eight months after our marriage, James was born, prematurely. Some incendiary set fire to my father's house one night. My parents were burned to death. I was actually there spending the night with them. I saw them die before my eyes on an upper floor. Next day, James was born and we've never been able to have children since. And ..."

She paused, as though bracing herself for the next disclosure.

"And, for years, Mr. Checkland doubted if James was his child. He wanted proof that he wasn't Walter's. Of late, now that James has shown certain traits which could only have belonged to the Checkland family, as well as a considerable likeness to his father, my husband seems really convinced. The return of Mr. Mason revived his old suspicions and accusations. They were quite untrue."

She poured out two more cups of tea. It was almost cold, but she didn't appear to notice.

"Then, five years ago, Bracknell arrived. We didn't know him until he'd been here almost two years. One morning, he came and asked to see me. In some way, he had come by a bundle of letters ... They were love-letters I'd sent to Walter

Mason. I thought them long ago destroyed. I must say, they were not the kind I would have wished anyone else to see. In fact, as I read the one Bracknell brought as a sample, I wondered however I'd been mad enough to put on paper all the intimate thoughts of my heart. Certainly, it would not have done for Mr. Checkland to see them. He was jealous enough without adding fuel to the fire. He always said I'd never loved him. I admit, I didn't ... Not in the way I'd loved Walter Mason. But I did love him in another, more reasonable and solid way. To have lived with him so long, shared his life, born his son, enjoyed his company ... yes, enjoyed, for he was quite a character and a kind and considerate man, in spite of his strange way of doing things sometimes. Now, I would not change Mason for him. All the love I had for Walter died long ago. Life goes on and we adapt ourselves. One can't be perpetually weeping and harrying one's self for a lost love ..."

"You bought the letters from Bracknell?"

"Some of them ... He sold them one at a time. He was a dreadful man. Hard, merciless, mercenary, cynical ..."

"Five thousand pounds?"

"There were over thirty of them ... His price increased. He had a scale of prices ... He was loathsome ... The passionate ones, the ones which read like pages from a novelette, cost me more. I heard of his death with joy. I even laughed and thanked God. You see, I thought some maniac had done it and that I was free. I was mistaken ..."

"Marcia Fitzpayne had come by the remaining ones?"

"Yes. How did you know?"

"We found her in Freake's Folly one day. She said she had been reclaiming a book and burning some of her own letters. Whether or not she was searching for your letters, or only wanted her own, I don't know. But she found yours, probably hidden with hers. She was a feminine counterpart of Bracknell. Hard as nails, unscrupulous, merciless... Did she call on you, too?"

"No. You see, between my paying another instalment to Bracknell and the Fitzpayne girl getting the letters, Walter Mason came. He said he could not remain in Australia any longer. It was like prison to him and he'd rather Mr. Checkland had him arrested and let him serve his term in gaol here than go on. He came to see me, secretly, as soon as he arrived here..."

She paused and sighed.

"Why, Superintendent, why do men who lose their first loves in their youth, always imagine them just as they were when they left them years ago? Walter said he'd never had me out of his thoughts all the time he'd been away. But his declarations lacked enthusiasm. It was obvious that he found me much changed. My hair is grey and my face is lined. I am twenty years older. He ended by professing eternal friendship and devotion."

She smiled wryly.

"I asked him about the letters. He said that Bracknell and he had been great friends in Australia. Bracknell had even stayed with him on his farm. But he'd no idea that Bracknell had stolen the letters. He admitted that, in conversation, he had spoken of me and told Bracknell how he had lost me to Mr. Checkland..."

She always spoke of her husband as Mr. Checkland. It was as though their conjugal familiarity did not extend beyond themselves.

"...It seems that shortly after one of Bracknell's visits, Walter's farmhouse—it was a wooden one—was burned to the ground and all in it. Walter thought the letters had gone with it... When I told him, he urged me to tell my

174

husband. He even said that if I wouldn't, he, Walter, would. I was afraid Mr. Checkland would be so furious at Walter's return, that he would call-in the police right away and have him arrested. So, I promised I would tell Mr. Checkland right away. I ought to have done it at the start, but I needed someone like Walter to persuade me."

"And you told your husband?"

"Yes."

"You mean that, having resisted the idea of telling Mr. Checkland about Bracknell's blackmail for so long, you immediately allowed Mason to convince you to confess at last?"

"Yes. There was another reason. I had used up all my ready cash by these payments. It would have necessitated selling investments. My share certificates are all in the company's safe and it would have meant asking my husband for them. He would certainly have insisted on knowing why I wanted them. I have always dreaded his finding out in some way the state of my balance at the bank. There is not much left there, I can assure you."

"And what happened when you informed Mr. Checkland?"

"There was a scene, of course. Strangely enough, he didn't seem particularly angry with me. In fact, he said the letters, after all that time, were of no interest to him. He was annoyed because he said he could hardly take it to the police. A man in his position being blackmailed on account of his wife's old love-letters would become the laughing-stock of the town if it got abroad. And, in any case, he wasn't going to wash his dirty linen in front of Herle and his men."

"So ... ?"

"He said he would see Bracknell."

"Did he?"

"Yes..."

She paused almost fearfully, as though afraid to go on. Then, she braced herself.

"He went to Freake's Folly on the night Bracknell was killed!"

Littlejohn sat upright in his chair.

"Why are you telling me this, Mrs. Checkland, when all the time it is seriously incriminating your husband?"

She smiled confidently.

"There are no witnesses. I could deny I ever said it. Also, I cannot give evidence against my husband. That's the law, isn't it? But neither of these is the reason. When my husband returned, he was completely stupefied. He came into the room and asked if I'd been to Freake's Folly myself. I said certainly not; I'd been indoors embroidering a chair cover all evening. Then, he told me when he arrived at the Folly, he'd found Bracknell dead—murdered. He was in no position to call in the police. Such a step would involve him in suspicions and not only that, the reason for his visit would come out and would ruin his position in Carleton. He comforted himself by saying the maniac who'd murdered the two girls must have been about. All the same, he was gradually losing control of himself, almost going insane, lest he'd left some trace there or been seen on his way to Freake's. He expected the blow to fall any day. I begged him to tell you, but he refused. Then came Marcia Fitzpayne's death..."

"What had that to do with it?"

"She sent me a note asking me to call on her at eight o'clock on the evening she was murdered. She said she had found some papers which would interest me, among Bracknell's effects, of which she was the owner now under his will. I knew that it was beginning all over again. I told my husband. He left to keep the appointment for me. He found her stabbed too. That was the second time. I urged him to see the police and he promised to send for you and talk with you. It seems he couldn't muster the courage, and he let you go without speaking of the affair. Nobody seems to have seen him there, however. I know he would probably enter the flats by the fire escape of which, as owner of the property, he had a key. Again, he's been expecting someone to tell you they'd seen him entering. It has been another nightmare on his mind..."

She rang the bell, but before the maid could answer had left the room and was calling downstairs.

"Have they not telephoned from the hospital, yet, Maudie?"

"No, madam..."

"They're taking a long time..."

She returned, her face convulsed now with anxiety.

"I do hope everything is all right with my husband, Superintendent. You must think me callous talking so much when all the time he is hovering between life and death. But there is a good chance he will recover, Doctor Harriman said. He did say it, didn't he? I'm not imagining it?"

"No, you're not imagining it. He said there was a good chance."

"To talk fully and freely to one so sympathetic as you, Mr. Littlejohn, has helped to stifle my own fears and anguish. But much more important, I must settle this matter right away now. It has preyed so much on Mr. Checkland's mind, that he has tried, in his fumbling way—and thank God it was fumbling—to take his own life. I know he did not commit the murders. He would never do such a thing. He is a kindly man beneath his veneer of... of bravado... If he lives, and his apprehension cannot be cleared away, what is to guarantee that he will not try it again, successfully perhaps? I wish you to know, Superintendent, and I would be so grateful if you could keep my confidences to yourself until you have discovered who really committed the crimes. Mr. Checkland will be in hospital for some time. He will be helpless and, if you would have had to arrest him on suspicion through what I've told you, you can surely regard him as being as good as under arrest now. I beg you, please help me..."

"Your husband told you after he'd discovered the body of Miss Fitzpayne?"

"Yes. And for the same reasons as before, he said he could not bring in the police, but had to leave the crime for someone else to discover."

Telephone.

Mrs. Checkland ran from the room and down the stairs. There was a brief conversation and she was back.

"Mr. Lapage was at the hospital, it seems, when my husband was taken in. He is operating now and it is almost certain that Mr. Checkland will recover. I must go to the infirmary right away..."

"I will come with you, if I may. I'll see to a car whilst you are getting ready. But, just one thing before we go, Mrs. Checkland. I will, for the time being, keep to myself the matter of the letters and your husband's discoveries of the bodies. But, as soon as he is fit to be moved or to make a statement, I shall have to tell my colleagues. I shall continue the investigations and I hope some useful lead will come to light."

She turned to go to her room to get her outdoor clothes.

"Just one more word, madam..."

Littlejohn spoke seriously and with great emphasis.

"Perhaps, after all, Mr. Checkland was *cleaning his gun* when it went off. For his sake and for your own, you must ask him if that is so before the police get his statement. You understand?"

She paused, with a puzzled expression on her fine face, and then she smiled and gave him a look of gratitude which answered his question.

CHAPTER XIII
TWO CALLERS

It was turned nine o'clock when things simmered down and then Littlejohn and Cromwell remembered they hadn't had a meal since noon. They could only give them cold food at the *Huncote Arms,* but they had the comfort of the *salle à manger* to themselves. All the crowds prophesied by the waiter had gone, leaving the place deserted.

"It's been quite a busy day, sir," said Cromwell, adding pickles to his cold beef.

And there the commentary ended, for Bertha appeared and apologetically announced that Littlejohn was wanted.

"I don't know why they should disturb you, sir. They look like a courting-couple in from the country. Shall I tell them you're busy?"

"No. We'd better see them, Bertha. Any name?"

"They wouldn't give one. They're not the kind who usually come here."

She was right, for she returned followed by Lucy Jolland, the girl who had combined delivering the milk and mild flirtation with Sam Bracknell.

"Come in, Lucy."

It was like a breath of fresh air after the ragtag-and-bobtail work of the past day.

Lucy had a frightened look. It wasn't that she was scared of Littlejohn and Cromwell, whom she had placed in her category of 'ever so nice', but the *Huncote Arms* was, according to her father, the abode of the devil. She hoped that nobody would see her there and tell her dad about it. Otherwise ... As usual, he would first pray over her and then ... She was too buxom to chastise now. So it would mean locked in her room until she expressed contrition.

She was not as pretty as when they'd first met her. Her brown tweed ill-fitting coat didn't become her like her clean white overall. She wore a touch of lipstick and powder, which she would need to wipe off before entering Pinder's Close, otherwise her dad would call her Jezebel. Now, she hovered round the door, smiling nervously.

"Come in, Lucy ..."

"Can Charlie come in, too? We called before on our way to the pictures, but you'd gone out. So, we said we'd be back when it was over. Dad doesn't let us go to the pictures as a rule, but it was 'The Ten Commandments' tonight, so ... We can't stay long. Dad said we'd to come straight back."

"Where is Charlie?"

"He's waiting in the passage. I wanted to come before, but he couldn't make up his mind. Now he's decided."

"Bring him in, then."

She left them and returned followed by a huge, shy, awkward young man with a bullet head of stiff fair hair, a calflick, and a stubborn expression.

"Come and sit down, both of you. Will you have some food ... ?"

Charlie looked hungrily at the beef, pickles and beer, but in spite of his size, Lucy was evidently the boss.

"No, thank you. We might take a cup of coffee, though."

Charlie looked at her dumbfounded. At Pinder's, it was always tea or non-alcoholic hop-ale. Dad regarded coffee as a drug, and, since someone told him it was extensively consumed in Turkish harems, sinful as well.

The drinks arrived, Charlie allowed himself to be relieved of his cap and raincoat, and Lucy took off her coat, revealing an emerald green frock, firm flesh and brawny arms.

"And now...?"

They didn't know where to begin. Charlie started to stare furiously ahead.

"We said you'd tell him."

"Well, let me think what to say... It's about the night Mr. Bracknell died. I'd left my gloves there that morning. We called back on our way home, but the place was locked up. I said I'd go for them at night when he was sure to be in."

Charlie started to mutter. He had drunk half his coffee and was expecting the stimulation foretold by dad. Instead, nothing had happened. He looked angrily at the waiter who was clearing away the first course.

"There's ice cream to follow, sir."

Lucy and Charlie began to take interest. Soon all four of them were eating peach melbas.

"Tell him about me, like you said you would."

Lucy sighed. Was there ever such a stubborn man! Charlie's mind ran on tramlines, each idea slowly emerging and expressed without deviation, according to plan.

"Charlie told me last night after he'd spoken to dad... Not about Mr. Bracknell, but about us getting married..."

She paused as though she'd remembered something joyful. Meanwhile, Littlejohn was imagining Charlie putting into words a request to the unctuous dad for his daughter's hand!

"I forgot. We're engaged to be married! Charlie said I wanted someone to look after me after Mr. Bracknell ... Well, you know what I mean."

Congratulations all round. Even Charlie smiled a slow, self-congratulatory smirk in between hissing with pain as the ice-cream punished his hollow tooth. They ought to have had champagne but, out of deference to dad, they had another course of ice-cream.

The interlude delighted the happy pair, if Charlie's grimaces and doleful lapses could be interpreted as signs of felicity.

"Charlie told me last night, that since the two girls were murdered, he'd never let me out of his sight. I didn't know he was there, but he was."

"I was that," echoed Charlie with emphasis.

"Every time I went to Mr. Bracknell's with the milk, he followed me down and peeked in at the window, protecting me, even when I didn't know it."

She was proud of him.

"Tell 'em what I said, Lucy. Tell 'em. And I meant it every bit."

"He said he didn't mind me talking to Mr. Bracknell. I'd a right to talk to intelligent people, a girl with my education."

"That's right. A clever girl like you, you've the right. But what else did I say ... ?"

Charlie leaned back ready to contemplate his own words again.

"He said it was only to be talk. If Sam Bracknell had so much as laid a hand on me, or tried to ... tried to kiss me ..."

"Tell 'em ..."

"He'd have come in the house, torn the arms and legs off Sam Bracknell, and thrown them over the fields like manure."

Charlie nodded, smiling proudly at his metaphor, as though he'd composed a verse from the Song of Songs. And then his stubborn face softened as he looked at Lucy and he gently touched her arm.

"I meant it, too. A chap like Bracknell to try to handle a fine girl like you. I meant it."

Cromwell cut a cigar he'd had in his pocket for weeks and lit it. Then he offered his packet of cigarettes to Charlie.

"No, thanks."

Only last night dad had made him promise not to smoke, drink, utter foul language, or indulge in other sins with names he'd never heard before.

Littlejohn lit his pipe.

"But that isn't what you called to tell me, is it, Lucy? Was there something important about the murder?"

She gave Charlie a hasty look. He nodded consent.

"I went for my gloves the night Sam Bracknell was killed. There was somebody there with him. The lamp was on and the curtains weren't drawn. I peeped in. Then, I went away. Charlie had followed me, as he'd said he would. We went back to the farm, then. I only hoped dad wouldn't ask where was my gloves. He didn't."

"What time would that be?"

"About half-past seven when we got to Freake's. Dad goes to chapel at seven and we went out soon after..."

"What did the man you saw with Bracknell look like? Did you know him, either of you?"

"No. We'd neither of us seen him before. Had we Charlie?"

Charlie, whose surname was Space, shook his head decidedly.

"Never seen him in my life before. He wasn't a local chap."

"Can you describe him?"

Then began a duet between the lovers.

"He'd be middle-aged..."

"That's right. Fifty or a bit more."

"Was he grey-haired, Lucy, or black, or fair...?"

"Grey, I'd say, and rather plenty of it."

"I never noticed his hair. I on'y took a bit of a peek after Lucy had come away from the window, like. He was thinner than you are. Not quite as tall as you, either. He was standin' up when I see him."

"What kind of a suit?"

Charlie Space was stumped. Dress wasn't much in his line.

"Grey, it looked like... Lighter than Charlie's suit..."

Which made it light grey.

"Did you get a full-face look at him, either of you?"

"I didn't, sir. He was standing side-faced. I could see he'd thick dark eyebrows, that's all."

Charlie said the same.

"And that's all you can both remember?"

"Yes."

Charlie nodded.

"You wouldn't be able to recognise him again, then?"

Lucy didn't answer and the obstinate look returned to Charlie's face.

"We aren't going to have to go to the police-station, are we? I don't think either of us would recognise him. I don't know what Lucy's dad would say to our going to the police. A lot would come out he doesn't know. It 'ud be awkward. In any case, we'd better be goin' home. It's nearly ten..."

"Is that all you have to tell me?"

"No. There's more. Charlie, you ought to tell it. It wasn't me."

"But you said you'd do the talkin', Lucy. You know I'm no good at words."

"Oh, very well. Charlie said he felt so sorry for me not gettin' my gloves, that he went again to Freake's after we'd got home. He saw me indoors and went off right away. He didn't say where he was goin'. He wanted to surprise me with the gloves."

"I went over the fields. It's only ten minutes that way."

He paused, waiting for Lucy.

"When he got to the house, the light was still on, the man who was there had gone. There didn't seem to be anybody in, though. So Charlie tried the door. It was loose. He went in ..."

Her voice faltered.

"You finish it. I can't bear what you told me."

"Nothin' in it. Old Bracknell was stretched on the floor. I could see he was dead. There was a knife in him. I couldn't see the gloves and I went off like a shot. I didn't want to be caught there. They'd have said I'd done it."

Littlejohn put down his pipe.

"You didn't do it, did you, Charlie?"

"Who? Me? Course I didn't. He'd been stabbed when I got there. Why should I have done it?"

"Because Bracknell was trying to steal your girl."

Charlie looked at Littlejohn as though he'd gone mad.

"Haven't I told you before, what I'd have done to Bracknell if he'd made a pass at Lucy? Tore him limb from limb and thrown him about the fields like manure. I'd 'ave let the crows pick Bracknell. That's what I'd have done."

Lucy felt she was called for the defence.

"Charlie wouldn't do such a thing. He's a kind man, is Charlie. Even can't bear ill-treatment to animals. Couldn't even stick a pig."

A hostile look crossed Charlie's ruddy face.

"Well...? What of it? Pig-stickers don't make the best husbands, do they? You don't want a pig-sticking husband, do you? If you do, you've only got to say so."

"Don't be silly, Charlie. It's because you're so kind and gentle that I like you."

In spite of tearing Bracknell limb from limb and the crows pickings, she understood him!

"What time would that be?"

Charlie gave it up and cast enquiring eyes on his girl again.

"As I said, it would be about half-past seven when we were at Freake's the first time. Charlie would be back there just before eight."

"Meanwhile, Bracknell had been killed."

"Yes."

"Do you think the man you saw with him killed him?"

"We both talked about it, didn't we Charlie? And we both said he did it."

"Why?"

"Because when we saw him, he seemed to be bullying Mr. Bracknell."

"Tellin' him off, you mean."

"If you put it that way, Charlie, yes."

"And that is all?"

"No."

Charlie said it stubbornly, as usual, as though the detectives weren't going to let him finish his tale. He was determined to do it dad or no dad, waiting at home with his watch in his hand.

"I hurried out of the house..."

"Just one question more, Charlie...Why didn't you tell the police that you'd found a murdered man?"

Lucy leaned and touched Littlejohn's arm gently, and then in a quiet voice defended her boy-friend.

"He did it for me. If he'd told the police, dad would have been awfully mad. It would have come out about us being down at Freake's after the gloves. Dad might have said there was something between me and Mr. Bracknell and asked what I was doing at the house at all when he'd forbid it. Also, the police might have said it was Charlie himself who did it on account of me. Everybody knows how Charlie was mad about me."

"I never said so. I never told nobody."

"But you were, and you behaved..."

"I always behaved decent."

"We know, Charlie, we know. Get on with your tale, then, if there's more. Otherwise, you'll be here all night. Then what will dad say?"

"Aye, Mr. Littlejohn. Besides, on top of what Lucy says, I knew the other man would tell the police. After all, he was the mayor and, as such, it was his duty."

"The mayor. What do you mean?"

"I was goin' to say, I thought when I see Mr. Checkland going to Freake's, like, he'd find the body and report it. So that lightened my conscience about telling the police myself."

"You met Mr. Checkland at Freake's Folly?"

"I said so. When I come out of the house, in a hurry, too, I can tell you, I heard footsteps comin' down Dan's Lane. So, I nipped into a dark corner till they'd gone. Mr. Checkland appeared. I could see him in the lamplight as he passed the window. Plain as I'm seein' you now. He went in. I didn't wait. I ran out of my hidin'-place and I didn't stop till I'd got back to Pinder's."

"Were you surprised when you heard nothing about Mr. Checkland being there."

Charlie looked crafty.

"No. I knew the mayor was connected with the police. That Herle's as cunnin' as a basket o' monkeys. I was sure he'd told Mr. Checkland to keep quiet about it, as a matter o' policy, like. Sort of trap they were springing on somebody."

Littlejohn lit his pipe again.

"So, Charlie, you are prepared to state that when you visited Freake's Folly at about half-past seven, with Lucy, you found Bracknell alive and in conversation with a man of the type you've both described...?"

"Yes."

"And when you returned about half an hour later, you found Bracknell dead and alone, and, as you left the house, Mr. Checkland was arriving and entered whilst you were hiding?"

"That's right."

"You're both agreeable to sign a statement to that effect?"

The two lovers looked at each other in alarm.

"It would mean everybody would know, Mr. Littlejohn?"

Lucy had grown red-cheeked and fearful and Charlie Space was beginning to look stubborn and hostile again.

"Couldn't it be kept secret?"

"I'm afraid not. You see, you two have just provided some very vital evidence about the murder of Samuel Bracknell. It will probably clear of suspicion someone who might have been accused of murder. Your evidence might be very necessary to bring the criminal to justice."

"I don't know what my dad'll say about all this. Such a lot of things will come out along with it."

"Nothin' 'll come out."

Charlie sat up suddenly, a determined look on his face. He wagged a huge forefinger at his blushing bride-to-be.

"If your dad says a word about us bein' home late, or about us talkin' to the police, or about anythin' you and me does together, I'll tell him where he gets off, take you away, marry you, and get myself a fresh job somewhere where we can 'ave a bit of peace. I'm sick of dad, dad, dad, everythin' we do. And that's flat and you know when I says a thing, I means it, and nothin'll change me."

He paused for breath, wondering at his sudden gift of inspired speech.

Lucy's face wore a new expression as she faced him.

"Yes, Charlie."

"And now we'll have a drink with these two gentlemen, if you please. We want 'em to wish us congratulations, happiness and long life, and children to bless us. You can have tea, Lucy, or herb-beer, if you want. But I'm having a pint of ale in a pewter tankard like my own dad used to drink from. Now, what'll you all have...?"

When later, Mr. Moses Jolland, watch in hand, opened the door to his two fly-by-nights when they arrived home at eleven, he called their attention to the hour, to his own instructions, to the evils of loose living, to the punishments for disobedience. His mobile nose moved as he detected the scent of strong drink in the air, too.

"So what?" asked Charlie Space, gently, and the tyranny of Mr. Moses Jolland crumbled in the dust.

Chapter XIV
The Better Man

It was exactly half-past ten when the telephone rang. The young couple from Pinder's Close Farm had hardly got through the doorway of the hotel before Bertha was in the 'scale à manger'.

"Superintendent Littlejohn is wanted on the telephone. It's the police station."

"Upshott's given us the slip again!"

It was Herle and he sounded very annoyed. He almost said 'I told you what it would be.'

The man on duty keeping an eye on Upshott at the *Barley Mow*, had, it seemed, spent a very comfortable Saturday night. Upshott had been a model suspect. He'd passed the evening after dinner in drinking, making friends, and standing drinks here and there. Then, suddenly, he'd left the group round the bar, casually walked into the hall, nodded at the man who was trailing him, as though he might have been an old friend, and, before the plain-clothes constable had realised what was happening, had walked through the front door and lost himself in the dark.

"It's time we arrested him, or else let him go altogether," said Herle.

"Did your man enquire of the group at the bar, what they'd been talking about just before Upshott gave him the slip?"

"I didn't ask him. What has that to do with it?"

"Quite a lot. I'll ring up the *Barley Mow* myself."

The manager of the hotel was an Irishman. He seemed to have formed a good opinion of Upshott.

"A nice, sociable kind of a fellow," he told Littlejohn.

"What were he and his friends talking about just before he left the hotel?"

"Somebody had just come in and reported that the mayor had met with an accident and was in the infirmary seriously ill..."

"Thank you very much, Mr. Maloney."

"Don't mention it, sir..."

And Mr. Maloney went to chuck out two men who were drunk and wouldn't go home.

"Could you get us a taxi, Bertha?"

"Of course..."

She went to the front door and blew a whistle. Three taxis drew up and Littlejohn chose the first to arrive. They left the other two quarrelling with Bertha.

"The infirmary, please..."

It was just on the outskirts of the town. A tall new building made of concrete and towering in the darkness. The mayor, they told Littlejohn, was doing very nicely, thank you. He'd had his operation and it looked as if he might recover.

"Is Mrs. Checkland still here?"

"No, sir. She left about ten minutes ago."

"Was there anyone with her?"

"A man arrived just before she left..."

"Tall, grey haired?"

"Yes. He asked if he could see the mayor. Of course, he couldn't. Then he asked if the mayoress was here. We said yes. She was just having a cup of tea in the sister's office. He went to see her there and they left together in Mrs. Checkland's car."

The night porter, a red-haired, cadaverous man, recited it all without a trace of emotion or curiosity. They were used to far worse things than that at the Carleton Infirmary.

"Take us to the mayor's house, please."

"He won't be at home. He's had an accident, I hear."

The taxi man knew all about it. Presumably it was all over the town by this. The morning papers would be full of it. There was a reporter being shown out of Checkland's house as Littlejohn and Cromwell entered.

"Hello, Super. You on the case, too? Is it connected with the murders? It's said the mayor shot himself. Is that true? Come on, now. Give us a break. We've got to live, like the police ..."

"Don't pester me now, that's a good chap. I don't know any more than you."

"Sez you."

The elderly maid seemed surprised to see them.

"Mrs. Checkland's engaged, sir. I don't think she'll be able to see you."

"We'll go and find out for ourselves, shall we, Maudie?"

And before she could reply, Littlejohn led the way upstairs. He tried the door of the library with which he was now familiar. Mrs. Checkland and Upshott were inside and both of them rose with startled looks. Then Upshott got nasty.

"What the hell do you mean breaking in here at this time of night? It's intolerable. It's exceeding your duty, Superintendent."

"If you persist, Mr. Upshott, in giving our man the slip and wandering away from your hotel, we're bound to seek you out and remind you that you promised to stay put."

"This is exceptional. The mayor's been shot. Mr. and Mrs. Checkland are friends of mine. I'm surely allowed to make enquiries as to what's happened and how the mayor is."

There were two glasses half-full of whisky on the table. Mrs. Checkland had been sitting in her usual wing chair. Upshott had apparently been standing, talking with her when the detectives interrupted.

"May I ask you, Mrs. Checkland, if you rang Mr. Upshott to tell him of the accident?"

"No."

"Of course she didn't. I heard about it at the *Barley Mow*. I hadn't time to explain or argue or ask permission to go from that flatfoot who's there seeing that I don't run away. I just left the place and found Mrs. Checkland at the infirmary. Now that I have found out that the mayor's likely to recover and brought her home, I'm quite satisfied and ready to go back to the hotel."

Littlejohn seemed to feel the heat of the room. He removed his raincoat and placed it across a chair with his hat. Upshott's coat, too, had been thrown across the same chair.

"You proposing to stay a bit, Superintendent? Mrs. Checkland ought to go and get some sleep. She's played out. She's been through a lot today."

"I quite agree. Before we go, however, madam, may I ask you one or two more questions? I won't take much of your time."

"Certainly. Won't you sit down, both of you."

She looked tired out, but as tranquil as usual.

"Thank you, but we must be going. I wanted to ask you and Mr. Upshott why he suddenly decided to come back to Carleton after more than eighteen years' absence? Did you both keep in touch all that time? Did you write to each other?"

"No, we didn't. I was in no mood for writing to her, or to anybody else when I left Carleton for Australia."

Upshott answered before Mrs. Checkland had quite understood the question. Now she passed her fingers across her forehead and looked at him as if asking him to tell the rest.

"The reason I came back was to see Bracknell. Eileen ... I mean Mrs. Checkland, wrote to me asking why I had given Bracknell her old letters, written before I went away. It was the only letter she ever wrote to me in Australia. She said she got my address from a letter I sent to her husband asking if he'd allow me to return to Carleton."

"But Bracknell had been blackmailing her for years. Why write a mere few weeks ago?"

Mrs. Checkland spoke in a weary defeated voice.

"My ready money was running out. I was desperate. I'd promised my husband I would never see or get in touch with Walter again. I broke my promise because I couldn't go on. I wanted to know why Bracknell had the letters ..."

"Mrs. Checkland's letter followed me about Australia. I'd had a good offer for my farm, sold it, and was travelling about a bit in search of a new job. The letter caught me up at Canberra. I decided then and there that I'd had enough of being on the run through Ben Checkland's malice. Besides, I wanted to know what Bracknell was up to. I took the next 'plane. I arrived in England probably three months after Mrs. Checkland wrote."

"You saw Bracknell?"

"I told you so. On the afternoon before he was killed."

"Are you sure you didn't go to Freake's Folly again after that?"

"Certainly. What makes you think I did?"

"You were seen there that night, just before Bracknell was found dead."

Mrs. Checkland covered her mouth with her hand as though to hold back a scream.

"You weren't there, Walter...?"

"Of course not. I was back in London by then. I've already told the Superintendent. Who's been telling yarns about seeing me at the Folly? Because it's all lies..."

"We have a reliable witness who saw you through the window indulging in high words with Bracknell. Are you sure your timing isn't wrong, Upshott, and you were there at night, not in the afternoon?"

"I'm dead certain. Someone's trying to frame me. Someone who's responsible for the murder. If I were you, I'd just keep an eye on that informant, Littlejohn."

"May I ask you, Mrs. Checkland, if your husband said *when* he proposed to visit Bracknell after you'd told him about the blackmailing?"

"He said he'd some arrangements for a finance meeting to make with the Borough Treasurer. It would take about half-an-hour. After that, he was going straight to Freake's Folly."

"What time would that be?"

"He'd fixed to see the treasurer at 7.30."

"Did you telephone, or otherwise let Mr. Upshott know that Mr. Checkland was going, and at what time?"

Upshott flushed a dull red.

"What is all this? Still pursuing the tack that I'm the murderer?"

"Please let Mrs. Checkland answer my question."

"Yes. I rang up. I'd arranged with Walter that if my husband wouldn't call and see Bracknell about the letters, Walter would do so. I said I would telephone when I'd got my husband's promise."

"So, you knew Mr. Checkland was going to Freake's Folly and at what time, Upshott?"

"Yes. But I didn't rush down there, kill Bracknell, and then leave it to look as though Checkland had murdered him..."

"Nobody said you did, Upshott."

"You insinuated it. I resent the way this interview is going. Before I know where I am, I'll be in gaol accused of the two crimes. If I'm a suspect, say so, and then I'll know what to do."

"Tell me, please, why you and Mrs. Checkland arranged to meet earlier today at the *Marquis of Granby*? It seems a strange thing to me that, knowing Mr. Checkland's attitude towards you, you should begin to pester his wife and make secret assignations with her..."

"Now don't be offensive, Littlejohn. You seem to think that because you're a policeman, you can be as insulting as you like. There are ways of dealing with people like you..."

Mrs. Checkland rubbed her brow with her fingers again.

"Please stop quarrelling, Walter. The Superintendent is only anxious...as anxious as we are...to find out who committed the crimes. Why don't you tell him...?"

Upshott seemed suddenly to go mad. It was as if he couldn't interrupt her and speak for himself fast enough. He almost shouted the place down.

"All right. I'll tell him then. Don't you say another word. It's my affair. I asked her to meet me to say goodbye. I escaped from your flatfoot who was shadowing me, and was going to beat it to London and off to Australia again out of the way. I'm sick of the whole business. As soon as I arrived here, I found myself mixed up in this crazy Bracknell affair, and, for makeweight, the murder of a woman I didn't even know. All I came for was to ask Bracknell for the letters and the money he'd extorted from Eileen. I saw him, he said he'd not got the letters with him, they were in his box at the bank, and that if I'd return next day, he'd have them."

Mrs. Checkland's mouth opened in surprise.

"But..."

"Will you let me speak, Eileen? Before I could get the letters, Bracknell had been killed. At first, they said it was a lunatic who was wandering around murdering people. Then it was somebody else... Then, it was me. I gather now that I'm suspect number one."

"Nobody said so."

"You've all but said it."

"And then, having met Mrs. Checkland at the *Marquis of Granby* and said goodbye, you didn't leave after all..."

"No. You and your police arrived and put me under house arrest again."

"It wasn't very stringent, was it, if you could escape as easily again as you did tonight?"

"No, it wasn't. You think I don't know that you laid it on lightly with an eye to trapping me. You thought if I found out I could break away easily, I'd lead you off somewhere and incriminate myself. Well, I saw your game. I'd nowhere to lead you. When, however, I heard that Mr. Checkland had had a gun accident... It's charitable to call it that, isn't it...?" He spoke through his teeth. His nerves were now so much on edge that he was growing vicious.

"When I heard our worthy mayor had had an accident, my first thought was of Eileen. I'd asked her to come back to

Australia with me. You might as well know it. She refused. I wouldn't take an immediate no. I said I'd wait until tomorrow. When, as I said, I heard Checkland was in hospital, I had to see her. I wanted to know if she needed any help. Also, I wished to tell her that I wouldn't leave tomorrow after all. I'd give her more time to decide ... time until Checkland was out of danger and himself again. And that's all I've got to say. And it's all Mrs. Checkland has to say, too, and I'll thank you to leave her alone now. She's had enough trouble without your adding to it."

There was a dead silence for a minute after this outburst. Littlejohn was quite unperturbed. He seemed to have forgotten the turmoil of the case and looked anxiously at Mrs. Checkland to see how she was taking it.

"Did you manage to have a word with your husband, Mrs. Checkland?"

"No. He was still under the anaesthetic. They promised to let me know as soon as I could see him. It will probably be some time tomorrow."

"I'm glad all has gone well. Is your son still at the hospital?"

"Yes. He said he would stay all night, just in case there was any change. He is very fond of his father."

Upshott watched them agitatedly, as though Littlejohn and the mayoress might, in some way, have been speaking in code and exchanging information in which he could not join.

"Did you know he owned a revolver?"

"Yes. He was an officer in the first war. He used to keep it in his desk and had cleaned it in view of there being so many robberies. I had no idea ..."

"Perhaps he was cleaning it again when it went off ..."

Upshott could bear it no longer.

"Are you keeping up this small-talk all night, Littlejohn? Please remember, it's a great strain on Mrs. Checkland. She needs a good night's sleep..."

"I'm all right, Walter. Please mix Mr. Littlejohn and Mr. Cromwell a drink before they go. They've both been very kind."

Cromwell wondered why Littlejohn didn't refuse. Perhaps it was to stretch Upshott's nerves even further and then trap him into giving more information.

Upshott poured out two whiskies. His hand trembled as he did so. Then he passed the syphon.

"Add your own soda." He almost snarled it.

Littlejohn sipped his drink slowly. He didn't seem ready for leaving at all. On the contrary, he started chatting to Mrs. Checkland again.

"It's surprising the steps they've made in brain surgery these days, Mrs. Checkland. Your husband will be all right, I'm sure."

"Thank you for being so kind, Superintendent. I shall be grateful to you both, always."

Upshott was pacing up and down the room like a caged animal. All the time he kept his eyes glued on Mrs. Checkland, as though she might melt away, or else divulge some queer secret she shared only with him.

Littlejohn finally turned on him.

"My dear Upshott, you seem very agitated. There's no reason for you to stay here. You have less right than my colleague and I. In fact, you've no business here at all. One appreciates the fact that you've seen Mrs. Checkland safely home, but to stay on drinking the mayor's whisky and all the time to be trying to persuade his wife to run away with you, seems to me to be a bit impudent, to say the least of it."

"I don't care a damn what you think, Littlejohn, I'm staying here until you go. If I leave you, you'll be here, putting Mrs. Checkland through a third-degree until dawn. You're going first. Then I'll follow."

"To the *Barley Mow*, I hope?"

"As you say, to the *Barley Mow*. And now, will you kindly go and let Mrs. Checkland settle for the night."

"We'll all go together."

"We won't. After tonight's session and your lack of consideration, I prefer my own company as far as the hotel."

"Very well..."

Littlejohn took up his raincoat, flung it across his arm, and then picked up his hat from the chair.

"Good night, Mrs. Checkland. I hope there will be better news for you in the morning."

"Good night, Superintendent...and Mr. Cromwell. Thank you both again."

Upshott even saw them to the door of the room and closed it behind them. They could hear him ring the bell for Maudie in the kitchen.

Maudie must have retired. There wasn't a sound in the house. A single light burned over the stairs, and outside, the hanging lamp over the main door and the one in the tunnel were still alight. Littlejohn descended slowly, fumbling in the pocket of his raincoat, fiddling with something in his hand. Cromwell, who couldn't see what he was doing, thought he was taking out some handcuffs.

"I forgot something. One more question for Mrs. Checkland. Let's both go back."

Littlejohn tapped on the door and flung it open.

Upshott was standing over Mrs. Checkland who was still sitting in her usual chair. Her eyes were wide with alarm and it was not due to the return of Littlejohn.

"Can't you see it was a trap...? If you'd..."

Upshott turned and faced Littlejohn.

"What the blazes do you want now? I'm sorry I can't chuck the pair of you out. I can't even send for the police to remove you! But I tell you this..."

Littlejohn put down his hat and coat on the same chair again. It looked as if he was preparing for another session.

"I tell you there are ways of dealing with people like you. Eileen, go up to bed right away. Don't heed these policemen... If they so much as dare to lay a hand on you..."

Littlejohn actually smiled at him.

"We don't propose to touch Mrs. Checkland at all. I've no more questions for her or for you, Upshott. I changed my mind on the stairs. I can't trust you at the *Barley Mow* any longer. We're going to take you with us to the police station and lock you up for the night."

Upshott laughed harshly.

"On what charge? You'd better be careful. You've nothing on me. You've no ground at all for detaining me. I warn you..."

"Come along, Upshott... We don't want to handcuff you."

"Handcuff me! Don't be funny. This isn't a melodrama. It's something that's going to put paid to your career, Littlejohn, when I report it to the proper quarter..."

Mrs. Checkland looked ready to faint. Cromwell poured her out some whisky and handed it gently to her.

"Thank you. Must you really...?"

"Don't worry, Eileen. We're going to the police station now, whether or not. We'll soon see who's in the right. Me or this meddling fool of a bobby..."

He crossed the room and took up his raincoat from beside that of Littlejohn.

"Are you ready?"

Littlejohn faced him smiling still. It was as if he expected something.

And Upshott snatched out a revolver from his coat pocket and pointed it at Littlejohn. It was another Army model, like Checkland's. Cromwell took it all in and looked ready to run the risk of pouncing across the room.

"Steady, old man. Don't do anything rash. Stay where you are."

Mrs. Checkland stifled a scream.

"Don't, Walter. No more, please. We've had enough trouble and bloodshed. Give the Superintendent the gun and go quietly with them."

"Not on your life. Don't interfere, Eileen. Leave this to me. Now, Littlejohn, stay where you are, and none of you move until you hear I'm through the tunnel and in the street. Then you've got a sporting chance. One move and I'll fire. And I warn you, I'm a good shot with a revolver."

"Give it to me, Upshott..."

Littlejohn took a step towards the gun.

Mrs. Checkland tried to scream and couldn't. Cromwell's eyes bulged, and drops of sweat like peas burst out on his forehead.

Upshott's face grew grim, his chin tightened, he aimed at Littlejohn and pulled the trigger. As he did so, he winced. His damaged right hand had not fully recovered.

Anti-climax. A silly little metallic click. And then another. No explosion at all.

Littlejohn took another step forward, his fist shot out, and Upshott measured his length on the carpet. Cromwell snapped the handcuffs on his wrists and hauled him up.

"Take him below and wait for me, old chap. Sorry, I didn't mean to scare you. I thought it a strange thing he didn't leave his raincoat in the hall below, like an ordinary caller, but brought it in the room with him. I touched the pockets as I put my own coat beside it and felt the gun. So I swapped coats when we left and emptied the magazine."

He turned to Mrs. Checkland who was regarding the scene horrified.

"I'm terribly sorry, madam. But this had to happen. I knew he was bullying you. Now you can retire to bed in peace. I think, though, you ought to send for Mr. James back from the hospital. You need him most just now."

"I think I do, Superintendent. Thank you for coming back. I was so terrified ..."

"I knew."

"You knew?"

"You were going to tell me why you met Upshott at the *Marquis of Granby*. Was it not that Upshott told you to call for the letters and you burned them there together?"

"Yes. How did you know?"

"I guessed from the way he behaved. He was afraid that you'd tell. He shouted you down and wouldn't let you speak again. Then, when we had left, he began to explain, to bully you, to tell you why you mustn't mention the letters."

"Yes. That's true. But why? If he'd taken them from Bracknell ... ?"

Her eyes opened wide in horror and her mouth fell.

"Oh ..."

"Exactly. Marcia Fitzpayne, not Bracknell, had the letters. How did Upshott obtain them?"

"He killed her?"

"It seems very much like it."

"But why bring the letters to me and incriminate himself?"

"I don't know whether or not he still loves you ..."

"God forbid!"

"But I think it's something else. He hates your husband. He's anxious for you to run away with him to complete the ruin and unhappiness of Mr. Checkland. He wanted to show you what a poor fish your husband is. If Mr. Checkland couldn't recover the letters for you, he, Upshott, was made of better stuff. He would do it. And he did. He thought you'd be grateful, admire him, leave your husband, and follow the better man."

"He must be mad."

"Exactly. Years of nursing hatred and plotting revenge have driven him out of his mind. Now, everything is going to be all right, Mrs. Checkland. Your husband will soon be back, and this nightmare will be over."

And for the first time since Littlejohn had known her, Eileen Checkland began to weep.

CHAPTER XV
IN THE SMALL HOURS

From midnight onwards the police station at Carleton Unthank was a blaze of light. Not that the arrival of Cromwell with a suspected murderer caused all the staff to be called out, but that Sergeant Dalrymple, who was on night duty, grew so excited that whenever he entered a room, he forgot to put off the switches. Several empty offices, therefore, were illuminated whilst all the work went on in Herle's sanctum.

Superintendent Herle had been roused from his bed.

"These Scotland Yard men will drive me daft," he told his wife as he drew on his trousers and tucked-in his shirt. "They don't seem to have any idea of the relative importance of events. I'll bet this is another mare's nest."

"Yes, dear," replied Mrs. Herle, and immediately fell asleep again, which made her husband all the more furious.

When he found Cromwell waiting for him with a handcuffed Upshott he was flabbergasted.

"What's going on?"

"We'd better wait for Superintendent Littlejohn, sir. He'll be over any minute. He's just having a few words with Mrs. Checkland..."

Herle sat down heavily in his chair.

"It beats me. And why have you got the handcuffs on Upshott?"

Upshott who had been behaving like someone in a trance suddenly awoke.

"When I get hold of a lawyer someone's going to get it in the neck for this. Littlejohn's made up his mind to arrest somebody and he's picked on me. Take off these ruddy handcuffs. I might be a criminal. And, by the way, you'll be made to bear witness that Littlejohn hit me, too. That's against the law. I'll..."

"Shut up, Upshott, or I'll sock you on the jaw, as well. You haven't told Superintendent Herle, yet, that you pulled a gun on Superintendent Littlejohn. Not another word from you."

"He pulled a gun...?"

Herle placed both hands on the top of his thinning crown.

"He pulled a gun! Am I dreaming? I give it up..."

But he was trying not to look like a man in the wrong. He'd said all along that Scotland Yard were kicking up a lot of fuss and getting nowhere. Now things were moving with a vengeance.

The outer door of the police station banged and Littlejohn appeared. He was filling his pipe and glanced at the *No Smoking* notice beneath the portrait of Winston Churchill over the fireplace.

"You don't mind my smoking, Herle?"

Herle shrugged. Why the sudden burst of good humour?

"I think you can take off the handcuffs, old chap."

Upshott didn't say a word as Cromwell relieved him. He was looking the worse for wear now. No longer dapper and smiling, he seemed to have lost weight, his cheeks were sagging, and two deep lines had appeared at the corners of his mouth. He looked at Herle as though he saw in him an ally.

"All this because I gave your sleuth the slip and went to enquire about the mayor at the hospital."

Herle, too, had lost his bite. He could hardly look Littlejohn in the face, but sat at his desk laden with documents and files and started to fiddle with some papers. He had treated Littlejohn with little civility now and then, and sometimes he'd been openly hostile. He'd even talked about him behind his back. He was wondering now if he was going to have to eat his words.

Littlejohn lit his pipe and threw away the spent match.

"Let's clear up the case right away and then we can get to bed."

"You've solved it?"

"I think so. Upshott, I'm sure, will differ, but there seems to be only one explanation ..."

"I did it! Go on! I've just been telling Superintendent Herle you've made up your mind to pin it on somebody and *I'm* the one you've chosen."

Littlejohn didn't seem to hear him.

"To begin with, Upshott, then called Mason, was a clerk years ago in Checkland's office. He and Mrs. Checkland, then Miss Eileen Huncote, were in love and hoped soon to be married. But Upshott was one who lived above his means, spent a lot, indulged in betting, and finally began to make up his differences by robbing the till."

A sturdy policeman had entered silently and stood by the door taking it all in. The harsh white light from the large bulb hanging in the middle of the room shone down on them all. It looked like an unreal scene in a waxwork show. Herle suddenly became aware of the newcomer and shouted to the sergeant.

"Well? Don't stand there doing nothing. One of you had better take all this down."

Littlejohn spared them the trouble.

"We'll get a proper statement later, Superintendent Herle ..."

"If you're lucky ..."

Cromwell dug Upshott in the ribs with his elbow.

"That'll do from you."

"Better all sit down, hadn't we?"

The constables started to run about for extra chairs and soon they were all seated, even the constables. Herle had given it up. They could all sit on the floor as far as he was concerned. It was like a nightmare to him.

"Mr. Benjamin Checkland was also in love with Miss Huncote, but didn't seem to have much of a chance. The theft by Upshott of his firm's money was just the opportunity he'd been waiting for. Checkland told Upshott that unless he left the country at once and didn't return, he'd prosecute him. Upshott fled to Australia right away."

Upshott's face suddenly changed. His features tightened, he began to take interest in what was being said, and then he produced a little pocket diary and a pen and began to jot down notes in it.

"It is quite possible that when he made his bargain with Upshott, he also made another with Miss Huncote. He insisted that they should be married right away. Within a month, Miss Huncote became Mrs. Checkland."

"Wonderful! You talk as if you'd invented it all yourself. Actually, anybody living in Carleton at the time it happened, could have told you the same ..."

"Nobody knew about your theft, Upshott. They only knew that you cleared out, left Miss Huncote apparently in the lurch, and Checkland married her."

For some reason, it made Upshott start busily writing in his little book again. He even smiled sarcastically as though he'd found a chink in Littlejohn's armour.

"From time to time, he wrote to Checkland, asking for pardon and to be allowed to return. The answer was always the same. A cable. *If you return... gaol.*"

"That's not true! I wrote and offered to pay back the amount I'd been wrong in my books. I'd be the last man alive to grovel to Checkland. He was a swine. However... Go on. This is very interesting. I'll tell you where you're wrong later."

Through the great window of Herle's room which overlooked the square, they could see the vast stretch of asphalt, shining in the rain with the dim figure of some dead and gone Huncote in bronze in the middle of it, pointing heavenward to emphasise his oratory. Not a soul about. The street lamps had been cut down and only one in three was illuminated. At the far side of the square, the lights over Checkland's door and in the passage were still burning. A night 'plane buzzed overhead and the noise finally died away leaving the silence deeper than ever.

"Upshott settled down, took to farming, made some money. All the time he was thinking of Carleton. Not perhaps of the woman he'd had to leave behind so much as the man who had brought about his ruin. He hated Checkland more and more, revenge became an obsession with him, and he lived for the day when he could get back and pay Checkland what he owed him, not in cash, but in hate."

As Littlejohn spoke, Upshott stared straight ahead, his face set, his hands jerking as from some inner tension. Then he awoke.

"You ought to write thrillers, Littlejohn. You make it all sound true."

"Then, Samuel Bracknell began to take a hand. Upshott and Bracknell had been friends in Australia, where Bracknell was born. They found they'd a mutual interest.

Bracknell had inherited some ruined property in Carleton, was getting tired of farming in Australia, and decided to come to England and inspect his patrimony. He seemed to like it over here, settled down, and took up his permanent residence at Freake's Folly. The only drawback was he was greedy for money. He soon found the way to get some. During his stay with Upshott in Perth, he grew curious about his friend and took the opportunity of having a look through his papers. He found a batch of letters from Mrs. Checkland, then Eileen Huncote. They were love-letters of a very private and revealing sort. Bracknell, a dirty dog at the best of times, saw a chance of blackmail in them. He was proposing to return to Carleton and might seek out the writer and cash in on them if possible. He took them with him. After all, by the time Upshott found them gone, Bracknell would be far enough away. Upshott, however, didn't miss them. His farm took fire, was burned to the ground, and he thought the letters were destroyed with it."

Upshott was writing furiously now. What about, they couldn't guess. Now and then, he raised his face and gave Littlejohn a sardonic smile; otherwise, he showed little emotion.

"Bracknell arrived in Carleton, settled down at the Folly, and started to make it habitable. His money came regularly from Australia and was sufficient for a while. Then it began to run out. He thought right away of the letters. The blackmail started. He put the screw on Mrs. Checkland mercilessly and hard. Bracknell was a ladies' man, it seems. And he found someone of expensive tastes among the good-looking girls of the town. Marcia Fitzpayne. She seems to have had some idea of the existence of the letters and perhaps she encouraged him in his demands. These eventually became so extortionate that Mrs. Checkland reached the end of her resources. She was afraid if she didn't pay, her husband would be approached. Somehow, Mr. Checkland had never lost his suspicions of his wife. He fancied she still nursed a love for Upshott. He even suggested that his own son might have been Upshott's instead..."

Upshott laughed harshly and wrote something else in his book.

"It would never have done for him to get hold of the letters. Mrs. Checkland had promised never to write to Upshott again. But the strain made her break her word. She wrote to him, told him what was happening, and presumably accused him of disposing of her letters instead of returning them. The letter settled matters for Upshott. He decided, Checkland or no Checkland, gaol or no gaol, he was returning to Carleton to find out what Bracknell's game might be. Since I've known Upshott, I wouldn't be surprised if he didn't think, too, of claiming a share of the loot..."

"Thank you, Littlejohn. I appreciate your good opinion. By the way, cut it short. It's getting late... Nearly half-past one. It's time I got back to the *Barley Mow*. They're respectable in Carleton, you know. Not like London, where it doesn't matter what time you turn in..."

"One thing was uppermost in Upshott's thoughts, however. He was going to take his revenge, somehow, on Checkland. He turned up here just as Carleton Unthank had receded from the newspaper headlines. A maniac had killed two local girls, but some little time had passed and the news had ceased to be hot. The first thing he did was to call and see Mrs. Checkland. She told him about Bracknell. He gave her some advice, which seemed sensible enough. He told her to tell her husband. She should have done so in the first place and risked the consequences. As it was, when she did tell the mayor, he treated the matter of the letters very lightly. He said he'd see Bracknell, however, and put a stop to the whole business. Upshott had arranged for Mrs. Checkland to let him know how the mayor reacted. It sounded a reasonable request. After all he was an old friend, anxious for her welfare. Actually, he wanted to know exactly when Checkland was going to Freake's Folly, because it was part of his plan for revenge."

Suddenly, Upshott's voice broke in.

"I'd prefer you to say all this in front of a lawyer, Littlejohn. You're making accusations against me. It's not right. I want proper advice, because I'm going to make you eat your words later."

He was as white as a sheet now. His nostrils were pinched and his features drawn, but he had enough energy to charge his words with menace.

"You can have a lawyer later, if you want one. As you say, it's getting late. I'd better finish as quickly as I can."

One of the constables arrived with tea. Six large, thick cups full of dark brew which he gingerly dispensed.

"There's at least one gentleman among us..."

Upshott never missed a chance of being nasty. The constable blushed to the roots of his hair and looked at Herle as though he expected a rebuke. Instead, Herle smiled sadly at him. He was feeling dazed. Dragged out of bed, bewildered by events, wondering what was coming next, he blew absent-mindedly on his tea. He was out of his depth.

"...It must have been on the morning of Bracknell's death that Upshott arrived in Carleton in his hired car. As I said, his first call was on Mrs. Checkland. He avoided the mayor himself, otherwise Mr. Checkland might have sent for the police and Upshott might have found himself involved in a defalcation case many years old. Next, he called on Bracknell. It was after dark, for, as Mrs. Checkland had told him either over the telephone or in some other pre-arranged way, the mayor could not get down to Freake's Folly until about eight o'clock. Now, the subtlety of Upshott's move becomes apparent..."

Littlejohn plodded on and on, speaking rather rapidly now in an earnest quiet voice. As he spoke, Upshott regarded him with a hostile, sneering look. He made more notes, but he didn't interrupt. He seemed in a mood of absolute self-confidence.

"...He planned to murder Bracknell and make it appear that Checkland had done it. He had previously, it seems, during his visit to Mrs. Checkland, asked her to leave Mr. Checkland and return to Australia with him. That would have paid for all! It would have made the mayor look a public fool and settled the account. But Mrs. Checkland refused. She preferred her husband to the returned embezzler whom time had not improved."

Upshott sprang to his feet.

"Really, Superintendent Herle, are you going to allow this. I've not been arrested or charged with murder. Nobody can prove I murdered anybody. I simply came over here in response to an appeal for help from an old friend. Now, Littlejohn heaps every kind of crime on me. Murder, violence, attempting to seduce another man's wife. I'm innocent of the lot and I'll prove it later. But I won't stay here and be insulted any longer. I'm going back to my hotel."

Cromwell didn't give Herle any time to reply to the appeal. He rose and pushed Upshott back in his seat.

"Shut up, Upshott! Or else I'll handcuff you again."

"Very well. Now I'm being manhandled by the police. Right. It'll be my turn soon..."

Littlejohn knocked out his pipe at the grate and began to fill it slowly.

"Before Mr. Checkland arrived at Freake's Folly, Upshott was there. I don't know whether or not he'd seen Bracknell before..."

"I had. In the afternoon. The only time I called at his place. I wasn't there the night you mention."

Littlejohn didn't seem to hear it. He went on with his tale.

"...He called at the Folly in the afternoon, found Bracknell out, and was told by a passer-by that he might be at Marcia Fitzpayne's flat. He went there but found it locked up. That night, Charlie Space, a farm-hand at Pinner's Close, went to Freake's with his girl to retrieve a pair of gloves she'd left there. They found Bracknell in, and there was a man answering to Upshott's description with him, as well. They were quarrelling. The time was about seven-thirty. Charlie and his fiancée went back to the farm. Charlie returned alone about eight o'clock. Bracknell was stretched out on the floor. knifed and dead. The visitor had gone. Charlie hurried away, scared and without the gloves. But, before he got away, he had to hide to avoid meeting another visitor. It was Checkland. The mayor didn't report the crime but left it for the next caller. Checkland not only feared he would be accused of the murder; he also didn't wish to stir up a hornets' nest which would involve his wife and her letters. He was the mayor and had to preserve his dignity."

"I wasn't near the place that night. Besides, how could the farm labourer and his girl know me. They couldn't identify me. It might have been anybody. This is just another trick to involve me in the whole shabby affair."

"Let me get on with the story... Upshott didn't bring away Mrs. Checkland's letters. Neither did Checkland. Upshott and Bracknell must have quarrelled about them.

They may have come to blows and Upshott, the less robust of the pair, used a knife ..."

"This is fantastic! All lies! All lies!"

"In any event, he spoke to Mrs. Checkland again. He told her Bracknell had said he hadn't the letters with him. They were in the bank for safe-keeping. That wasn't true. Bracknell had told Marcia Fitzpayne about them. She was his mistress and he was in the habit of confiding in her, especially when he was drunk and maudlin. She knew of the letters and where they were kept. After Bracknell's death, she went to Freake's Folly and took them from their hiding-place. She couldn't wait to put the squeeze on Mrs. Checkland. She wrote to her at once and there began again the blackmail Bracknell had started."

Upshott was now sitting so rigidly in his chair that he looked as if he'd been turned into a block of wood. He gave Littlejohn a stupified look and started to write furiously again.

"But Marcia wasn't aware that Mrs. Checkland had told her husband and Upshott about the blackmail. Here was a supreme chance to underline Checkland as a murderer with an obvious motive. The mayor quietly fled from the Folly after finding Bracknell's body. Nobody reported seeing him and he left no trace. That wasn't what Upshott wanted. He prepared a repeat performance, only this time in a block of public flats where the mayor's visit was sure to be seen. The same plan was unfolded. Mrs. Checkland, having told her husband, sent another message to Upshott that the mayor was going to see Marcia Fitzpayne about the letters. Again, the mayor was keeping matters dark because he didn't want to tell the local police and make a fool of himself to his underlings..."

Herle didn't like the word and gave Littlejohn a nasty look.

"Upshott saw Marcia in the flat. How he got in without being seen, I can't say. But he did. Nobody saw any visitor entering Marcia's flat that night. He must have seized his opportunity and been lucky. He got the letters from Marcia, either by threats, promises, or force, and then killed her. Then he left her body for Checkland. He forgot one thing. The mayor owns the flats and has a key for the door of the fire escape. So Checkland, too, got in and out without a soul seeing him. Upshott had taken all his trouble for nothing! He turned to his second line of attack. He began to beg Mrs. Checkland to run away with him again. In his frenzy for revenge, he tried to prove himself a better man than her husband. He produced the letters when they met for what Upshott intended to be a final talk, at the *Marquis of Granby*. He hoped she'd be grateful to him, despise Checkland, and go to Australia with him. He could never bring himself to believe that she'd ceased to love him and hate Checkland for forcing them apart and compelling her to marry him. Instead, he found that she'd grown at least to respect her husband, and refused to leave him. Just before we arrived at the *Marquis of Granby*, Mrs. Checkland burned the letters, the ashes of which were visible in the fire when I examined it."

"This is all theory, mere fiction. You've not uttered a word you can prove. I've noted down all your fallacies and when I see my lawyer ..."

Cromwell yawned.

"You'll be given a chance. Listen to the Superintendent. It's rude to interrupt."

"We don't know where Upshott lodged during his stay here and before we found him. On the night Marcia Fitzpayne was killed, he didn't return to his hotel. He thought he'd better be off. He slept in a church and slipped away in a football bus, lost in the crowd and, in the hope that if the worst came, he'd not be traced. He got off the bus at a station on the route instead of going to Northampton. He ditched his hired car which he feared to use in case it might be recognised and stopped. I think he intended making for London, persuading Mrs. Checkland to join him there— for, you recollect, he still had the letters he'd taken from Marcia in his possession. If Mrs. Checkland had met him in London, he'd have tried again to persuade her to return with him to Australia. He just couldn't believe she'd grown to prefer the mayor to him. The years didn't seem to count. He still thought he was the better man and Mrs. Checkland could be convinced that it was true. Brooding on the matter, alone and far away, had driven him a bit dotty..."

As if to confirm this opinion. Upshott laughed. It was like the baying of a dog at the moon. He consulted his book.

"All through this crazy story, Littlejohn, you've treated me as the guilty party, and you're wrong. You're off the beam. My lawyer'll make mincemeat of all you say. And why? Because I never committed any crime. I was in London at my hotel the night Bracknell was killed. I told you so. I'd no alibi. I was at the Piccadilly Hotel. It's so busy that none of the staff would remember me, I'm sure. I went out for a meal, returned about eleven, and went up to bed. I'd kept my room key in my pocket as I expected to be back in an hour and didn't want the fuss of handing it in and asking for it back again in such a short time."

"I see. Did you go up in the lift?"

"No; I walked up. I was on the second floor and didn't wait for the lift."

"Unlucky for you, Upshott."

"Perhaps. But as I didn't commit any crime, you can't need an alibi. It's as simple as that. You can prove nothing."

"You were here the night Marcia Fitzpayne died. We know that. In your thirst for revenge, you couldn't keep away. You had failed once; you were going to try again."

"Nothing of the kind..."

"Why did you sleep in a church, instead of in your hotel as before? And why did you sneak off by bus, get off it half-way, and wait for a London train in an obscure little station? You began to feel guilty, that's why. In spite of all your protests you *felt* like a murderer. Guilt was beginning to press on you. Constant thinking about the murders prevented you from being sure that your own guilt was quite unknown. You began to behave like somebody guilty, when, all the time, an out and out lie would have been accepted as the truth. If you'd driven up to a hotel in the hired car you abandoned, told them you were a commercial traveller, spent the night, and left early in the car, you'd have been on the way back to Australia now. But you temporarily lost your head and behaved like a criminal, sleeping out, trying to cover your tracks, and, when the police found you, you adopted a smiling cocksure attitude and overdid it. You're overdoing it now. There's guilt written all over you. If the mayor had died tonight, one part of your scheme would have been a success. But he's going to get well..."

Upshott rose to his feet.

"I'm glad he's going to get well, for the sake of his wife. All your theories are cooked-up and my lawyer will soon put you where you belong. On the scrap-heap of also-ran detectives. And now I'll be going, if you please. We've heard enough."

"Your lawyer will have to face the testimony of Mrs. Checkland, before whom, in your vanity, you burned the letters you'd got from Marcia Fitzpayne when you killed her. Charlie Space and his fiancée will describe the man they saw at Freake's Folly just before Bracknell was killed. Charlie will give Mr. Checkland an alibi, too, if he needs one. All your comings and goings will be gone into, the reason for your return to England, the strange death of Bracknell almost as soon as you arrived, your past association with him and, finally, the story of the blackmailing of Mrs. Checkland and how you were involved in it."

"That won't be enough. I never committed any crime and you can't prove a thing. Your case is purely circumstantial and imaginary. You'll make a fool of yourself. I've no time to argue any more with you. I'm going..."

He thrust out his jaw and smiled aggressively.

"Going to stop me?"

"Yes. Walter Upshott, I arrest you for the murder of Marcia Fitzpayne and I warn you that anything you say may be taken down and used in evidence..."

Upshott moved back a step in astonishment and Herle and Cromwell both rose. Cromwell had been thinking the case was a bit thin and Herle had been waiting for cast-iron proof and it hadn't come. Perhaps, at this time of night, Littlejohn had hoped to wear down Upshott's resistance and force a confession. No confession seemed likely. Upshott was gathering himself together and almost looking pleased with himself.

"So, you want to try your luck, Littlejohn, and have a go at pinning it on me. Very well. Lock me up. You'll see how it all ends."

Littlejohn turned to Herle.

"Lock him up for the night."

Herle made a sign to the sergeant, who was still in the room, out of his depth, too, but dazzled by the majesty of the law. He longed for the day when he could caution and arrest a murderer.

Upshott was led off, still making threats and swearing to bring about the downfall of Littlejohn.

"You're sure, sir?"

Herle, although he doubted that Littlejohn had a clear-cut case, had grown much more respectful and subdued.

"I hope to clear it all up shortly. Young James Checkland is coming from the infirmary, as soon as possible, to look after his mother, who needs him. I've asked her to send him across here immediately she can spare him. He'll probably be able to help us."

Herle didn't even ask, How? He had so much to ask about the affair that one question more or less didn't matter.

"I couldn't finish the investigation with Upshott on our hands. Now we're rid of him, we can clear up one or two doubtful points."

"Are we right in keeping him under arrest?"

"It's not safe to let him go. He seems to be a kind of Houdini in getting away from your men ..."

Herle winced.

"And, more than ever, since he pulled a gun on us, it's not right to put him back in circulation. What about the man who was keeping an eye on him tonight? Will he be off now?"

"No. He's on duty till 2.00 a.m. When we'd finally found Upshott again, he went off to Fenny Carleton police station. It's under this one, and on Saturday night we usually have a plain-clothes man there. The local teddy-boys congregate at a dance-hall on Saturdays, so we give them an extra when we can spare one. Why?"

"I'd like to speak to him."

"His name's Walker. Constable Walker. A nice chap, in spite of tonight's little slip."

Walker was in. When Herle told him Littlejohn wanted him, he stammered a bit. He thought he was in for a reprimand.

"Is that you, Walker?"

"Yes, sir. Sorry about tonight's mistake. I'm afraid there is no excuse..."

"Forget it. We've got him safely in the cells. I want your help. What was he doing about 7 o'clock?"

"As far as I remember, he was in the lounge with a crowd of others, standing cocktails before dinner."

"Did you keep an eye on him all the time?"

"Well... I'm sorry, sir, but I'm not what you might call an expert at trailing people. It's a bit embarrassing, like. You see, I couldn't very well follow him about closely. I mean, when he was in the crowd round the bar drinking, I couldn't just stand by his side and see he didn't disappear, could I? I wasn't expected to do that, was I?"

He sounded strained and anxious.

"Of course not. You let him out of your sight; is that it?"

"He was among the crowd. There must have been twenty or more of them. There were a lot back from the football match, celebrating. Carleton beat Northampton, 3—1. I sat in the outside lounge and kept an eye on the crowd in case Upshott came out."

"Anything else unusual?"

"There was a telephone call about seven o'clock. I kept the box in view and was ready in case he tried any tricks. We were caught that way before. He didn't go out. Went back to the bar and drank along with the rest."

"And then did he come out to dinner?"

"At about 8.00."

"Now think carefully, Walker. Is there another way out from the cocktail bar?"

Heavy thinking at the other end.

"Yes. Into the storeroom behind the bar. That's the only other door in the place, except the one I was watching out into the hall."

"Is there an exit from the storeroom?"

A pause.

"Don't hesitate, Walker. There's no trouble brewing for you. As a matter of fact, you're being a big help."

"Thank you, sir. There is a door from the storeroom leads to the alley behind the hotel. It's where they unload some of the wines."

"Now, this is most important. Between seven and say half-past, did you *see* Upshott among the crowd? Think carefully."

"I couldn't swear to it, sir. I was seeing that he didn't leave the room and get away…"

"Thank you, Walker. That will be all."

"Everything all right, I hope, sir."

"Of course. Thank you for helping us."

Walker hung up as bewildered as the rest of his colleagues.

Meanwhile James Checkland had entered. He was pale and drawn, but nevertheless had the relaxed air of one who has been relieved of great anxiety.

"How's your father, Mr. James?"

"Much better, sir. He has a very good chance of pulling round."

He looked questioningly at Littlejohn, as though wondering if he'd sent for him at this unearthly hour to enquire about the mayor's health.

Littlejohn took the revolver Upshott had used from his raincoat pocket and put it on the table.

"Do you recognise that?"

James Checkland winced.

"It's my father's..."

"Sure?"

"Of course, I'm sure."

He picked it up. Then he pointed to two notches on the handle.

"I recognise it by those. My father used to let me play with it when I was small. Unloaded, of course. I'd been to a film where an outlaw used to chisel notches on his gun for every man he shot. I did the same. Pretended I'd shot someone and cut a notch. When my father saw them, he took the gun away and locked it up. It was one he had in the first war. He was an officer in the Midshires."

"You have the revolver you found on the carpet beside the mayor's body, Herle?"

Herle, more bewildered than ever, crossed to a safe, opened it, and took out another gun, almost exactly like the first.

Littlejohn examined it.

"I suppose it was a general issue for the Midshires. Upshott must have been an officer as well."

"But what is all this about, sir? That's not my father's gun, but it was found by his body. You mean to say...?"

"Yes. He didn't shoot himself. He was shot... Bring Upshott in again, please."

"He's asleep," said the sergeant-in-charge apologetically.

"Bring him in all the same."

Upshott, shoes unlaced, without collar, was led in. He was sulky this time.

"Chalking up a heavy score, aren't you, Littlejohn? Is this a new kind of third-degree? Keep waking-up a man to extract a confession. What do you want now? And be damned quick about it. I'm losing my beauty sleep."

"I forgot to finish the story, Upshott. We'll all sit down again..."

"I'm damned if I will. I'll stand, and if you're more than a couple of minutes I'm going back to my cell to bed."

"I forgot to ask you, why you shot Mr. Checkland tonight."

"Well, I'll be damned! He's thought up another!"

He looked at the rest of them with a pitying look on his face.

"Checkland rang you up about seven, asked you to come over to see him, arranged to let you in himself unknown to his family. So you gave the plain-clothes man the slip by mixing with the crowd in the cocktail-bar of the *Barley Mow,* creeping round the counter, and out into the street behind."

"This is getting very tedious, Littlejohn. I don't need any bedtime stories, you know. My cell's comfortable enough."

"You paid a visit to Mr. Checkland. You'd already called on him the night before. On that occasion, Upshott, you beat him up... Don't deny it. You're in better condition than he is and you gave him a punishing... Keep your temper, Mr. James. We're going to give Mr. Upshott his dues, now. Mr. Checkland made out he'd had a fall. He didn't wish to upset his wife or the fact to become public that his former rival for his wife's hand had returned and thrashed him..."

"Another fairy-tale..."

Littlejohn seized Upshott's right hand and twisted the fingers gently backwards. Upshott winced and almost screamed.

"You were so vindictive that you knocked back your wrist and barked your knuckles in your efforts. You're not much of a boxer, Upshott. Just a vicious swine! Luckily for the mayor you *did* injure your wrist. When you shot him, you fumbled the gun, because you couldn't handle it properly on account of your injury. You fired too high and that saved his life. Be quiet! You're not getting out of this one. Mr. Checkland had something to say to you. His wife had told him you'd obtained the letters and burned them. She was explaining your rendezvous at the *Marquis of Granby*. Mr. Checkland wondered about the letters. How had you come by them from Marcia Fitzpayne, the woman you said you never knew? He saw it all. You were the murderer of both Bracknell and Marcia. He accused you. This time, you couldn't use your fists on him. He had his revolver on the desk and told you what he'd do if you tried any tricks. A pity he didn't know you had your own gun in your pocket. You were quick to see that your revolvers were alike. The same issue, in fact, from the first war. You shot Checkland, took his gun away with you, and left your own with the body, looking as though it had slipped from his hand as he fell. I don't know where you hid until you'd a chance to creep out by the window in the confusion. There were thick curtains, drawn, when we were there. Did you get away whilst Mr. James and his mother were out of the room? We'll probably find traces of your descent from the window. Then you ran back to the *Barley Mow*, where your drinking companions probably thought your slipping out and in were some joke or other..."

Littlejohn turned his back on Upshott.

"Take him away. Perhaps he and his lawyer can get away with that one, too."

The trial of Walter Upshott caused quite a sensation at the Midshire Assizes. The jury chose to take the word of a string of reputable witnesses, including the mayor and mayoress of Carleton, against the denials of Upshott and the forensic eloquence of his lawyers. He was found guilty.

Upshott was sentenced to life imprisonment. True to the nickname of Houdini, which Littlejohn had given him, he escaped twice from gaol, and was re-captured. In his third attempt, he fell from the high prison wall and broke his neck. It was a pity the hangman hadn't been able to do it more painlessly for him long before.

Death in the Wasteland

George Bellairs

Chapter I
A Body Vanishes

The Maid wakened Littlejohn and told him he was wanted on the telephone. No peace for the wicked! He removed the newspaper which covered his face, eased himself out of the long lounge chair in which he had been extended, took a quick almost furtive swig from the glass of *Pernod* at his side, and followed the girl, down the long cool corridor like a cloister, to the instrument.

'Allô!'

An English voice answered.

'Is that Superintendent Littlejohn?'

Littlejohn and his wife were staying with his friend Dorange, of the Sûreté at Nice. Dorange, a bachelor, lived with his parents in their villa at Vence in the hills behind Antibes. His father was a wholesale grower of roses and carnations and their home stood in the midst of his gardens, bathed in the fragrance of flowers. Behind, the ground rose steadily to the barren forbidding peaks of the Basses-Alpes; ahead, it slowly descended to the Baie des Anges and the fabulous blue Mediterranean.

It was August and the air vibrated with the heat. Grasshoppers and cicadas were chirping in the fields and cars and motor-bikes kept up an incessant hum along the distant roads.

Littlejohn was on his own. His host was on duty in Nice; his father was in his rose-fields; and Mrs. Littlejohn and Dorange's mother had gone on a shopping expedition to Antibes. Littlejohn had propped himself in a chair in the shade of the loggia, cursorily scanned a three-days-old English newspaper, and then spread it over his face and fallen asleep.

'Is that Superintendent Littlejohn?'

'Yes.'

'My name's Waldo Keelagher...'

No wonder the French maid hadn't been able to pronounce the name! She'd called him Monsieur Kay, and then given it up.

'My name's Waldo Keelagher. You won't know me, but I happen to be a cousin of Inspector Cromwell...'

What next! Somebody on holiday who'd found himself at a loose end or else short of ready money. However, Littlejohn had heard of him. Cromwell had spoken of his cousin Waldo a time or two. He was a London stockbroker, who now and then gave Cromwell hot tips which didn't come off. Impossible to forget a name like Waldo.

'He's mentioned you from time to time. You're a stockbroker, aren't you?'

The voice grew full of eager relief.

'That's right. Thank God you've heard of me, and I don't need to start proving that I'm genuine. I'm in a mess with the police in Cannes. I'm there now. My car's been stolen. But that's not the worst. My Great-Uncle George's dead body was in it.'

Littlejohn mopped his forehead with his free hand. Either he or Waldo must be suffering from the heat.

Trundling his Great-Uncle George's dead body around the Côte d'Azur in a car! It just wasn't possible.

'Say that again ...'

'I know you won't believe me. It's fantastic, but ...'

There was someone else on the line, too, to add to the confusion. It sounded, judging from the arithmetical conversation, like a maître d'hôtel of a large establishment arranging his rake-off with the local grocer.

'Please hang-up. This line is engaged. Police.'

Littlejohn smiled as he said it. He could imagine the receiver of the unknown intruder being very softly replaced. There was a click and they were free of him.

'You were saying ...?'

'I'm sorry to bother you, sir. But, you see, I'm on holiday here with my wife and we don't know anybody. I'm in a fix. We were in a caravan. I ought to tell you that my Great-Uncle George insisted on coming with us, and died suddenly last night. We were miles from anywhere, and well ... I thought we'd better bring the body to the nearest town and report it to the police. It seemed the best thing to do at the time, but now I have my doubts. I brought him to Cannes, parked the car near the police station, and my wife and I came in and told them about it. They wanted to see the body. When I went out to the car, it had been pinched and the body with it. I swear that's the truth. The police here think I'm either mad, or playing a practical joke on them, or else perpetrating some hideous crime or fraud. They won't believe the car was stolen ...'

No wonder! Littlejohn wondered if he were having a nightmare and would wake up when it grew too horrible to bear.

A pause.

'Excuse me. The policeman here's saying something ...'

Littlejohn could overhear it. The quick-spoken French of the policeman was almost loud enough to be heard down in Vence. Then, Keelagher asking him in halting French to speak more slowly.

'He says I'd better ask you to come here and discuss the matter. He says he's sorry to trouble you. He's a friend of Commissaire Dorange and has met you before, but it's a rather awkward matter to settle over the 'phone.'

Awkward! If he hadn't been Cromwell's cousin...

'All right. I'll come. It will take me about an hour. How did you know I was here?'

'I saw in the paper that you were in Vence staying with Commissaire Dorange. That'll be Cromwell's boss, I said to my wife...'

Littlejohn might have known! The papers had got it and inserted it in the *Comings and Goings* column between a notice of the arrival of an oil magnate in his yacht and that of a film-star who'd run away with a conjurer's wife.

Superintendent Littlejohn and wife, of Schottland Yard, arrived yesterday, to stay at Les Charmettes, home of Commissaire Dorange at Vence...

The trouble was, it was too hot altogether for undertaking a wild-goose chase after Great-Uncle George's body. It was only out of affection for Cromwell, who, for some reason, always seemed proud of cousin Waldo and his Stock Exchange, that Littlejohn bestirred himself and took out the little Floride which was at his disposal and snaked his way down to Cannes. He was almost killed twice on the way. Once by a car with a large G.B. on the back, driven by an Englishman who seemed to have gone berserk and reverted to driving on the left. The other was by a Frenchman, driving at sixty and trying to make love at the same time.

When he reached Cannes, he wished he'd stayed at home. The streets were packed with holidaymakers manipulating every possible kind of vehicle, one main street was blocked by a religious procession and, in the other, a milk lorry had apparently collapsed beneath its load of bottles and scattered milk and broken glass all over the shop.

The police were therefore fully extended and the disappearance of Uncle George, deceased, had become a side issue. He found Waldo Keelagher sitting with his wife, despondently neglected and waiting in a small room for attention. Even the good looks of Mrs. Keelagher, a straight-haired, blue-eyed blonde, with a skin the colour of honey and next to nothing on, had failed to stimulate the local officials, the bulk of whom seemed to be noisily concerned with the milkman who'd blocked the Rue d'Antibes.

Waldo himself looked as excited as he probably did in Throgmorton Street after a substantial change in the Bank Rate or the collapse of Wall Street. He was tall, fair and slim, and his thin yellow hair was plastered across his head as carefully as if he'd just returned from the City. His features were distorted by a huge pair of sun-glasses, which he removed when Littlejohn entered to reveal his panic-stricken eyes and eyebrows so pale that he didn't seem to have any at all. He was dressed in a sleeveless buff shirt with shorts to match and his body had the boiled look which arises from too much sun.

The arrival of Littlejohn was like water in the desert to Waldo. He flew at the Superintendent, too full of emotion to speak, and wrung him heartily by the hand.

'So good of you,' he said in a broken voice.

Waldo's wife, who was very beautiful, and seemed intelligent with it, too, was taking it all very calmly. After all, it wasn't *her* Great-Uncle George who'd died and been stolen. Also, she was of a different temperament from Waldo, nervously exhausted by the ups and downs of stocks and shares. She provided the morale of the partnership and Waldo the money. Besides, Great-Uncle George, now, they hoped, with God, had been reputed to be worth a quarter of a million, to say nothing of the goodwill in the stockbroking firm of which he had, until lately, been senior partner and in which Waldo carried on the family name. The thought of Uncle George's estate gave her a comfortable, warm feeling inside.

'So good of you to come, Superintendent. We do appreciate it. I'm in a real mess. I don't know whether or not it might end-up with my being accused of murder...'

'Don't be silly, darling. Of course it wasn't murder. Uncle George ate far too many mushrooms last night and his heart gave out. Now that the Superintendent is here to help us, everything's going to be all right. Isn't it, Superintendent?'

It just depended on what you meant by all right. Little wonder the Cannes police had been incredulous... Here they were now, in the shape of a *brigadier*, who, as soon as he saw Littlejohn tactfully vanished and was replaced by an Inspector. Littlejohn had met the Inspector before. His name was Joliclerc.

Joliclerc, who had once worked with Littlejohn in Cannes on a case of a murdered English antique dealer, was delighted to see him. So much so, that Waldo Keelagher's dilemma seemed forgotten and the meeting took on the form of a social function. Joliclerc shook hands with Littlejohn three times before they finally got down to work.

'Yes; the matter of Monsieur Valdo... Valdo...'

Inspector Joliclerc looked at the card on his desk.

'Valdo Kaylayjay...'

It would do! Anything to get down to business and get away.

The Inspector confessed that he didn't understand English. And Monsieur Valdo's French was a bit difficult. He thought that perhaps the Superintendent Littlejohn wouldn't mind coming to interpret and help Monsieur Valdo.

So, the three-cornered interview began. Waldo to Littlejohn in English. Littlejohn to Joliclerc in French. And then the return journey to Waldo.

As Littlejohn expected, it took some time to convince the French police that Waldo wasn't drunk or mad. This formality finally overcome, Joliclerc sent for a male stenographer to take down a statement. He politely allowed Littlejohn to do the questioning, only intervening now and then to elucidate a point.

It turned out that Waldo Keelagher was a great do-it-yourself votary and over the past two years had been building a luxury caravan in his spare time. He had finished it in the Spring, tried it out at Easter to Swanage and back, and he and his wife had voted it good for a trip to the Riviera in August.

Late in July, Waldo had committed the folly of boasting about his handiwork to his Great-Uncle George, the wealthy head of the firm in which he had made Waldo a junior partner. Anticipating the ultimate arrival of a family, Waldo had prudently planned accommodation for four in his vehicle.

'The very thing!' Uncle George said when he heard of it. 'I'll come with you.'

Waldo paused in his narrative at the horror of it, and Littlejohn paused for breath in his marathon translation to Joliclerc.

'You see, Uncle George, who is about 65 ... or *was* ... besides being a stockbroker has for a long time very vigorously carried-on a hobby and since he went into semi-retirement, it's become a sort of mania. He's a naturalist and writes books about it. He's just started another. It's about what's called the praying mantis ...'

Praying mantis ... It stumped Littlejohn as interpreter. However, Waldo had a note of the French for it in his diary among a lot of other phrases supplied by Uncle George.

La mante religieuse! Joliclerc and his stenographer threw up their hands in chorus, shrugged, and looked more stupefied than ever at the mad tale. Waldo continued as though it were an everyday occurrence. He seemed to be talking to himself.

'... It seems that, although Uncle George had closely studied these insects in captivity ... he had a sort of praying mantis zoo in a gauze cage ... to study them properly he wanted to see them in their natural habitat, as he called it. He said the fully developed adult mantis made her appearance on the Riviera in August, like the rest of us. He said with a caravan, we could camp right among them, so to speak. He was bad on his feet and said the hotels were too far away ...'

'He was too greedy to pay his hotel bills, in spite of his money. He was a miser,' interrupted Mrs. Waldo, whose name, by the way, was Averil.

'What does madame say?'

Littlejohn translated and Joliclerc smiled for the first time during the tale. And, seeming to notice Averil, too, for the first time, he twisted his little moustache and straightened his tie. The more acute stenographer had already done this half-dozen times.

238

'He insisted on coming. It was difficult, in fact impossible, to say No to him. You see, I work for his firm and, well, he's a very wealthy man.'

He paused and coughed.

'Go on, Waldo. You may as well tell them. You have expectations...'

Waldo turned pale and then flushed and, as though dazzled by his forthcoming good fortune, put on his dark glasses again.

Littlejohn thought it high time to control the narrative. After all, they couldn't be at it all day. It was nearly lunchtime, too.

'He came with you?'

'Yes. We tried our best to persuade him out of the idea, but he was always a stubborn old man. Do you know, the praying mantis eats its mate in a most revolting manner...'

No wonder all the hot tips Waldo gave Cromwell always ended in a washout! He simply couldn't concentrate on the business in hand.

'When did you set-out?'

'Last Saturday. We stayed on Sunday outside Beauvais. On Monday...'

'When did you arrive in Provence?'

'Tuesday. We camped just outside Aix-en-Provence. Yesterday, we arrived very early in the Estérel, where uncle proposed to spend some time studying his damned insects. It's wooded there, and stony, and we'd no trouble finding a spot for the night. Averil and I went down to the coast for a bathe at Théoule and left uncle hunting for mantises. We got back around six in the evening.'

'You found him safe and sound.'

'Yes. He said he'd had a splendid afternoon. The place, according to him, was teeming with mantis. He'd also gathered a lot of mushrooms. They looked lethal to me, but both Averil and uncle said they were all right. He ate a lot after Averil cooked them in milk and I think that's what upset him.'

'What time did you retire?'

'About nine o'clock. It was dark then and there was no pleasure sitting out of doors with a light. The place was infested by every kind of winged insect, especially mosquitoes.'

'Your uncle slept in the caravan?'

'Yes. There are two bunk-rooms, a kitchen, and a bathroom and toilet.'

At the translation of the sanitary arrangements, the two Frenchmen threw up their hands again. Joliclerc looked baffled and interjected a private question at Littlejohn in in an undertone.

'Do they have water-tanks and do they carry the water to them to operate the bath and the W.C. in the wagon?'

'Yes.'

Joliclerc shrugged his shoulders sadly. He was obviously dealing with madmen and told the shorthand-writer in a whisper to take account of it.

'You passed a good night?'

'Averil and I are good sleepers. We'd had a heavy day. We slept till eight. Then we got up and found uncle had passed away.'

His tone suggested that if Waldo had been wearing a hat, he'd have bared his head. It seemed to rile his wife.

'He was *dead*,' she added.

'Was he a normally healthy man?'

'Generally speaking, yes. He never ailed anything for as long as I can remember. But lately, he'd been under the doctor with a weak heart. He pooh-poohed the idea, of course.

He was like that. He fancied himself as a quack-doctor, as a matter of fact.'

Littlejohn was beginning to build-up a picture of Great-Uncle George. Quite a character!

'He died in bed?'

'No. He was lying on his face outside the caravan, as though he'd been taken ill and gone out for fresh air.'

'Fully dressed, or in his pyjamas?'

'He didn't wear pyjamas. He said they made him feel suffocated. He had a nightshirt.'

'Was he wearing it?'

'No. He was fully dressed. We thought he'd had a heart attack. He must have been dead for some time. He'd gone cool.'

Gone cool! Joliclerc leapt to his feet.

'Why didn't you leave the body as it was and go to the nearest telephone and notify the police?'

Littlejohn translated, but Averil replied.

'Waldo lost his nerve and went all to pieces. I don't blame him. You'd feel the same. Miles from anywhere in that appalling country with nobody about. I believe it was once the haunt of brigands and cut-throats.'

'But that was no excuse for packing-up the body and bringing it to the police in that way. If death wasn't natural, you've destroyed all the evidence.'

Averil suddenly seemed to understand Joliclerc's angry, authoritative French.

'You can tell him he needn't get in a tizzy about it. I offered to go for help, but Waldo wasn't fit to leave or to drive either. We couldn't leave the body out there. It didn't seem decent. We seem to have done the wrong thing and got ourselves in a rare mess. I think we ought to have buried and left the body there, after all.'

Littlejohn translated a revised version of that. No use annoying the French police. Things were bad enough as it was. Averil was thoroughly annoyed with them all.

'I know it sounds silly to all of you now. Actually, it seems silly to me, too. But Waldo's had two nervous breakdowns since the war. He'd a bad time with the Gestapo as a prisoner in Germany. I wasn't going to have him down with a third breakdown. He's more precious to me than all your Uncle Georges. What did Uncle George want foisting himself on us, any way? He'd no business coming.'

'So, you made a parcel of him and put him in the caravan?'

'No. We locked the caravan, left it where it was, and brought him here by car. We knew he'd died a natural death. We're not medical experts, but who'd want to murder Uncle George at that time in the morning?'

Joliclerc put his head in his hands. It was getting beyond him.

'Go on ... *Continuez*...'

'Well, that's all. We brought the body in the car, as I've already told you. We parked outside and came in to report it. We knew there'd have to be some sort of post-mortem but it seemed simple to us then. We explained to the sergeant here, who brought in someone who understood English. Then we took them to where we'd parked the car. It was gone!'

Averil told it all in a very matter-of-fact way. Waldo kept trying to get a word in edgeways, but she wouldn't stop. She seemed to have made up her mind to get it over.

'And that was where you came in, Superintendent Littlejohn. Waldo had seen in a paper we bought at Aix that you were staying near Nice. We felt we needed some help.'

That was the end. Averil had been wound-up and now she'd run down. She burst into tears.

Waldo trembled, wrung his hands, hung over his wife and tried to comfort her. At first, Littlejohn thought he'd attack the French police. Eventually, he managed to quieten down the pair of them.

Joliclerc sat back and sighed deeply. He was a heavy man with a small moustache and sad, pouched brown eyes. A most polite and civil officer whose patience had been badly strained. He was moved by Averil's tears. He looked at his watch. One o'clock.

'We must send someone to the caravan and the spot must be examined. Also, give me details of the stolen car, which we will circulate. Do you happen to have a portrait of the dead man, too?'

Waldo produced various papers covering the car, as well as a photograph of it, coupled to the caravan, with Waldo proudly at the wheel and Averil with her head through the window. He also produced their joint passport and everything else he could think of. His driving-licence had been endorsed. Dangerous driving two years before! He seemed to think he owed them an explanation.

'It was the night before my wedding...'

Finally, Waldo probed in his wallet and produced a postcard photograph of Uncle George. Whether he carried it for good-luck or duty he didn't say.

Uncle George was dressed in academic cap, gown and hood. A small, shrivelled-looking man, with a hatchet face, Roman nose and shrewd piercing eyes. He had a tough, stubborn look about him and, on the occasion of the photograph, must have achieved some long-sought triumph, for he looked self-satisfied.

'That was taken nearly ten years ago. He got an M.A. degree for a thesis on Ants when he was nearly sixty.'

Come to think of it, Uncle George looked a bit of an ant himself! Industrious, persistent, a confounded nuisance ...

Joliclerc swept the papers in a file and gave his orders to the secretary. He was quite unimpressed by the cap and gown.

'And now...'

He looked sternly at Waldo and his missus.

'If what you say is true, you are both in a delicate position. We ought to detain you until the matter has been cleared-up ...'

Littlejohn told them in English what it all meant.

Waldo made a noise like a sob.

'In gaol?'

'Yes.'

His first thoughts were of Averil.

'I'm sorry, darling. It was all my fault. I ought to have been firm with him.'

Averil seemed to know how to handle him.

'Of course it's not your fault. It's your Uncle George's for insisting on coming and then dying on our hands. It serves him right.'

She turned to Littlejohn.

'I didn't mean that, but it makes me so mad. Could you help us, Superintendent? You've been wonderful, but there's one thing more. Could you sort of go bail for us? After all, you can trust us. Waldo's your Inspector Cromwell's cousin on his mother's side. Could you?'

Littlejohn couldn't refuse, could he? Cromwell's cousin! He spoke with Joliclerc, who seemed glad of a chance to do him a good turn.

'I'll have to speak with Commissaire Dorange to begin with.'

It took a bit of ironing out. They had to go higher up the ladder than Dorange for a final decision. Littlejohn ended-up in charge of Waldo and Averil. They were in his hands, *sous caution,* under bail, pending the clearing-up of the affair.

Littlejohn didn't mind being responsible for them. They were nice young people. Cromwell's relations. But, he had them on his hands until Great-Uncle George turned-up. And, perhaps after that, too.

He invited them to lunch as his first duty as godfather. It was like being guardian to a couple of kids in distress.

LOVE GEORGE BELLAIRS? JOIN THE READERS' CLUB

GET YOUR NEXT GEORGE BELLAIRS MYSTERY FOR FREE

If you sign up today, this is what you'll get:

1. A free classic Bellairs mystery, *Corpses in Enderby*;
2. Details of Bellairs' new publications and the opportunity to get copies in advance of publication; and
3. The chance to win exclusive prizes in regular competitions.

Interested? It takes less than a minute to sign up, just go to www.georgebellairs.com and your ebook will be sent to you.

Made in the USA
Las Vegas, NV
11 February 2022

43735673R00152